CW00547886

The Kiss On The Cliff

Ivy Lovestone

Published by Ivy Lovestone, 2023.

This is a work of fiction. Similarities to real people, places, or events are entirely coincidental.

THE KISS ON THE CLIFF

First edition. July 18, 2023.

Copyright © 2023 Ivy Lovestone.

ISBN: 979-8223200307

Written by Ivy Lovestone.

To my late husband Damien, you were there with me for my own journey...

Chapter 1

The English countryside rolled by in a blur of vibrant green as Elizabeth stared resolutely out the carriage window. Inside the plush interior, the air felt stifling, amplified by the stern gaze she could feel upon her without even turning. "Do sit up straight, Elizabeth," her mother chided. "You are slouching most unbecomingly." With a silent huff, Elizabeth obeyed, smoothing the folds of her dress. As the carriage jostled along, she fixed a pleasant smile on her face that belied the restless energy churning within. At nineteen, she felt certain she should be out living life to its fullest, not trussed up in finery on the way to yet another insipid social event intended to showcase her marriageability. If she never attended another stuffy high society ball, it would be too soon. As the vehicle rolled to a stop before an imposing stone manor, she steeled herself, donning the mask of the demure young gentlewoman she was expected to be. If only her parents and peers could see past the facade to the bold spirit underneath that longed to break free! Inside, Elizabeth endured the usual barrage of greetings and inane small talk with practiced grace. As the chamber ensemble struck up a lively reel, couples began lining up for the dance. Out of the corner of her eye, she spied her friend Charlotte beckoning eagerly. Glad for any excuse to avoid her other potential suitors, Elizabeth hurried over. "Thank heaven you are here, Lizzie! These events are so frightfully dull otherwise," Charlotte whispered conspiratorially. Though from a respectable family herself, Charlotte shared Elizabeth's disdain for the rigid expectations placed upon them. Together they whirled through the steps of the dance, keeping up a steady stream of hushed, irreverent commentary that helped make the evening bearable. Elizabeth was nearly breathless from suppressing laughter by the time the music concluded. As Charlotte was promptly whisked away by her next partner, Elizabeth felt a light touch on her elbow. Turning, she found herself face to face with James Huntington, the insufferable son of a

1

prominent local family. His thin lips curved into a smirk as he regarded her. "Miss Elizabeth, you are looking well this evening," he purred, the compliment sounding almost sinister. Before she could protest, he was steering her relentlessly back towards the dance floor. Elizabeth barely restrained herself from rolling her eyes in disgust as Huntington confidently led her through the steps while carrying on a self-absorbed monologue. Did the man not realize how ridiculous he appeared, fawning after her for her family's status? The interminable dance finally ended to Elizabeth's profound relief. But as she attempted to offer Huntington a perfunctory curtsy and retreat, his clammy fingers closed over her wrist. "Surely you can spare another dance for me?" He blinked at her imploringly with a poor imitation of charm. This time, she did not restrain her glare. "Forgive me, my dance card is rather full tonight," she replied coldly, wrenching from his grasp. Ignoring his sputtering protest, she slipped away into the crowd and out onto the balcony for a much-needed breath of night air. Leaning against the balustrade, Elizabeth gazed up at the velvet sky glittering with stars. How she wished she could escape the confines of this world - set off on some thrilling journey to discover what lay beyond the familiar English countryside. Or even just meet someone with whom she genuinely shared a spiritual connection, rather than polite social niceties. But her parents had already begun assessing her portrait to some of the local families well-regarded in society's eyes. Like Charlotte, her fate seemed sealed to become some fortunate gentleman's ornamental wife. The image made Elizabeth's stomach turn. She had no intention of being auctioned off like cattle to the highest bidder! But as a young woman, she possessed little power to shape her own destiny. I cannot accept this as my lot in life! she thought fiercely. There must be more than endless monotonous days confined within the roles society deems proper. Somewhere out in the vast world, the life she truly deserved awaited. She need only find the courage to seek it. Squaring her shoulders, Elizabeth cast one last scornful look over her shoulder at the glittering ball inside before slipping off into the night. The grounds were deserted and eerily still, save for flickering lamp light from the manor windows. Making her way stealthily across the lawn, she ducked through an opening in the towering hedge bordering the property. Once safely on the other side, she broke into a breathless run. Wheels of carriages crunched faintly in the distance carrying the revelers home as Elizabeth raced on alone under the moonlight. At the crest of a hill, she finally paused, chest heaving, turning her gaze northward. Out there somewhere, her destiny called. She imagined herself aboard a great clipper ship, salt spray on her face, sailing towards fabled lands. Or perhaps finding a cozy cottage nestled deep in the countryside far from prying eyes, a beloved companion by her side. One day she would have it all - love, adventure, above all freedom. For now, she could only glimpse that brilliant future through the haze of duty and expectation engulfing her. But she would find a way forward. Taking a deep breath of the sweet night air, Elizabeth gathered her skirts and turned back towards the manor glowing like a jewel box in the distance. For now, she must resume playing her tedious assigned role. But the fire in her soul would not be dimmed. She had tasted freedom under the stars, and its siren call could never again be ignored.

Chapter 2

Elizabeth picked listlessly at her breakfast, dreading the conversation to come. Last night after the ball, her parents had mentioned George Wilson's imminent proposal and strongly implied she should accept it. George came from a well-established family and had a promising career in law ahead of him. On paper, he was the ideal match. But Elizabeth harbored no affection for him. At social events, his discourse focused on banal pleasantries or his own career aspirations. He did not share her thirst for adventure or pushes against tradition. A marriage to him would be a lifelong sentence of boredom. Yet as an obedient daughter, how could she refuse this opportunity her parents had arranged? Women of her station had few options outside of marriage. Defiantly rejecting George would create an ugly scandal that would close doors for her throughout local society. Elizabeth was roused from her brooding by her mother's voice. "The Wilsons will be joining us for tea this afternoon. I trust you will be on your best behavior?" It was more command than question. Elizabeth replied only with a mute nod, eyes downcast. As the afternoon wore on, her feet felt weighted with dread as she paced the manor halls restlessly. She had narrowly avoided proposals from other respectable suitors like James Huntington so far. But her parents' patience was evidently at an end. At precisely four o'clock, the Wilson family carriage pulled up the drive. Stomach churning, Elizabeth arranged herself decorously in the parlor beside her mother. This was it - the death knell of her independence. Stilted pleasantries were exchanged as tea was poured. Elizabeth kept her gaze fixed on her teacup, responses barely more than murmurs. Eventually, talk turned to the future as the elder family members strategized. "George's law practice continues to flourish," Mr. Wilson declared. "Why, just this week..." Elizabeth let his words fade into a drone as despair threatened to swallow her. She was merely a pawn in this negotiation, her desires inconsequential. As she stared blindly into her

4

tea, she found herself longing desperately for some dramatic intervention - a tremor to split the ground beneath her, a shrieking gale to shatter the windows. Anything that would put a halt to this relentless machinery carrying her towards captivity. But the sun continued to stream serenely through the windows as polite conversation buzzed around her. No one remarked upon the anguish in her downcast eyes. At last Mr. Wilson broke decorum. "My boy, why don't you take Miss Elizabeth for a turn about the garden?" George started, then flushed. "Ah, yes. An excellent idea." Stiffly offering his arm, he guided a numb Elizabeth out through the French doors onto the veranda. For a few tortured paces, they walked in silence through the rose garden. Finally George halted beneath a carved archway tangled with vines. Turning nervously to Elizabeth, he began fumbling in his pocket. "Miss Elizabeth...that is to say, I hope you will permit me to call you Elizabeth..." Elizabeth's lungs constricted as he dropped awkwardly to one knee, brandishing a silver ring set with a modest pearl. This was the moment she had dreaded. "Would you do me the honor of becoming my wife?" George peered up at her entreatingly. Elizabeth's tongue felt leaden in her mouth. How easy it would be to scream her refusal, fling the ring into the bushes and fly out the gates forever! But she knew the reality - such dramatics would leave her destitute, shunned by society with nowhere to turn. However stifled she felt now, ruination would surely be far worse. Swallowing the lump in her throat, she slowly extended a trembling hand. "I accept your proposal, Mr. Wilson," she forced out in a strangled tone. Relief broke across George's face as he slid the ring onto her finger. It felt like an iron manacle binding her to this fate. "Oh my dear, you've made me the happiest of men!" Standing awkwardly, George wrapped her in an embrace. Over his shoulder, Elizabeth glimpsed her parents beaming proudly through the parlor window. It was done. The cage had closed around her. That evening as she prepared for bed in her childhood room, Elizabeth numbly twisted the ring upon her finger. She had bought herself some time by requesting a long engagement period before the actual wedding. But soon enough, she would be ensconced in George's respectable home as his wife. A pretty caged bird. Bile rose in her throat as she regarded her pale reflection in the vanity glass. Was this demure passive countenance truly her? Or just the face society demanded she wear? She hardly recognized herself. But perhaps it was better if the fiery girl who had yearned for freedom faded away entirely. That Elizabeth could only beget more pain. With a choked sob, she buried her face in her hands. She must accept that from here on, her life was not her own. All she could hope for now was peaceful resignation. In the darkened manor, no one heard her muffled cries of despair.

Chapter 3

Candlelight glimmered off crystal goblets and the gems of the ladies in attendance as the string quartet soared into another sweeping waltz. Laughter and merriment filled every corner of the opulent ballroom. Yet at the center of it all stood Elizabeth, the bride-to-be, feeling utterly hollow. She had smiled until her cheeks ached, received countless well-wishes, and danced every obligatory turn. But it was all a performance - inside she was screaming. In one month's time, she would be leg-shackled to George Wilson. The date loomed before her, inescapable as the tides. Tonight was meant to be a celebration of their impending union. To Elizabeth it felt like a lavish funeral for the girl who once dreamed of freedom. Needing respite from the cloying ballroom, she slipped out onto the terrace for a breath of fresh air. Away from the revelry, the night was tranquil. Elizabeth leaned against the balustrade with a shaky sigh, letting the cool quiet settle over her. How easy it would be to keep walking right out of this gilded cage and never look back. But where would she go? A young unmarried woman alone had no prospects. Better to swallow her fate gracefully than face the harsh alternative. Blinking back tears of defeat, she made to turn back inside. But a glimpse of movement in the gardens below gave her pause. A lone figure was standing motionless beneath the rose arbor, half-obscured in shadow. From his fine dress, Elizabeth surmised he must be one of the wedding guests who had also stepped outside to escape the commotion. He did not seem to have noticed her presence on the terrace above. But something about his solitude and stance of quiet melancholy resonated with her own conflicted heart. Before she could think better of it, she called out softly. "Good sir? Is all well with you?" The stranger started, peering up to meet her gaze. As he stepped forward into a shaft of moonlight, Elizabeth stifled a small gasp. He had perhaps the most arresting face she had ever seen - strong jaw, roman nose, and piercing eyes that seemed to see straight through to her soul. She felt oddly exposed under his penetrating stare, frozen in place against the balustrade. When he spoke, his voice was rich and smooth as velvet. "Forgive me if I caused alarm. The ball within was somewhat... overwhelming." Elizabeth nodded in instant understanding. "I could not agree more. I confess I came out here for the same reason, even though this ostensibly celebrates my engagement." She did not know what prompted her to share that personal detail with this stranger, yet she felt compelled toward honesty. The stranger's dark brows lifted in surprise. "You are the bride then? My sincerest congratulations." Elizabeth thought she caught a glint of pity in his eyes. She looked away, unable to hold that searching gaze any longer. "I had better return within. My future husband will be looking for me." With a final conflicted glance at the handsome stranger, she slipped back inside, heart pounding inexplicably. Why had she bared even a small piece of her soul to this man she did not know? Surely it was only the isolation of her situation that left her so starved for real connection. Back in the glittering ballroom, she quickly located George in his formal attire, surrounded by a circle of eager well-wishers. As she joined reluctantly him, his face lit up with relief. "My dear, there you are! I had quite despaired of finding you in this crush. Come, there are several important gentlemen I would like you to meet." As he steered her about the room on his arm, Elizabeth kept searching the crowd for a glimpse of the intense stranger from the garden. But his dark eyes and chiseled features were nowhere to be seen. After being paraded before what felt like every influential family in attendance, Elizabeth's feet ached intensely in their dainty slippers. Mercifully, George was engaged in an animated debate about local politics with several gentlemen, giving her a chance to slip away unnoticed again. Weaving through the crowds, she ducked behind a silk drapery into an empty alcove. Pressing a hand to her throbbing temple, she sank down onto an elegant brocade chaise. Finally alone with her thoughts. Those piercing eyes and melodic voice from the garden filled her mind unbidden. She shook her head sharply.

It was foolish to dwell on a chance encounter with a man she did not even know. In a month, she would be bound to George forever. Best not to indulge in pointless daydreams. A sound in the passageway outside her hiding spot made her glance up warily. But it was not George come to drag her back to the ball. Framed in the alcove entrance stood the stranger, eyebrows raised in surprise at finding her there. "Apologies, miss," he said. "I did not mean to intrude upon your solitude." Elizabeth's pulse quickened. "No need to apologize, sir. In truth, I came here to escape the revelries for a moment. But I should return before I am missed." Yet she made no move to rise from the chaise, finding she had no desire to leave this man's presence. Beneath his penetrating gaze, the constant ache inside her eased, just fractionally. Seeming to sense her ambivalence, the stranger spoke gently. "These affairs can be tedious when one feels...out of step with the crowd." "Precisely," Elizabeth breathed in grateful wonderment. How had he discerned so easily the alienation isolating her, even here in a ballroom surrounded by her peers? She stared at him in frank appraisal. "Forgive me, but I do not believe we have been introduced." The man grimaced apologetically. "You must think me rude. I am Peter Maxwell, a longtime friend of your betrothed." He held himself with an air of restrained power, yet his eyes glinted with something wilder beneath. "I have been abroad for many years, only just returned." "Well, Mr. Maxwell." She inclined her head graciously though her pulse raced. "Any cohort of dear George's is most welcome here." The lie tasted bitter on her tongue. "I am Elizabeth Harlowe, George's intended." "Miss Harlowe." He spoke her name like a caress. "I hope we shall have the chance to further our acquaintance, if you can bear to escape the festivities again." Mischief lurked at the corner of his lush mouth. Despite herself, Elizabeth felt an answering smile touch her own lips. "I believe that could be arranged." Footsteps echoed suddenly down the corridor, and Peter melted back into the shadows just as George appeared around the corner. "Ah, here you are, my dear! Our guests are eager to begin the traditional toast." Oblivious to her racing heart, he drew her to her feet. "Come, let us join the celebration." Elizabeth cast a final, desperate glance over her shoulder, but Peter had vanished as mysteriously as he appeared. With a pang of regret, she let George usher her back into the ballroom, her mind reeling from the strange encounter. For the remainder of the interminable ball, she kept one eye trained about the room, hoping for another glimpse of the compelling stranger who seemed to see all the way into her weary soul. But Peter did not reappear to relieve the tedium of wedding pleasantries. When the last guests finally stumbled out in the hazy hours before dawn, Elizabeth had never felt more drained. Trudging up the grand staircase ahead of the servants still cleaning up, she pushed open the heavy door of her bedchamber. Stepping inside, she found a single red rose laid across her pillow, so dark a crimson it appeared almost black. Elizabeth lifted the bloom to her nose, breathing in its rich scent. There was no note, yet she knew at once it was from him. A secret token binding them in this fleeting moment of understanding, before propriety forced them apart again. She pressed the mysterious flower to her heart, unaware that elsewhere in the night Peter did the same. Though they inhabited different worlds, some ethereal thread connected them - if only for a few stolen hours. Whatever tomorrow brought, Elizabeth would carry the memory of this night and the stranger who saw her lonely soul. For now, that would have to sustain her. With a bittersweet smile, she laid the rose gently atop her vanity before sinking into exhausted slumber.

Chapter 4

Sunlight filtering through the curtains stirred Elizabeth from sleep. As consciousness returned, so did remembrance of the previous night's enchantment - and the maddening stranger responsible for the irrepressible hope now rising within her. Sitting up, her gaze fell on the black rose atop her vanity, proof she had not dreamt the charged encounter. She had scarcely exchanged two words with this Peter Maxwell, yet his piercing eyes haunted her still. With a determined sigh, she rose and dressed for the day ahead. Such fanciful notions were dangerous indulgences that would only wound her further. In one month she was to be George Wilson's bride, and that was immutable fact. Yet try as she might to quell thoughts of the mysterious Mr. Maxwell, they crept unbidden to the forefront of her mind throughout the day's wedding preparations. As the modiste circled her taking measurements for her gown, Elizabeth imagined she felt Peter's dark eyes watching her discerningly even from afar. When the florist presented elegant white rose centerpieces for her inspection, in her mind they transformed into the single passionate bloom Peter had left like a secret pact between them. Its heady perfume seemed to envelop her again whenever her resolve weakened. But she could not allow herself to be tempted astray from her duty, no matter how her lonely spirit might yearn for the connection she had glimpsed. So she banished all mention of the stranger from her speech and actions, though never from her private thoughts. Several afternoons later, Elizabeth sat in the parlor working on her embroidery - a task which chafed at her soul but was expected of a dutiful bride-to-be. Sunlight streamed in gaily at odds with her inner turmoil. A knock interrupted her gloomy thoughts, followed by the entrance of Reginald, the household butler. "Pardon me, miss. A Mr. Peter Maxwell is here requesting an audience." Elizabeth nearly fumbled her stitching at the name. Drawing a steadying breath, she forced nonchalance. "Please show him in." Moments later Peter appeared in the doorway, his tall form seeming to fill the room. Elizabeth hastily rose to her feet, pulse skittering. She had not allowed herself to hope he would seek her out again. "Mr. Maxwell. This is an unexpected pleasure." Peter bowed gracefully, but there was a roguish glint in his eye. "My sincere apologies for calling unannounced. I wished to pay my respects to the lovely bride-to-be." His smooth voice washed over Elizabeth like a physical caress. But she steeled herself against its effect. She could not let him sway her from the path of duty, however much he might make her long to. "You are too kind, sir. Please do sit and take tea." She gestured to the wingback chair opposite her own. Peter settled languidly into the proffered seat while Elizabeth busied herself pouring tea with slightly unsteady hands. But as she passed him the fine china cup, their fingers brushed, sending sparks dancing along her skin. She quickly withdrew her hand. "I must thank you again for the honor of your company at the ball," she said, willing her voice not to tremble. "It was a delight to make your acquaintance." "The delight was mine, Miss Harlowe." Peter's gaze bored into hers over the rim of his teacup. "I find you a most singular woman. Much more complex than you first appear." Elizabeth's breath caught at his boldly perceptive comment. Once again he seemed to see through to the truth of her that she kept so carefully hidden, like a flower blooming only in darkness. She glanced down, abashed. "You are too perceptive by half, Mr. Maxwell." "Please, call me Peter." He leaned intently towards her. "I speak only the truth that others are too blind to see." Elizabeth's heart thrilled at his words, yet deeper instincts warned he could be her undoing if she let him sway her from her principled path. Giving in to his allure would only lead to further sorrow. Setting down her teacup firmly on its saucer, she met his mesmerizing gaze. "You are most kind to take interest in me. But in one month's time, I shall be a married woman. My duty will then lie solely with my husband." Though the words burnt bitter on her tongue, they erected a necessary barrier between them. One she prayed would hold firmer than her fragile resolve. Peter's eyes darkened, but he simply inclined his head. "As you say, Miss Harlowe. You are to be admired for your steadfast loyalty. But if you ever have need of a friend, I remain at your service." Rising gracefully to his feet, he took her hand and raised it to his lips in a lingering kiss. As much as Elizabeth tried to calm her racing heart, she could not deny the connection kindling between them. It both thrilled and frightened her in its intensity. After seeing Peter to the door, she crumpled into her chair with a shaky sigh. This was dangerous ground she trod. He was not hers to covet. And the lure of throwing aside duty's chains to grasp fleeting happiness seemed reckless beyond measure. Yet the right path had brought her nothing but unending sorrow. Perhaps the only way to emerge from this shadowed forest was to follow the light in her soul, wherever it led. Even into the darkly magnetic eyes of a mysterious stranger. Over the next weeks, Peter called often upon their home, always presenting a respectable facade. But regularly their façade of cordial discourse fell away to reveal the fire simmering beneath, tangible as lightning. In his presence the world became charged with new possibility, the fetters binding Elizabeth loosening if only temporarily. When she was with him, iron certainties wavered and shifted like mirages. The lure was intoxicating - yet frightening in its power. She knew she stood poised upon a dangerous precipice which would alter her forever once leapt from. But the breathless plunge called to her soul too profoundly now to resist. One crystalline morning when dew still glittered on the grass, they found themselves alone again, the air ripe with unspoken longing. When Peter captured her hand unexpectedly, caution finally failed Elizabeth. "You must know," he murmured fervently, "I have never met another like you. Together we could live a grander life than either could alone. Say you feel the same, Elizabeth. Say you will be mine." His smoldering eyes seared her, igniting the reckless flame within that she had suppressed too long. This was her watershed moment. She could still retreat back into the refuge of convention, or abandon all for the breathtaking freedom she had dreamed of. Drawing a shuddering breath, she gave her answer. "My heart is already yours, my love. For you hold the key that awakens my spirit as none else ever has." They came together then like two stars colliding, all reticence burned away in an inferno more brilliant than any she had dared fathom. Elizabeth knew she could never return from this blazing pinnacle. The timid girl who had bowed obediently to duty was gone. All that remained was the woman standing radiant in the light of her own making, reckless heart untamed. She had stepped off the precipice forever. And though the landing lay veiled, she did not fear. The chains of others' expectations had melted away, leaving her unfettered and alive. Whatever came, she would face it boldly, guided only by the wild longings of her own soul. For one transcendent moment, she had touched true joy and freedom. That would sustain her through any darkness yet to come.

Chapter 5

Moonlight filtered through crystalline panes as Elizabeth sat awake long past decent hours, unable to find rest. Ever since that fateful morning in the garden when she had thrown caution aside and pledged herself to Peter, sleep evaded her. Her mind was too afire with possibilities, her skin prickling with the phantom warmth of his embrace. Propriety and her long-held principles seemed hazy as distant stars compared to the searing nova their joined souls had ignited within her now. A faint click at the window made her start. Peering outside, she could just discern a tall figure standing on the lawn below, face upturned expectantly. Joy leapt within her chest. Slipping on a robe, Elizabeth eased open the window. Peter's hushed voice drifted up out of the darkness. "My love, will you walk with me tonight?" Thrill tingling along her spine, Elizabeth nodded wordlessly and crept downstairs on silent feet. The great house was still around her, all its inhabitants asleep. She felt like a wayward spirit gliding through the shadows toward her divine appointment with the night. Peter's strong form materialized through the moonlight as she slipped out a servants' door into the garden. No words were needed as he took her hand and guided her into the silver-limned meadow beyond. To simply stand hand in hand beneath the stars felt deliciously wicked. Elizabeth's old life of dutiful conformity seemed to fall away until nothing was left but her pounding heart and the warm solidity of Peter's palm against hers. At length he turned to her, eyes searching her upturned face intently. "Have I awakened your spirit, my love?" His voice was husky, pleading. "I could not bear it if this were merely a fleeting fancy for you." Elizabeth reached up a hand to caress his cheek, thrilling at her own boldness. "You have unlocked something within me I thought long dead. My soul is bound irrevocably to yours now." Peter let out a shuddering breath and pulled her close against him. They stood entwined beneath the indifferent moon as it traced its endless path

– two flame-seared hearts daring to beat to their own rhythm. When finally Peter withdrew, reluctance shaded his features. "You should return before your absence is noted. But I will count the hours until we meet again." He pressed one last searing kiss to her willing lips before stepping back into the shadows of the trees. Elizabeth watched until even his silhouette faded from view, already longing for his return. So began their clandestine midnight rituals away from prying eyes. Whenever Peter tapped at her window, some primal instinct woke within Elizabeth, guiding her unerringly into his arms no matter how unseemly. They wandered moon-drenched meadows and groves of ancient trees, speaking passionately of life's injustice and those who dared resist it. Peter's world-weary wisdom called to her own wild spirit, too long tethered by expectations. With him, she could voice her most radical dreams of independence and self-determination. The future unfurled before them like some mythical landscape they would discover hand in hand. "Just imagine, my love," Peter whispered as they lay upon a midnight hillside gazing at the spangled heavens. "We could voyage beyond these constraining shores, behold wonders these small minds cannot fathom." His vivid visions painted a grand mosaic of what her life could become if only she would take the leap. The restless longing that had simmered inside Elizabeth blazed into a hungry flame. Peter rolled onto his side to gaze at her, his eyes twin meteors burning through the darkness. "Say you will turn your back on this society forever and be truly free with me. We will find a way, I swear it." Heart crashing against her ribs, Elizabeth opened her mouth to answer him in the affirmative. They would cast aside outdated mores and carve their own path, two fearless souls matched in fierce purpose. She would finally become who she was meant to be. But in the end, only strangled words emerged. "I want that with all that I am. But not yet...not yet..." Some last shackle of inner doubt bound her still to the familiar. If she spoke the words that could never be unsaid, the course of her life would shift irreparably in this very moment. Peter's face fell, but he pressed a fervent kiss to her knuckles. "When you are ready, my love. I will wait." But as he walked her back towards the great house where her cage sat waiting, the distance between them yawned palpably wide. The next evening as Elizabeth picked halfheartedly at her dinner under her family's oblivious gaze, she felt Peter's absence like an ache. She regretted her hesitation now with every fiber of her being. Unable to bear the stifling confinement any longer, she pleaded a headache and fled to her room. But no sooner had she changed for bed than a faint rap sounded at the window, unmistakable in its intent. Rushing to unlatch the pane, she inhaled sharply to see Peter perched on the ledge, eyes blazing. Without awaiting invitation, he slipped catlike into her bedchamber. "Forgive my intrusion, my love. I could not stay away a moment longer." Before she could respond, his mouth captured hers with a desperation that stole her breath and swept all objections from her mind. She clung to him like one dying of thirst to an oasis. When finally they broke apart, chests heaving, he kept her head cradled fiercely against his racing heart. "Say you are mine utterly, Elizabeth. I cannot bear living only in our midnight fantasies. Let us make them real." Elizabeth knew she stood at the crux of her destiny. This time, she did not hesitate. "Yes, my love. We will leave this place forever and live the life we have dreamed. I will follow you to the ends of the earth." A ferocious joy blazed up in Peter's eyes. With a ragged cry, he lifted her in his arms and spun her around the moonlit room. Their mingled laughter pealed out brightly, leaving no crevice for doubt or remorse. As he slowly set her down, Elizabeth knew she would never sleep again in this cold, cloistered room that had contained her youth. Tomorrow they would fly into their future, come what may. Peter pressed reverent kisses to her upturned face. "I swear to you, we will never look back. Our life begins on the morrow." Their whispered plans danced on the night air until the small hours when Peter scaled down the exterior wall with a final ardent look. Alone again, Elizabeth stood wrapped in her robe in the center of the room that had sheltered her since childhood. No sadness or regret pierced her; only soaring anticipation. She had made her choice at last. The cage door was flung open, and the fledgling about to take wing. Come the dawn, she and Peter would disappear into their new existence. For once not duty but the wild longings of her own heart would guide her path. Tonight had been her true wedding ceremony, pledging herself unreservedly as she never could to any ordinary suitor. Let society shake its collective head over the scandal. She would gladly bear that small cost for the unfettered life stretched out before her now, waiting only for her to claim it. Sinking onto her bed, she closed her eyes and dreamed of a smiling, dark-haired youth who grasped her hand confidently. "Come, my darling sister, it is time for your greatest adventure..."

Chapter 6

Dawn's rosy fingers crept across the room, stirring Elizabeth from fitful dreams. As slumber retreated, so did the intoxicating visions of the night prior. In their absence, cold reality crept in. Today she was meant to become George Wilson's bride. Sitting up with a gasp, Elizabeth clutched the bedsheets as the walls seemed to close in around her. How could she have let Peter's tempting promises distract her from the inevitability of this day? They had been no more than fantasy - dangerous, beguiling fantasy. A tentative knock came at the door - her mother and sisters bustling in eagerly to help dress her for the ceremony. Their cheerful bustle battered against Elizabeth's pounding heart. She must not reveal a hint of her inner turmoil. Numbly, she stood motionless as the maid laced her into her wedding gown. The exquisite satin bodice felt like hands clutching at her throat. She averted her eyes from her wan reflection crowned in lace. Somehow she survived the carriage ride to the village chapel through sheer force of will. All around her, guests mingled happily in the Autumn sunlight - while she remained locked in her private anguish. It was not too late. She could still turn and flee this fate, if only she could find the courage... But then the organ swelled within, and her father took her elbow to lead her firmly down the aisle. Step by helpless step, her choices fell away until all that remained was the altar and George waiting to claim her. Elizabeth moved through the ceremony in a daze, the vicar's dull intonations sounding far away. None but she and Peter knew her vows were empty words with no power to bind her. Only at the final moment did the magnitude of it all crash over her. As George leaned in expectantly to seal their union, she averted her face in panic. His kiss landed awkwardly on her cheek before she schooled her features to careful neutrality. If anyone noted her odd behavior, they hid it well behind sunny smiles and applause. As Elizabeth took George's arm to process back down the aisle, she kept her eyes trained straight ahead over the sea of approving faces. The deed was done. She was now Mrs. George Wilson in the eyes of the world. The wedding breakfast passed in a blur of cloying scents, clinking glassware, and endless hollow pleasantries. When finally the last guests took their leave, Elizabeth nearly collapsed in exhaustion. The day had leeched what little spirit she still possessed. George's hand at her elbow made her flinch involuntarily. Oblivious, he smiled down at her with patient fondness. "Come, my dear. It is time we retire and commence our new life together." Elizabeth swallowed back a wave of nausea. She had no choice but to follow where honor and duty commanded. Head bowed beneath her suddenly cumbersome bridal veil, she accompanied her new husband obediently upstairs. But as they reached the bedchamber door, her courage failed entirely. Wrenching free of George's light hold, she blurted some excuse about changing from her dress and fled down the corridor into an empty guest room. Slamming and bolting the door behind her, she tore the suffocating veil from her head with shaking hands. The pristine bed and polished furnishings of this unused space only emphasized the sterility of the life now awaiting her. Collapsing to the floor, Elizabeth finally allowed the tears to come. They were not merely for her lost freedom, but for dear gentle George whose happiness she could never truly share. He deserved a wife who could love him fully, not one whose heart pulled inexorably elsewhere. She wept until night fell and a hesitant knock came at the door. "Lizzy?" George's concerned voice carried through the heavy wood. "Was today too taxing for you, my dear? We can wait to fully join our lives until you are ready." His selfless patience wrenched Elizabeth's heart anew. George was a good man. In time, perhaps she could even grow to love him after a fashion. She owed it to them both to try. Drying her eyes, she unbolted the door. George still hovered there looking worried, but his expression softened as she managed a tremulous smile. "Forgive me, darling. My nerves simply got the better of me today." She reached for his hand. "But I am ready now." Allowing him to lead her back down the shadowed corridor, Elizabeth bid a silent farewell to the girl who had dreamed wild dreams of freedom and adventure. Tonight she would perform her final duty as a proper wife should. But as George's fingers fumbled gently with the fastenings of her gown, she squeezed her eyes tight and saw only Peter's face hovering above her. The days trickled by in monotonous routine. By night, Elizabeth lay stiffly beside her sleeping husband pretending not to feel the cold space between them. By day she played the dutiful wife, slowly growing accustomed to her new privileges and responsibilities. Outwardly she knew she appeared content. Yet inwardly her soul crept numbly through colorless hours, awaiting some reprieve she could no longer define. Of Peter there had been no word or sign since her wedding. She told herself that was best - a clean break to avoid further temptation. But loneliness gnawed at her nonetheless. One dreary evening as rain lashed the windows, Elizabeth sought solitude in the library, running her fingers idly over leather spines. Her former passion for reading had abandoned her along with all other girlish joys. A slip of paper wedged between two books suddenly caught her eye. Heart lurching, she plucked it free with trembling fingers. Unfolding the note, she instantly recognized Peter's bold scrawl. My Dearest Elizabeth, Not a moment passes I do not think of you. The memory of your touch haunts me ceaselessly. Say you will meet me at our spot beneath the old oak tonight if your heart still burns for mine as mine does for yours. I will wait all night if I must. Yours eternal, Peter Elizabeth's pulse roared in her ears. How easy it would be to steal into the night again, back to those moonlit meadows where they had spun their private dreams away from watchful eyes. But the tendril of ivy engraved on her new signet ring seemed to burn reproachfully on her finger, binding her to duty's path once more. As much as her soul might ache for what could have been, she had made her choice. Blinded by tears, she watched the note blacken and curl in the library grate. Her dreams turned to ash, but honor remained intact. George deserved at least that, as did any children they might someday have. Yet she had loved the Elizabeth who burned so brightly in Peter's company - more than the pale ghost she had become. That Elizabeth she must mourn tonight, along with the man who had awakened her. At the stroke of midnight, she slipped from the house shrouded in black, a single red rose clasped in her hand. The grounds were silvered under a full moon as she made her way to the ancient oak. Laying the bloom at the tree's gnarled roots, she bowed her head and let the tears flow freely. Here she buried all lingering hopes and might-have-beens. The chill autumn wind would erase even this small token by dawn's light. Turning her back on what could never be, Elizabeth walked slowly back towards the cold set of rooms that comprised her new cage. From this night onward, she must harden her heart to all childish fancies. But just as she reached the terrace, she glimpsed a lone figure on horseback silhouetted at the edge of the estate. He raised a hand in silent farewell before disappearing into the murk. Elizabeth's breath caught in her throat. Even now, Peter continued keeping vigil over her like some brooding guardian angel. Perhaps she need not bar the doors of her heart entirely just yet. The memories at least she could cling to in the colorless days to come. Wrapping her shawl tighter against the night air, she slipped quietly back inside. The house was still around her, its sleeping occupants oblivious to her midnight requiem. She had laid her ghosts to rest; no one need ever share in her lingering sorrow. In the sanctuary of her room, she unpinned her hair and let it fall long about her shoulders like the girl she once was. Tonight, for a few precious hours until dawn, she would permit herself to dwell in what might have been. Tomorrow the dutiful wife would resume her placid mask. But tonight, she would allow the dream to live on just a little longer within the haven of her heart. Somewhere, she liked to think Peter was gazing up at that same moon, knowing its distant light still shone upon her. Linked by memory and muted longing, under separate night skies they kept their own small vigil. And though their paths had diverged, each could still feel the phantom tread of the other's footsteps somewhere out in the dark. For a few stolen hours more, that spectral connection persisted.

Come daylight, they would go their separate ways - one path toward passion, the other resigned to duty. But perhaps someday

Chapter 7

Sunlight filtered through gossamer curtains, rousing Elizabeth from restless dreams. For a moment she forgot where she was, expecting to open her eyes to her familiar childhood bedroom. Instead, the unfamiliar elegant furnishings of the honeymoon suite met her gaze. Today was her last as a single woman before becoming George Wilson's bride. The thought chilled her blood. Rising mechanically, Elizabeth moved through the motions of dressing and breakfasting with the staff bustling eagerly around her. But even the savory meal turned to ashes in her mouth. In just a few short hours, her freedoms would be lost forever. The bridal preparations passed by in a blur - floral aromas, rustling silk, her mother's delighted fussing over each detail. Yet through it all, Elizabeth felt like a prisoner awaiting the hangman's noose. At last, she was enclosed alone in the carriage to make the short journey to the village chapel. Villagers lined the routes tossing flower petals in celebration, cheering for the young couple's bright future. Elizabeth kept her gaze fixed straight ahead. None but she knew the true turmoil roiling beneath her placid mask. She had come so close to fleeing this fate with Peter. Now escape was impossible; she must accept her sentence with dignity. The chapel doors loomed up before her, a portal into the next phase of her life - one which would be irreversible once crossed. As Elizabeth took her father's proffered arm, she summoned every ounce of poise she had been taught since girlhood. But just as she made to set foot over the threshold, a shriek shattered the festive air. "Liar! Scoundrel!" A lithe figure in scandalous scarlet dress had broken through the crowd, eyes aflame beneath lush dark curls. Elizabeth froze in shock as the woman stormed straight for her, venom distorting her otherwise beautiful features. "Do not take another step, you fool!" She rounded furiously on Elizabeth whose father was attempting to interject. "This blackguard you think to marry is naught but a callous seducer!" Dazed murmurs rippled through the gathering crowd. The venomous woman pointed an accusatory finger at Elizabeth. "Ask him about Mary, the tavern girl he wooed and ruined without a second thought!" The name jolted Elizabeth from her stupor, kindling foreboding recognition. She turned slowly to George who had gone deathly pale. "What is this woman talking about?" she asked in a strangled whisper. "Who is Mary?" George's mouth opened and closed helplessly. Before he could find any words, the scarlet-clad woman gave a scornful laugh. "Cat got your tongue, George? Shall I tell her myself then?" She turned her blazing eyes back to Elizabeth. "He won poor sweet Mary's heart with gifts andpretty words, had his way with her, then cast her off to raise their babe alone." A collective gasp arose. George seemed to wilt beneath the judgmental stares, but still no denial passed his lips. Only pained guilt. Elizabeth's mind reeled. Dear gentle George, a rake? She had known he sowed some wild oats before their courtship, but this? Bile rose in her throat. She thought she had known his character to the core. The woman's fury subsided into righteous vindication. With a tug of her cloak, she revealed a tiny dark-haired boy clutching her skirts. "This is Andrew. The boy your betrothed left me to care for alone in poverty and disgrace." At the sight, the last traces of color drained from George's face. He swayed on his feet, all pretensions crumbling before the child's uncanny resemblance to him. Elizabeth's pity warred with revulsion. George's abandoned son - flesh of his flesh - stared up at them with innocent curiosity, oblivious to his role in ruining this day. In that moment, she knew with cold certainty she could not join her life to this man. Wrenching her arm from George's limp grasp, she backed away with a cry. "I cannot... I cannot..." Whirling, she fled blindly from the chapel, heedless of the stares drilling into her back. The surrounding vista swam dizzyingly through her tears as she ran on and on. At last her foot caught on an abandoned wagon rut and she collapsed hard to her knees in a meadow. A ragged sob tore from her throat. Her life lay in shattered pieces around her, her reputation ruined. But the only sweetness she felt was relief at evading a marriage built on lies. She stayed there until the distant church bells tolled the hour when she was meant to have become George Wilson's bride. Hugging her knees, she let her tears mingle with the wildflowers. Everything once certain had dissolved to chaos in one fell swoop. As the sun dipped low, Elizabeth's thoughts turned reluctantly back toward the village. She could not linger here overnight unchaperoned. Slowly she picked herself up, brushing the dirt from her now-ruined gown. But which way should she turn? The village with its inevitable scorn, or the open road leading who knew where? She wavered indecisively as dusk deepened. A horse's whinny in the distance decided her. Turning her back on the chapel bells' mocking echoes, she struck out for the narrow ribbon of road visible through the trees. Each step away from the life she had known felt like a small freedom. Darkness fully enveloped her, but she walked on as if in a daze. If anyone came searching, they would assume she had returned home chastened. Not imagine the spurned bride wandering the night in her tattered finery. When fatigue finally forced her off the road to rest, Elizabeth curled up beneath a tree and wept again, this time for herself. She was well and truly ruined now. Even her family would surely turn her out. Perhaps she could hire herself out as a seamstress or governess in some far-flung place where her disgrace was unknown. At least then she could support herself honorably, however reduced and lonely her life would become. Lost in melancholy thoughts, she did not notice the approaching horse until it was nearly upon her. Looking up with a frightened gasp, she saw only a looming masculine silhouette in the moonlight. "I mean you no harm, miss," said a blessedly familiar voice as the rider hastily dismounted, hands raised peaceably. "Are you hurt?" "Peter?" she whispered, hardly trusting the evidence of her own senses. But as he crouched down, the beloved features became unmistakeable in the silvery light. "What are you doing out here alone?" Worry creased his brow as Peter helped her gently to her feet. As Elizabeth wavered there, the events of the day crashed over her anew. A ragged sob escaped her as she collapsed into his arms. "Oh Peter, everything is ruined!" Between heaving breaths, she recounted the terrible events at the chapel - her abject public humiliation and subsequent flight. By the time she finished, she was trembling violently in Peter's embrace. He made no immediate reply, simply held her close and stroked her hair until her tears slowed. At length, he pulled back just far enough meet her eyes, his own gaze serious. "You were right to flee such deception, Elizabeth. Though I wish I could have spared you this pain, perhaps there is purpose in it." He took a deep breath, as if steeling himself. "Come with me tonight as we once planned. We shall find a new life together, somewhere no scornful eyes can follow." He reached up to cup her cheek tenderly. "I yet have savings from my seafaring days. Enough to book us passage out of England, if you are willing." Elizabeth's heart stilled, then quickened. Not twenty-four hours ago, this offer would have thrilled her. But the comfort and familiarity of home still held some appeal, even one stripped of finery and privilege. "Could I not simply take up some quiet occupation here?" she asked uncertainly. "Fleeing the country seems rather extreme..." Hurt flashed across Peter's features. "You would return then to live beneath the judgmental eyes of those who condemn you?" He studied her intently, as if glimpsing her anew. "Or are your dreams of freedom extinguished?" Stung by the accusation, Elizabeth jerked back. "Of course they are not! But have I not sacrificed enough today without losing all I have ever known? Can you not be content here with me?" Peter raked a hand roughly through his hair. "I cannot linger in this place that has brought us such grief. I beg you, Elizabeth, do not spurn this chance for liberation." His eyes burned with fervent urgency, but also desperation. "We can find meaning together, far from these paltry lives." Elizabeth wavered, tears threatening again. "Just allow me some time to think..." But Peter had already withdrawn into himself, his outstretched hand falling dejectedly to his side. When he looked at her again, the warmth in his eyes had frosted over. "So be it."

Chapter 8

A bone-chilling breeze stirred Elizabeth from her fitful slumber. Sitting up on the hard wooden bench, she winced as every muscle protested. After Peter had stormed off last night, she'd taken refuge in this abandoned shepherd's hut rather than face potential scorn in the village. Pale dawn light filtered through chinks in the walls. She had passed her first night as a ruined woman. The full weight of that now crashed over her, bringing tears that could not warm her shivering frame. A scraping at the door made her scramble to her feet. Had someone from town come searching? She cast about for somewhere to hide just as the door creaked slowly open. Framed in the entryway stood the woman from yesterday, the one who had shattered Elizabeth's wedding. Mary, Peter had called her. She was wrapped in a threadbare shawl, any residual fury now absent from her pretty features. "Forgive the intrusion," she said neutrally. "I saw you enter here last night. Only wanted to ensure you were unharmed." Elizabeth blinked in surprise at the uncharacteristic concern. In truth, she had feared the woman might return to berate her again. "That is kind of you. I have had better lodgings but am adequately sheltered." Mary nodded, hesitation plain on her face. She glanced behind her furtively before stepping inside the hut and closing the door. Taking a deep breath, she met Elizabeth's puzzled stare. "In truth, I came to speak with you privately. What I revealed yesterday was but half the story." She wrung her hands, seeming to choose each word with care. "George Wilson wronged me, yes. But another man shares the burden of truth." A sense of foreboding rose in Elizabeth's chest. "What do you mean?" Pity shone from Mary's eyes. "You seem a good woman. I should hate for you to be deceived as I was." She reached tentatively to clasp Elizabeth's hand. "Beware Peter Maxwell. His charms hide a darker nature." Elizabeth's breath caught sharply. She tried to pull away, but Mary held firm. "Hear me out," she implored. "I know Peter's allure - his magnetic air. I too once mistook it for virtuous. But he wooed me only as diversion from his true aim - my friend George's betrothed." The words sank like stones in Elizabeth's gut. She searched Mary's face for any trace of dishonesty, but saw only grave sincerity. "That cannot be," she whispered weakly. "Why should I believe you over him?" Sympathy filled Mary's eyes. "I understand your resistance. But reflect - did Peter not first pay court after you were promised to George? Does he not press you to cast aside all else for him?" At Elizabeth's conflicted nod, she squeezed her hand. "You are not his first such conquest, nor his last I fear." Elizabeth's thoughts spun drunkenly. She recalled Peter's ardent pursuit even after her engagement was announced. How he had seemed to materialize conveniently whenever her fortitude wavered. Was it all calculated pretense? Shakily, she pulled away from Mary's grasp and turned her back, seeking composure. This woman had already proven truthful about George's dishonor. What cause had she to lie about the rest? Behind her, Mary spoke gently. "I tell you this not from bitterness, but womanly compassion. Peter Maxwell nearly ruined me, but you need not share that fate." Slow footsteps retreated towards the door. "My sincerest hope is you find the life you seek. But I urge you - seek it wisely." The latch clicked softly, leaving Elizabeth alone again in a world upended. She sank back down on the rough bench, Mary's revelations swirling dizzyingly in her mind. Facts she had tried ignoring now glared accusingly - Peter's mysterious past, his convenient appearances when she was vulnerable, the secrecy of their trysts. Had it all been choreographed manipulation by a skilled rake? Hot tears coursed down Elizabeth's cheeks. She had spurned convention and reputation for a beguiling fantasy - one perhaps constructed solely to serve Peter's base appetites. The betrayal cut crushingly deep. Worse yet, Mary had hinted at other victims. How many other hearts had Peter ensnared and discarded? How foolish Elizabeth had been to believe herself special! Blindly she stumbled from the hut into the morning sun, welcoming its warmth on her tear-stained face. The countryside lay before her now, empty of promise or refuge. She was well and truly alone. Her flight from the village had burned all bridges. Returning home was impossible, even if her family would still accept her. Which left only an uncertain future making her own way however she could. Resolutely, Elizabeth turned her steps down the lane leading away from town. Each stride built distance between herself and the credulous girl she had been. She was wiser now and would not again be swayed by pretty promises or smoldering eyes. Vengeful anger kindled inside her, burning away the last futile tears. She had been deceived by two false men, but the only ruin she would accept was that written by her own hand. Let society scorn her choices - at least they were hers alone. The road stretched ahead, endless and unknown. Elizabeth squared her shoulders and continued onward, leaving the shattered remains of who she had been behind her. What lay ahead only destiny could reveal. But she would walk forward proudly on her own terms, beholden to no one. The future unfurled before her, frightening in its freedom, but hers to claim. Raising her face to the sunlight, Elizabeth closed her eyes and whispered a silent promise to the girl who had dreamed of more. She would find meaning and purpose without reliance on any man. When she opened her eyes again, the horizon seemed to shine a little brighter.

Chapter 9

Dawn's rosy fingers crept over the cottage windowsill, rousing Elizabeth from restless dreams. For a moment, she forgot where she was, expecting to open her eyes to the familiar comfort of her childhood bedroom. Instead, the quaint furnishings of her grandmother's cottage met her gaze. Today marked one full week she and Peter had taken refuge here, fled from society's scornful gaze. One week since she had thrown caution to the wind and bound her fate to Peter's, for better or worse. Rising quietly so as not to wake Peter, Elizabeth moved to stand by the window overlooking the secluded garden. A light mist still clung to the ground, matching the hazy uncertainty in her heart. Had she acted rashly, allowing passion to overrule reason? Peter remained in many ways a stranger to her. What truly lay beneath his worldly charms and flattering words? As if conjured by her thoughts, she heard him stirring behind her. Turning with a smile she hoped did not appear too strained, she met his drowsy gaze. "Good morning, my love. I hope you slept well." Peter blinked groggily and beckoned her over with a lazy grin. "I always sleep well with you by my side." He drew her down and silenced any reply with a long, slow kiss. By the time he released her, lips kiss-swollen and color high, her doubts had scattered momentarily. But later, as she prepared a modest breakfast while Peter stepped outside to chop firewood, Elizabeth's misgivings crept back in. She had not forgotten the mystery woman's startling confrontation on what was meant to be her wedding day. The venomous accusations still haunted her, much as she wanted to dismiss them as jealous slander. What had Peter's life been before her? He often regaled her with thrilling tales of his travels and adventures abroad, but revealed little of past loves or heartbreaks. Jealously gnawed at her, try as she might to suppress it. Surely a man as worldly and charming as Peter had indulged in dalliances before her. But were there those who still mourned his loss? Those whose trust he had betrayed?

31

The pound of the axe outside paused, followed by approaching footsteps. Elizabeth smoothed her features hastily as Peter entered, cheeks flushed from exertion. His eyebrows lifted quizzically at her strained smile. "Is all well, my love? You seem troubled." "It is nothing," she replied lightly, turning aside to ladle porridge into bowls. But Peter came up behind her and turned her gently to face him, a furrow between his brows. "Come now, I know that look. What bothers you, Elizabeth?" She studied the rough floorboards, words sticking in her throat. At length she forced herself to meet his searching gaze. "On our ruined wedding day, the woman who confronted us...Mary. She made certain claims about you. I cannot banish them from my thoughts." Peter's expression shuttered. He released her and took a half-step back. "And you would give credence to the bitter lies of a jealous woman over the man who has devoted himself wholly to you?" There was an unfamiliar hardness to his voice that gave Elizabeth pause. But she had come this far and could not retreat. "She seemed quite sincere in her concern. Tell me honestly, did you...court her as you did me?" "Court her? Never!" Peter's laugh jarred hollowly in the small cottage. "We were naught but passing acquaintances. The poor girl became infatuated, but I spurned her advances." He moved to cup Elizabeth's face entreatingly. "You must believe me, my love. My heart has only and always belonged to you." His eyes burned with fervent conviction, and Elizabeth felt her reservations crumbling. Laying her hands over Peter's where they cradled her cheeks, she managed a tremulous smile. "Forgive me, darling. I know not why I gave such accusations any thought." She turned her face to press a fervent kiss into his palm. "Of course I believe you over a bitter stranger. Let us speak no more of this." The lingering shadows in Peter's eyes lifted and he drew her into a crushing embrace. "Wise lady, to put your faith in my love. I vow I shall never give you cause to doubt." His voice was thick with passion. And Elizabeth let his ardor wash away the last of her idle misgivings. Perhaps she did not fully know his past, but they had a future to build together. She would not jeopardize that for unfounded gossip. After they had broken their fast, Peter announced he was going into the village on errands. Though she knew tongues likely still wagged about their mysterious presence, Elizabeth longed desperately for some change of scenery after days cooped up indoors. "Might I join you, just this once?" She fixed him with her most entreating gaze. "I promise to keep to myself and avoid any unpleasant talk." Peter hesitated, but finally relented with a chuckle. "I suppose I cannot keep you locked away forever, as much as I might wish it. Just stay close and do not engage." Donning her plainest frock with the hood drawn low, Elizabeth clung to Peter's side as they traversed the muddy lane into town. She kept her eyes downcast, evading the curious glances of villagers going about their business. But it was heavenly just to breath fresh air and hear new voices around her. Peter left her on a bench outside the mercantile while he went inside to purchase supplies. Unable to resist, Elizabeth let her hooded gaze drift over the bustling market lane. Vendors called out their wares, women bartered for goods, and ragged children darted underfoot. It was all so wonderfully lively compared to the seclusion of home. One figure in particular caught her eye - a lady close to her own age, though far more richly dressed. Something about the proud bearing struck a chord of familiarity. As if sensing her stare, the lady turned. Elizabeth gasped. Mary! The woman from her ruined wedding! Alarm roused in Elizabeth even as Mary's eyes narrowed in recognition. Glancing hastily around, Mary circled through the market crowds toward Elizabeth's bench, coming to stand imperiously before her. "Come to gloat at the wreckage you have made?" Elizabeth kept her voice low but could not contain her surge of resentment. This was the woman who had shattered her world with poisonous words. To her surprise, Mary had the grace to look abashed. "I know you owe me no kindness. But I wish to make amends, if you will permit it." At Elizabeth's wary silence, she sighed. "Walk with me a short way. Grant me a chance to explain." Curiosity warred with simmering anger in Elizabeth's breast. But finally she nodded tersely and followed Mary down a narrow alley away from prying eyes. When they had reached a secluded corner, Mary turned to her somberly. "After our last encounter, I was racked with guilt. Whatever the truth of it, I played some role in your misfortunes and wish to atone." She spread her hands entreatingly. "I know nothing I say can undo the past. But I want to offer a friendly ear, from one woman to another." The simple kindness cleaved through Elizabeth's resentment, and she felt herself softening. "I appreciate the gesture, Miss...?" "Please, just Mary." The other woman managed a trembling smile. "I will not claim innocense. George Wilson did me grievous wrong, and I responded in anger. But one good act does not justify another." Her eyes grew distant with remorse before focusing intently on Elizabeth again. "Especially if I have exposed you to harm." A chill crept down Elizabeth's spine at Mary's ominous tone. "Whatever do you mean?" Mary's gaze turned pitying. "You are here with Peter Maxwell now, are you not?" At Elizabeth's instinctive nod, she pressed her hand urgently. "Then you must be careful. Peter has a shadowed past - one with many victims, myself included." Elizabeth jerked back as if scalded, panic rising. "No. I do not wish to hear this." She glanced around desperately for some escape from the conversation she now fervently regretted. But Mary followed, keeping her voice low and intense. "Please, you must listen! I tell you this not from spite, but concern for a fellow woman. Guard your heart, Elizabeth. Peter Maxwell is not who he seems." Just then, Elizabeth spotted Peter exiting the mercantile, and relief crashed over her. Turning a glare on Mary, she hissed, "I appreciate your concern, but I must go. Do not hound me with these accusations again." Without a backward glance, she rushed to Peter's side, linking her arm firmly through his. But as they walked briskly from town, the chilling seed of doubt had been planted. Had she aligned herself completely to a man with dark secrets? Only time would tell...

Chapter 10

The cottage door slammed, making Elizabeth jump where she sat tensely waiting at the rough-hewn table. Peter stormed in, dropping his parcels on the counter with more force than necessary. His face was like a thundercloud. "I warned you not to engage in town," he bit out. "But no, you spoke at length with that venomous viper Mary, did you not?" Elizabeth shrank back, which only seemed to fuel his temper. Peter paced the small kitchen like a caged animal, raking his hands through his hair. "Tell me, what lies did she feed you this time? Has she turned you against me with her serpent's tongue?" His eyes, usually so warm, were cold and hard as he loomed over Elizabeth. Shaking, she rose so they were at least on equal footing. "Do not take that tone with me, Peter," she managed to reply steadily. "I am your partner, not some pet to command." Peter looked momentarily taken aback. The icy fury simmered down into something more akin to desperation. Still, Elizabeth kept her spine rigid. She would not be cowed, no matter how chaotic her inner doubts. "You are right. I should not have lost my temper." Peter ran a hand wearily over his face. "It is only...the thought of losing you undoes me, Elizabeth. Your love is all I have." At his forlorn expression, the last of Elizabeth's anger melted away. Perhaps she had been too swayed by the bitter words of his ex-lover. With a deep breath, she closed the space between them and took Peter's hands in hers. "You have not lost me, darling. But I need you to be honest with me." She gazed up steadily into his conflicted eyes. "Mary said troubling things about your past. I cannot simply ignore them. Help me understand the truth." Peter's throat worked, emotions warring across his countenance. For a moment she thought he would refuse. But finally he gave a brusque nod and led her to sit beside him on the cot. He stared down at their entwined hands for a long moment before beginning haltingly. "You know I have led an...unconventional life. But much of what Mary knows, she has only gleaned from rumors." He finally raised his eyes to meet Elizabeth's uneasily. "I was not always the man you know. I have made grave mistakes, treated certain ladies ill in my youth. But I swear to you, since our first meeting I have been utterly devoted." The raw sincerity in his voice convinced Elizabeth as mere excuses would not have. Still, she gently pressed for more. "What sort of mistakes? I only want to understand where you have come from." With a heavy sigh, Peter delved further into his shadowed past. He spoke of losing his parents young and learning to survive on the harsh streets. Falling in with dangerous company, losing his way for a time. Dabbling in vices to dull his pain. "I was selfish and reckless in my dealings with women. I saw only conquests, not human hearts. But when I met you..." His voice roughened with emotion. "You were the light that showed me a better path. I strive to become the man you deserve." He lowered his head ashamedly. "I know I can never atone for my youthful sins. I can only endeavor to live nobly going forward. With you as my guiding star." When he hesitantly met her eyes again, they shone with remorse and devotion in equal measure. In that moment, Elizabeth saw the wounded boy beneath the confident exterior. Her heart ached at the trials he had endured alone. Impulsively, she drew him into a fierce embrace. "Thank you for entrusting me with this difficult truth," she whispered against his hair. "You are not defined by past mistakes, but the man you are today." Drawing back, she cradled his beloved face between her hands. "We all stumble in darkness at times. What matters is having the courage to follow the light when it comes. You have walked that hard road nobly." Peter grasped her wrists almost desperately. "You have always seen the best in me, even when I could not. I vow to spend my life proving worthy of your love." Leaning in, he rested his forehead tenderly against hers. The past and its shadows fell away, leaving only this haven they had built together. Whatever trials lay ahead, they would face arm in arm, hearts entwined. Over the next weeks and months, such moments of quiet intimacy wove into a new life. At times Elizabeth grew restless in their isolated refuge, longing for society or a less confining future. But Peter always eased her misgivings with kisses and pretty words until she forgot what had troubled her. When nagging doubts resurfaced, she pushed them firmly aside. Her lot was cast now for good or ill. Each day she rose to fulfill her role as helpmate and lover faithfully, letting the rough comfort of the cottage and Peter's passion fill the empty spaces within her. If at times her soul cried out for something more, she muffled its voice. Until one crisp autumn morning when Peter announced over breakfast his need to journey north to settle an old debt. "I should only be gone a week at most. Think of it as an opportunity to visit freely with your grandmother without me underfoot." He smiled teasingly, but Elizabeth felt only a swell of panic. "Cannot I join you? I should not care to remain here alone so long." Peter shook his head indulgently. "The roads are too treacherous at this time of year, especially for coach travel. I promise the time shall fly swiftly, my love." Seeing her crestfallen expression, Peter drew her onto his lap, nuzzling the sensitive spot behind her ear until she shuddered. "Absence only makes the heart grow fonder, sweet. And gives us something to anticipate." His lips found the hollow of her throat, effectively ending any protests. After he had loved her thoroughly, leaving her spent and sated, all her arguments for accompanying him seemed distant trivialities. Surely she could manage a few nights alone. The next morning Elizabeth bid Peter farewell bravely before watching his horse disappear down the lane. But no sooner had he gone than the empty cottage seemed to close in around her. Though usually occupied with chores, now the hours dragged endlessly with only her needlework and books for company. By the third day, she felt herself unravelling without Peter's anchoring presence. Everything around her took on a sinister pall. What secrets might he be keeping on this solitary journey? Was she a fool to so easily entrust him with her happiness? That evening she found herself at her grandmother's door, craving any friendly company to quiet her mind's troubling turn. Though Adeline seemed surprised by the unannounced visit, she welcomed Elizabeth in warmly. Over hot tea laced liberally with brandy, her grandmother's gentle queries drew out Elizabeth's darker thoughts - how stifled she often felt, and the worries that sometimes gnawed regarding Peter's devotion. It was a relief to give voice to them after so long silent. "There are always seasons of doubt in any marriage," Adeline said thoughtfully once Elizabeth had poured out her heart. "But only you can decide if this union still brings your spirit joy, or drains it entirely." She patted Elizabeth's hand. "Trust yourself. No choice that honors your true self is ever wrong, even if difficult." The simple wisdom bolstered Elizabeth's flagging spirit. As she returned home through the woods, she felt calmer and more sure-footed than she had in ages. Her life was hers to live freely, so long as she possessed courage and will. The next days passed swiftly until Peter returned flushed with high spirits. "Next time you must join me on my travels, my love. The open road stirs the spirit!" Though Elizabeth smiled and greeted him warmly, she made no promises this time. A newfound kernel of selfhood was taking root within her. If Peter noticed her new reticence, for now he did not press. But change was on the horizon - she could feel it in her bones. That night as she lay wakeful studying the ceiling beams, the choice crystallized before her. She could cling here forever to the parody of a life they had built and the safety Peter represented. Or dare to take up her own path, wherever it may lead. Elizabeth had tasted fleeting freedom once before in Peter's company and knew in her soul she thirsted for more. As much as she cared for him, a part of her would always chafe at the confines of this isolated existence. She was meant for so much more than waiting dutifully in some remote cottage. Turning to look at Peter sleeping soundly beside her, Elizabeth slowly traced the line of his bearded jaw. She would always treasure the refuge they had found together for a time. He had opened her eyes to bold new possibilities and been patient mentor to her wild spirit. But she sensed now their seasons were shifting, their paths diverging. To pretend otherwise would only breed secret resentment that poisoned what affection still flowed between them. Better to make a clean break now with generosity on both sides. She could venture forth on her own with head held high, taking strength from the ways their union had matured her. And Peter would remain safe here, the haven he had never known in his troubled youth. They would both have the freedom to write their next chapters unfettered. Elizabeth's decision settled upon her with calm certainty. Come morning light, she would gently tell Peter her intention to leave this place and make her own way. It would not be easy parting from one who yet held so much of her heart. But she must be true to the voice inside urging her on towards horizons unseen. Turning onto her side, she closed her eyes and let sleep overtake her at last. Dreamless rest carried her into dawn and her new beginning.

Chapter 11

Elizabeth stared at her pale reflection in the full-length mirror as the maid secured the final silk-covered buttons down the back of her wedding gown. The dress was exquisite - ivory satin overlaid with delicate lace, cinched at the waist before flowing out in a graceful train. It had been tailored to her exact measurements, but now hung upon her thin frame like an extravagant disguise. A farce for the farce of a marriage she was about to enter. Once the maid adjusted the veil just so and scurried off, Elizabeth found herself suddenly alone in her childhood bedroom, mere minutes before she was meant to leave for the chapel. Outside these walls, the household bustled with frenetic last-minute preparations. Inside lay only stifling silence. Elizabeth's eyes burned with unshed tears as she stared helplessly at this opulent trap about to snare her. Perhaps it would not feel so suffocating once said and done. She could slip into the role of demure wife as society demanded, don this exquisite costume daily until it became a second skin. Until the joyful girl who had spun in meadows perished entirely. A brusque knock interrupted her spiraling thoughts. "Lizzy?" her mother called through the door. "The carriages have arrived, my dear. It's time." Each footstep closer to that waiting carriage felt weighted with lead. This was wrong. She could not fade voicelessly into a passionless union. Not while her spirit still cried out for freedom. At the top of the staircase, Elizabeth froze. Below, the great front doors stood open to the sunny June day, a line of elegant coaches waiting to convey her to her new gilded cage. Her mother and sisters had already descended, but her limbs would not obey, rooting her to the spot. She should turn back, flee to her room and climb out the window as she had once as a girl late for lessons. Anything to evade the death knell ringing her today under the guise of wedding bells. But she had come this far playing the compliant bride-to-be. Such radical defiance would heap disgrace upon her family now. Elizabeth teetered agonizingly on the cusp of revolt, every muscle tensed... Commotion outside broke the paralysis of indecision. Men's raised voices rang sharply from the drive. Elizabeth scarcely dared to hope they heralded some miraculous deliverance. Heavy footsteps pounded up the stairs, and the butler's normally implacable face appeared, uncharacteristically flustered as he halted before her. "Pardon the intrusion, miss. But we have just received an urgent rider from the village. It seems Mr. Maxwell has absconded unexpectedly. His lodgings lie empty." For a stunned moment, Elizabeth could not process the meaning behind the hastily relayed news. Peter was...gone? Vanished without even a farewell on the very day he had pledged to rescue her from this fate? As the revelation sank in, her legs nearly gave way in a surge of anguish and disbelief. After all his pretty words and fervent promises, he had abandoned her to scandal and imprisonment. The bitter betrayal of it scorched through her soul like wildfire. Blinking fiercely against the threat of tears, Elizabeth managed to rasp, "Please inform the guests the ceremony will be delayed." As the butler hurried off, she sagged back against the wall, barely holding herself upright. Only yesterday Peter had sworn to her that nothing could keep him from her side today. Yet now that vow lay in tatters at her feet, her last desperate hope crushed. In the flurry of confused activity, nobody marked Elizabeth's solitary, hollow-eyed figure stealing away to her chambers once more. If they noted her disappearance, they likely assumed she required a moment to steady her nerves before the grand affair. But her family could wait in vain; she had no intention now of proceeding with this mockery of a wedding. One way or another, after today she would be free of this house and its stifling obligations. Even if that meant casting herself fully upon the harsh mercy of the world. With numb fingers, Elizabeth shed the extravagant wedding gown, letting it pool like an ivory serpent at her feet. She kicked it aside. Her mother could store it away for the next daughter she hoped to marry off into a respectable match. Moving mechanically, she stripped her opulent undergarments until she stood in only her threadbare chemise before the vanity mirror. The girl reflected back at her now appeared as vulnerable and lost as she felt inside. Where was that defiant flame which once had ignited her soul to reckless daring? You cannot rely on anyone else to rescue or define you, she admonished her crestfallen reflection. If you do not take hold of your fate, then you accept your cage. Leave this place with your head held high and live more boldly going forward. It is the only way back to yourself. Galvanized by the stern resolve in her own eyes, Elizabeth hurriedly washed then slipped on her most modest dress and cloak, tying her hair back simply. She moved with renewed purpose. The discarded finery and luxuries of her old life no longer held any appeal if she had to sacrifice freedom as their price. A plain canvas sack held the few items and mementos she wished to take - the practical clothes required for modest country life, her journal, the tattered hair ribbons from girlhood. She left no note for her family, having no adequate words to explain the necessity of this breach. They would not understand, but she knew now her destined bridegroom was not George or any man, but her own fiercely beating heart. Her hand was on the door when she paused, feeling the absence of her one small defense in the wide world. Returning to the vanity, she retrieved the pearl-handled silver letter opener, given as a gift by her father for her 16th birthday. It fit neatly into her dress pocket, lending some scant reassurance. Thus provisioned, she moved stealthily through the empty upper halls and down the servants' stair. The chaos below allowed her to slip unnoticed across the kitchen yard and through a small side gate, emerging onto the road where not long ago she had nearly breathed her last as a free woman. The waning afternoon sun dazzled her eyes after the dimness of the house's interior. For a moment she stood frozen, unable to believe her daring. Then resolve spurred her onward down the dusty lane. She did not look back. That first night Elizabeth walked until nearly dawn through moonlit countryside, fueled by equal parts fury at Peter's betrayal and exhilaration at her newfound liberty. When finally her legs would bear her no further, she crept beneath a hedgerow and collapsed into exhausted slumber. Rising with the sun's first light, she breakfasted on bramble berries and pressed onward, avoiding the main thoroughfare. Occasionally she spied another traveler in the distance and froze or hid herself in the brush until they passed from view. But none seemed to mark her solitary progress. When hunger gnawed sharper, she traded her silver letter opener at a roadside inn for a meal and a room. Though her entire body ached for rest, she lingered only a few hours to regain strength before resuming her wayfaring under cover of darkness again. Something within urged her ever forward. So began the pattern of her days over the next weeks - walking throughout the cooler hours, stopping at sundown to offer some useful labor in exchange for lodging, avoiding villages or anywhere her father might send searchers. Under the hot sun, calluses formed on her once delicate hands. Her face tanned and freckled, while unruly curls escaped her braid. The mirror reflected a sleeker, sinewy figure, with a new flint in her eyes. She grew lean but strong, her very spirit shedding gilded trappings to stand bare and proud. This unfettered existence was not without hardship or uncertainty. But it thrilled Elizabeth's long-dormant soul in a way her pampered life of comforts never had. Each dawn she rose eager to embrace the freedom of the open road and unwritten days ahead. Nearly a month into her travels, Elizabeth crested a hill midday and drew up short at the sprawl of buildings in the valley below. She had lost accurate track of how far north she had come, but the bustling town seemed more prosperous than most she had glimpsed in her wanderings. Unexpectedly, her road-weary spirit quickened at the sight. Perhaps there she could find proper shelter and occupation for a time. Questing alone could become lonely, and she had coin enough now to rent a humble room. Descending the slope, she followed a lively stream of merchants and townsfolk over a granite bridge towards the heart of the town. Elizabeth craned her neck, enchanted by the noisy commotion of commerce and community. How long it had been since she walked among others! Weaving through streets facaded with timber and stone establishments, she chanced upon a labor hall and stepped inside. Pinning notices shouted for seamstresses, laundry maids, milkmaids and more. Her prospects looked promising. Near a sunny window, a paper caught her eye advertising for a tutor. Elizabeth paused, intrigued. She could almost envision herself pouring her love of literature and passion for knowledge into the next generation. Shaping eager young minds as her own governesses once had. Stepping closer to the notice, she quickly read the details - a family called the Bartons sought an instructor in French, mathematics, botany and more for their daughter Caroline, age 12. The role included room and board. It seemed ideal. Elizabeth carefully memorized the address then set out into the bustling streets once more, newfound purpose quickening her stride. She had not permitted herself to consider anything beyond surviving each passing day. But perhaps here lay a chance to build a life on her own terms, humble yet meaningful. The Barton residence proved to be an elegant townhome near the city center. Taking a bracing breath, Elizabeth rapped the polished brass knocker, trying to ignore her travel-stained appearance. This chance was too precious to allow self-consciousness to hinder her. A liveried butler answered promptly and eyed her disheveled state dubiously. But Elizabeth stood tall under his scrutiny. "I am Elizabeth Harlowe, responding to the advertisement seeking a tutor. I wish to offer my credentials." If her boldness surprised the butler, he hid it smoothly. "Please come in. I will inquire if the master and mistress are available to interview you." Shown to a finely appointed parlor, Elizabeth tucked her hands in her lap to still their nervous trembling. This opportunity meant more than just employment - it represented hope of finally claiming her hard-won independence on her own merit. She scarcely dared dream the Barton family might accept her. Too soon, the butler returned and beckoned her to follow. Jaw clenched, Elizabeth trailed him upstairs to an airy study where a couple in fashionable dress stood from behind an imposing desk. The gentleman's beard and spectacles gave him a scholarly air, while the lady studied Elizabeth with barely veiled surprise at her unconventional appearance. Bobbing a quick curtsy, Elizabeth mustered all her long-engrained genteel manners. "Mr. and Mrs. Barton, I presume? I am Elizabeth Harlowe. I could not help but apply when I saw you were seeking an instructor." The silence swelled uncomfortably as they continued scrutinizing her travel-stained attire. But Elizabeth stood calmly awaiting their judgment. She had nothing to hide or be ashamed of. Either they valued her skills or not. At last Mr. Barton broke the taut silence with a thoughtful hum. "You are not quite what we pictured for the post, I admit. But you present yourself well. What is your background?" Over the next quarter hour, Elizabeth outlined her scholarly pedigree from her distinguished tutors, fluency in three languages, and passion for broadening young minds. The Barton parents listened closely, clearly impressed. Inwardly she breathed a sigh of relief. The rest was in fate's hands now. When the interview concluded, Mrs. Barton gave her a judicious look. "You seem qualified and I appreciate your...spirit. But you would require more appropriate attire. The fashions you left behind, I assume?" Gripping her hands tightly in her lap to still their trembling, Elizabeth nodded. She had sacrificed her fine wardrobe for freedom. But she would gladly work every hour to earn it back, if it meant claiming this new future. The couple exchanged a thoughtful look, seeming to communicate silently. After an endless moment, Mr. Barton smiled benevolently. "Very well. We shall offer you a probationary period as Caroline's tutor. She is a bright girl and will benefit from your guidance, I think." Relief crashed over Elizabeth in a dizzying wave. This family was giving her a chance despite her unorthodox situation. She blinked back grateful tears, managing a tremulous smile. "You shall not regret taking a chance on me. I intend to prove myself worthy." As the details were discussed, joy began to kindle within her. She had taken the first vital step towards building a new life through her own merits. Books and clever children awaited her. Her caged wings could finally stretch themselves again. This position was but the beginning, the first milestone on a long road yet ahead. Elizabeth did not know where it ultimately led. But now she walked it on her own terms, guided only by her spirit's inner compass - and that was everything. Whatever the future held, she would continue reaching boldly for each new horizon. The possibilities stretched as far as her courage and vision.

Chapter 12

Consciousness returned slowly, the rocking motion stirring him from dark dreams. Before even opening his eyes, the strange smells accosted him - salt, tar, unwashed bodies and rope. This was not his bed. Blinking against the harsh sunlight, he tried to sit up and immediately clenched his jaw to choke back a groan. His entire body throbbed mercilessly, along with a gash he could feel clotted with blood on his scalp. Gingerly twisting to survey his surroundings, he saw stacks of wooden crates and coils of thick rope. Some sort of cargo hold, he surmised. The creaking and fluttering above told him they were aboard a sizable ship. But his mind recoiled from that hazy deduction like a frightened horse. He could make no sense of how he had come to be here, aboard this vessel heading who knew where. Panic constricted his chest as he desperately tried to recall... anything. But only frightening blankness met his efforts. No memories or sense of self came to orient him. His own identity was gone, leaving only animal fear at this utter loss of anchor. Footsteps on the boards overhead jolted him from shock. Someone was approaching - whether friend or foe he could not say. He tensed, ready to defend himself barehanded if necessary. A hatch opened, flooding the hold with painful brightness. He squinted upwards as booted footsteps descended the ladder. A rugged, weathered man came to stand towering over him, sharp eyes assessing. "So our stowaway finally wakes." The stranger's voice was not unkind, merely gruff. "You've been raving with fever the past two days from that skull bash. Lucky to be breathing still." Words jammed in his dry throat. He had no explanation to offer of how he came to be here with no memories. But he sensed this man held the only answers he would get. "Where am I?" he managed to rasp out. "What is this ship?" Bushy gray eyebrows shot up at his ignorance. "You're aboard the Bonny Pearl, lad. My merchant brig bound for the West Indies with a cargo of cotton and tobacco." His shrewd eyes narrowed. "But you should know that. So how did you end up bloodied and tucked behind my stores?" Agonized frustration welled up and spilled out. "I don't know. I can't remember anything before waking here. Please..." His voice cracked shamefully. "Can you at least tell me my own name?" The captain rocked back on his heels with a low whistle. "Sweet Mary, you took quite a blow if it rattled your wits that soundly. You recall nothing at all?" At the mute head shake, he scrubbed a hand over his grizzled jaw. "Well you're no one I've seen before and had no belongings on you to hint at your story. Give me a moment to think on this conundrum." Pacing the small hold, he muttered half to himself. "Can't upend my voyage to return you to shore till we reach port in Havana. But hard labor might help knock some sense back into that skull of yours." Turning back, he eyed the man's ragged clothes and rawboned frame. "I'll bunk and feed you like crew. You work and maybe we unravel this mystery in time. For now..." He snapped his fingers decisively. "Samuel. That can be your name, since I'm giving you a new life of sorts." Samuel nodded humbly. The name felt no more or less his than any other. He had no alternative but to accept the captain's terms and trust this man's word that he belonged to no nefarious outfit. "Thank you for the kindness, Captain. I will earn my keep here until my memory returns." And so Samuel adjusted as best he could to life aboard the Bonny Pearl as it plied through summer swells towards lands he had no recollection of. The work was ceaseless and grueling, but honored the captain's faith in him and distracted from his predicament. By day he coiled ropes, swabbed decks, and memorized the intricacies of knots and rigging. At night he collapsed into his hammock too spent for troubling dreams. His hands grew calloused and back bronzed under the tropical sun. The crew remained wary at first, distrustful of his erratic memory and lost look. But in time Samuel proved his worth through tireless labor and deference. The men's standoffishness shifted to gruff acceptance of the foundling in their midst. Only the captain still sometimes watched him with a furrowed brow when Samuel unwittingly revealed unknown skills -

navigating by the stars or hand-drawing maps to pass the evenings. Evidence perhaps of whoever he had been before. Who was that man? Someone educated but possibly also dangerous if he'd ended up bloodied and without identification. Flashes surfaced in dreams but vanished upon waking, leaving Samuel adrift. Weeks flowed by without progress as the Bonny Pearl visited more ports - Antigua, Trinidad, Grenada. Samuel observed everything, hoping for some flicker of familiarity. But all remained foreign to his fractured mind. Passing a grim fifth month thus, he sank into black despair, plagued by nightmares of slowly dissipating into the sea's depths. If even his own name and face were lost, how could he claim himself human still? Then one sweltering noon at their Jamaica berth, as Samuel trudged back from a provisions errand, he halted abruptly in the thronged street. For a moment, he could not place what had seized his attention so - only an impression of dark curls and graceful neck. Then the lady shifted and he glimpsed her profile - sharp chin, fine-boned features, and proud eyes the color of a moonless night. Astonishment slammed into him with dizzying force. "Elizabeth," he whispered, the name both foreign yet achingly familiar upon his tongue. His heart hammered violently, not from exertion but recognition. Elizabeth. She was a vital piece of the shadowy past he could not grasp. But who exactly was she to him? By the time Samuel fought through the crowd to the spot, the lady had disappeared as if she were only another tormenting specter. Despair threatened to swallow him again at her absence. Somewhere deep in his lost memory, that face still lingered. The only definite thing he knew about his former life. He clung desperately now to the single image and name etched in his mind. Whatever other revelations still eluded him, somehow Elizabeth yet held the key. All he need do was find her again. From that day forward, new fervor possessed him. At every port of call, Samuel now wandered whenever allowed, hoping to glimpse her telltale curls and fine-boned features in the throngs. He pinned his hope to the slim chance providence might bring them crossing paths again. The crew whispered at his strange ardor, fearing it sign of encroaching madness. But Samuel persisted, driven by the promise of the past this wraith embodied. She alone could resurrect him from limbo. Two years after waking aboard ship, a few glimmers had returned to him but naught of true substance - a snatch of birdsong, the fragrance of lavender. He grasped at each one greedily, praying more would follow. The cracks were spreading in his prisoning void. Soon he might burst through. Then one foggy afternoon in Boston as Samuel heaved on the mooring ropes, a voice cut through his distraction - feminine, clear as a bell. "Sir! Please, I beg your assistance." Samuel turned and the years collapsed away between heartbeats. Approaching along the dock, clad in a modest blue dress, was Elizabeth. Older and wearier but unmistakably her beloved face. The longest fortnight of his life had ended at last. Her intelligent gaze fixed on him entreatingly as she drew up before the ship. "I hope I am not intruding, but I seek passage northward. Might your captain have need of a cook or maid for the voyage?" Samuel could scarcely speak around the pulse thundering like waves against a breakwater. She was here. His Elizabeth. The one still vivid ember remaining from his extinguished past. Somewhere he found his voice. "I know not what opportunities might exist. But come aboard and we shall inquire together." He extended his hand to help her onto the gently swaying deck. Her small hand still fit so perfectly in his. As their skin touched, a blinding cascade loosened in his mind. Fragments tumbled over themselves too swift and disjointed to grasp, but he sensed each held meaning. Elizabeth was speaking of her circumstances and need for employ. But Samuel could focus only on the maelstrom inside him. He must get her somewhere private to trigger full resurgence of his erased identity. With murmured excuses, he led her below deck to the cramped mess hall, every nerve thrumming. As soon as they were alone, he turned to her urgently. "Elizabeth, forgive my mystifying behavior, but I must tell you something incredible." He grasped her hands, willing her to understand. "Two years ago I awoke on this ship with no memories. Only your name and face lingering in fragments." Her eyes widened in shock, but Samuel pressed on. "The moment I saw you again on the docks, it was as if a dam collapsed. I still cannot grasp it all, but you are the key to unlocking my stolen past." Elizabeth looked understandably overwhelmed. "Sir, I...I do not know what to make of your tale." She studied him closer. "Your face does seem familiar, though I cannot place where we may have crossed paths. You have me at a disadvantage, knowing my name while I do not know yours." Samuel raked a hand through his shaggy hair in agitation. "I was christened Samuel by the captain, for lack of any other. But if you know my truer name, I beg you tell me." Her helpless silence rent his heart. For two years he had clung to the hope this woman could restore all he had lost. Yet fate had cruelly reversed their positions, leaving him beholden to Elizabeth for identity and history. Seeing his anguish, compassion softened her confusion. "I wish I could help unravel this mystery. Perhaps in time we may piece it together." She bit her lip pensively. "You seem a gentle soul. I shall vouch for your character to the captain on your behalf." Samuel's laugh held more despair than mirth. "You always did bring out the best in me." At her puzzled look, he shook his head ruefully. "Apologies. You remind me of things that never were." They remained in uneasy silence until footsteps heralded the captain's arrival. Despite feeling only more adrift, Samuel thanked Elizabeth sincerely for her assistance securing him a chance here. Some good might still come of their crossing paths again, if only within his disordered mind. Once she had disembarked for lodgings in port, Samuel retreated to his hammock and lay staring up at the beams as the ship rocked around him. Having her here so close yet just as far was exquisite torture. He was glutted with agony and revelation, hollowed out again. But tomorrow he would wake and she would still be real - not a taunting illusion. He must be patient, keep faith that Providence had some purpose for bringing them together again when all seemed lost. Perhaps she alone could resurrect the man he had been and somehow bridge the impossible distance still separating them. For her, he would gladly walk through fire or take on the sea itself. He would become whole once more. The creak of timbers and slap of water slowly lulled him to sleep, where a lovely, dark-eyed girl waited patiently to show him the way home.

Chapter 14

Elizabeth stared numbly at the vacant patch of earth where Peter's bootprints had marked his stealthy nightly visits to her window. He had vowed to steal her away from the insufferable marriage being forced upon her. Promised they would disappear into a new life together beyond society's scornful gaze. Now on the very morning he was meant to rescue her, he had vanished as if he were only a phantom all along. The bitter betrayal of it choked her. She had ruined herself for this man - defied her family, reputation, everything honorable - only to be cast off in her most desperate hour. What cruel twist of fate or coldness of heart had caused him to abandon her without even a farewell? Had his pretty words and fervent pledges been only calculated means to an end after all? A soft cough behind her made Elizabeth spin, quickly dashing the tears from her cheeks. But it was only George, shuffling his feet awkwardly and watching her with pity in his kind eyes. "Forgive the intrusion. Only, you slipped away so suddenly from the parlor, and I wanted to ensure you were...well." He grimaced at his foolish choice of words. Elizabeth's laugh held more despair than mirth. "Well? When I have thrown my future to the brambles for a scoundrel who fled as soon as fortune required an ounce of courage from him?" She turned away, wrapping her arms around herself tightly lest she shake apart completely. "Please just allow me solitude to collect myself, George. I will be inside shortly." Instead of retreating and allowing her to salvage scraps of dignity, she felt the hesitant warmth of George's palm come to rest gently upon her shoulder. When he spoke, his voice throbbed with quiet empathy. "You needn't hide your pain from me. Truly, I admire your spirit, Lizzy, even if it has led you down thornier paths of late." He exhaled heavily, as if debating his next words. "When you fled from our wedding, I confess my first response was anger. But I have had ample time to reflect since. I acted the petty tyrant, never appreciating that a good marriage means meeting of hearts, not demands." Bewildered,

Elizabeth finally turned to face him. "Why do you speak so earnestly to me now, when I have so disgraced myself and your family? You owe me no comfort." "No, it is I who owe you an apology." George's eyes glistened with sincerity. "I should have courted you in a manner to inspire affection. Made certain your heart was mine before pressing my suit." His head bowed regretfully. "Please know I hold you in the highest esteem, Lizzy, and care not what idle tongues may wag. If you would still do me the honor of being my wife, I swear to spend my life devoted to your happiness." Elizabeth stared, stunned by such selfless magnanimity after all she had put him through. But bitter experience had taught her to be wary. "I am moved by your gracious spirit. But I could not promise any sort of worthy partnership now, with my heart so scarred and chaotic." George's expression remained open and earnest. "I understand. I only ask that you consider my proposal with an open mind. I believe given time, we could find contentment together. At least more so than you wandering without repute or means." His concern touched her, even as his pragmatic words stung. He was right, of course - her wildly impulsive actions had ruined her good name. Returning to George's side would restore everything she had tossed heedlessly away. It would be the sensible choice to salvage her secure future. Yet the prospect of submitting again to that suffocating life, even with George's good intentions, made her throat tighten. She would be forever haunted by wild longings for something more. As if sensing her inner turmoil, George laid a supportive hand on her shoulder. "You need not decide this moment. Go, refresh yourself. But know I stand ready to help you rise above this darkness, when you are ready." Nodding numbly, Elizabeth turned towards the house as George slipped tactfully away. But her feet carried her past her own chamber to her father's study instead. Within lay her only means of escape from either a loveless marriage or life as an outcast. Hands trembling, she took a sheet of parchment and began scratching out a letter giving the barest details of her circumstances. She knew well her family would never accept such shaming explanations delivered in person. But like this, she could provide them closure. The note written and placed prominently upon her father's desk, Elizabeth slipped up to her room, where she neatly packed a single satchel. Into it went the few dresses and meager coins that were solely hers, along with the beloved books of poetry she could not bear to part with. Stopped before her bedroom window, Elizabeth turned back to slowly survey the space she had dreamed and hoped in since childhood. It already seemed to belong to a stranger, or a life left behind long ago. She breathed a silent farewell to the girl who had resided here - and the foolish dreams that had died here today. Stale air still lingered in her lungs when she had slipped out and marched briskly down the side lane leading away from the only home she had ever known. Each step took her further from the wreckage and constraints of her old existence. The future loomed ahead vast and frightening in its uncertainty. Elizabeth clutched her worn satchel tighter, felt the bulk of the books within. In these pages lived words crafted ages ago by those who had also dared to walk bravely away from the well-worn roads. Whatever befell her solitary path now, their bold spirits would help sustain her.

Chapter 15

Birdsong outside her bedroom window stirred Elizabeth from a restless sleep. For a blissful moment upon waking, her mind was blank, unaware of the date's significance. Then recollection crashed over her like a breaking wave. Today she was to become George Wilson's bride at last. The thought filled her with both dread and dull resignation. In the weeks since Peter's disappearance, she had wavered endlessly on whether to accept George's renewed proposal. Though her family encouraged it as the only viable path, Elizabeth struggled to silencing the small voice of defiance that remained. But refusing George's magnanimous offer after all the disgrace she had brought upon herself seemed more pride than principles. However circumscribed her future, she owed it to her family and her own good name to make the most honorable choice now. So she had agreed at last to proceed with the wedding, though her heart felt laden with stone at the prospect. George was a good man; perhaps with time she could find some modest contentment as his wife, if not the breathless adoration she had once dreamed. As the maids laced her into her pristine gown and arranged the lace veil just so, Elizabeth stared numbly back at the stranger in the looking-glass. This passive, hollow-eyed creature seemed to bear little resemblance to the irrepressible girl who had spun dreams of adventure, independence and fierce love in this very room. Well, she told herself sternly, that fanciful girl had gotten herself into woeful trouble. Today marked the start of a new chapter, where good sense ruled her head, not indulged passions. She must lay those reckless ghosts to rest. The ensuing wedding passed in a haze, voices sounding muffled and far away to Elizabeth's shuttered ears. With taciturn obedience she played the blushing bride, even as her spirit remained locked away and silent. There seemed scarcely anything of herself left to give George, but she must try. At the intimate wedding breakfast afterward with only family, Elizabeth forced down mouthfuls of cake that tasted of chalk. George watched her with unconcealed worry from the head of the table but did not press the issue. He would be unfailingly patient with her, she knew. The thought brought a pang of remorse rather than comfort. As soon as was seemly, she feigned a headache and returned to their bridal chambers to change into her traveling clothes for the journey to Bath. Here the newlyweds would spend a fortnight for society's sake, though Elizabeth wished only to retreat to some remote quiet place. Standing before the mirror, she unpinned her veil with nerveless fingers, watching the luxurious lace slither off herhair like a departing ghost. The clatter when she let it slip unheeded to the floor made her shudder involuntarily. Was that hollow echo all marriage would be for her now - pretty trappings cloaking two strangers merely playing at intimacy? A tentative knock interrupted her desolate reverie before George entered, his boyish features flushed with mingled excitement and uncertainty at this new dynamic between them. But upon glimpsing her distress, his brow creased in concern. "Lizzy? Are you quite all right, my dear?" He moved behind her to gently wrap his arms around her waist. "I know this has been an ordeal for you. But we will take things slowly." His simple comfort undid her fragile restraint. Turning in his embrace, Elizabeth laid her head on his shoulder so he could not see her face crumple. "Forgive me," she choked out angrily through her tears. "I do not mean to spoil this day. Only ... I cannot seem to escape this darkness haunting me. I had thought it fled." George tentatively stroked her loose hair. "Your feelings do me credit. But you must cast that scoundrel from your thoughts forever now. As your husband, it is my duty and privilege to bring you the happiness you deserve." Grasping her shoulders, he tilted her chin up gently. "I hope someday to see joy in your eyes again, my Lizzy." Seeing his tender optimism, Elizabeth was awash in fresh remorse that she could not yet reflect it. She had not married him dishonestly - truly believed herself prepared to leave the past behind. Yet here on the threshold of their new union it still clung to her like a ghost. Searching for some response that would not wound her sensitive new husband, her gaze landed on her discarded veil. An idea took sudden shape. Turning back to George with a fragile but sincere smile, she took his hands in hers. "I am blessed beyond measure for your patience and compassion. I cannot promise to blossom into an ideal wife overnight." She nodded towards the veil. "But tonight, I wish to symbolically leave behind that which has overshadowed me, so I might enter tomorrow unburdened." George's eyes lit at this positive step. Together they collected the veil, carrying it outside to the garden. In the gathering dusk, they released the silk and lace to drift away on the breeze like the last remnant of Elizabeth's carefree past. She kept her eyes fixed on it until the veil was lost from view in the gloaming. When she turned back to George, it felt akin to stepping aboard a ship bound for unknown lands. She drew a deep breath of the cool evening air. "Now we look only forward." Wrapping an arm around her, George pressed a kiss to her temple. "Well done, my dearest. I am proud to walk this journey beside you." With a playful glint, he scooped her up, making her gasp in surprise. "Shall we commence this adventure?" Carried giggling over the threshold, Elizabeth felt something ease ever so slightly within her heart. The pain of Peter's memory would fade, given time and care. She must let it, and look only ahead. True to George's pledge, their weeks in Bath passed pleasantly, filled with leisurely walks, boat rides, theatre, and easy conversation. Whenever her thoughts turned too melancholy, George would gently steer her back. At night, they slept chastely side by side, his nearness slowly becoming a comfort rather than an imposition. Away from familiar pressures, Elizabeth discovered facets of George she had not fully appreciated before - his dry humor and adventurous spirit, his genuine interest in her thoughts and feelings. The scabbed-over wounds where her wild dreams had been slowly began to mend. She would never again be the starry-eyed girl George first courted - too much had intervened. But if she could not give him ardent love, she could at least offer companionship and trust. For now, it was enough. The return to their new household brought another wave of trepidation, being back amid the familiar social circles and gossips who had witnessed her shame. But George's steadfast presence was her bulwark. Together they cultivated a life of contentment - hosting dinners, attending theatre, even occasionally dancing again. In the quiet moments before sleep, Elizabeth often thought of Peter, wondering what he had truly felt for her in those fervent midnight trysts. Had it merely been a game of capture? Or something real, but too wild to be contained? Yet such pining did no good now. Her choices had been made for better or worse. Each morning she continued to rise and embrace the gentle happiness offered by her new life's routines. Over time, the fiery dreams of that reckless season receded into mere willow-wisps among her memories. She and George would likely never share consuming passion, but had built something kinder - a refuge of loyalty and patient affection. It was a more modest life than the one she had once boldly imagined. But it was peaceful, and it was hers.

Chapter 16

Pale dawn light filtered into Elizabeth's chamber as she sat staring numbly at her reflection in the vanity mirror. Today was to be her wedding day at last. In just hours, she would become Mrs. Elizabeth Wilson, bound eternally to dutiful domestic life. The girl gazing back at her looked a stranger - eyes hollow, skin wan beneath her silk bridal robe. Elizabeth barely recognized the spirited soul who had spun wild dreams and drunk in poetry by starlight. But she had chosen this sensible path, and must walk it with head held high. A soft knock interrupted her melancholy musings. Before she could respond, the door creaked open to reveal her mother's kindly face. "Are you awake, dearest? We should begin your bridal preparations." Her mother entered, followed unexpectedly by the household maid bearing the dressmaker's exquisite gown. Elizabeth managed a faint smile. "You are early. The wedding is not for hours yet." "I know, but there is much to oversee before the guests arrive. We want everything perfect for your special day!" Her mother prattled happily about flowers and menu finalities as the maids helped Elizabeth into the stunning ivory gown. It fit like a glove, accentuating her graceful silhouette. When at last the bustling women took their leave, admonishing her to finish readying herself, Elizabeth turned reluctantly back to the mirror. It was silly to mourn the end of her unwed days when life as Mrs. Wilson promised comfort and security. Most young ladies would gladly trade places. Sitting down with a sigh, she opened the drawer to retrieve her hairbrush. But her hand froze as she noticed a small folded parchment within bearing her name in a bold scrawl. Heart lurching, she plucked it out with trembling fingers. Could it be...? Hands shaking, she unfolded the letter hastily. My Dearest Elizabeth, I can scarcely find words for this bitter sorrow. My ardent promises to you now lie in ruin, and you must believe yourself cruelly forsaken. But I swear to you upon my life and soul, I remain wholly yours. Dark forces beyond my control have intervened. Know you were ever the bright compass of my spirit. If Fate wills we cross paths again, I shall devote all remaining days to your happiness. Until then, you remain in my thoughts and prayers. Your most ardent admirer, Peter A small gasp escaped Elizabeth as emotions crashed over her - shock and anger that he had dared contact her, but overwhelming relief that she had not been so callously discarded. He yet cared for her, but was somehow prevented from fulfilling his pledge. Clutching the letter, she paced the room, thoughts churning chaotically. She had vowed to go through with this marriage despite inner misgivings. It was the proper choice now, however bitter. Yet this letter crackled like lightning through her mind, changing the landscape entirely. It offered hope the dream she had been forced to bury still lived, merely delayed. Could she in good conscience bind herself to George when her heart pulled so strongly elsewhere? The sound of the carriages arriving to convey her family to church returned Elizabeth abruptly to the moment. Time was slipping away, and she must choose. Should she proceed as planned to the altar where George awaited? Or seize this chance to flee to an uncertain but liberated future with Peter, trusting his promises had been sincere? Mind racing frantically, Elizabeth snatched up the letter and her satchel of possessions. With shaking hands she tore a page from her diary and hastily scrawled a farewell note to her parents. It was barely adequate, but there was no time for eloquent explanations. She must fly. Pausing only to press a final kiss to her mother's embroidery hoop laid out for the next project, Elizabeth slipped downstairs and out the servants' door unseen. And then she was racing down the back lane, the wind tearing the pins from her neatly coiffed hair like scattering leaves. Reaching the edge of town, she slowed to an urgent but dignified walk, buffeted by emotions. She mourned causing distress to those she loved on her wedding day. But the chains of convention had fallen away, and her spirit soared at the impossible second chance she had been given. The road's end was uncertain, but she did not fear. Locked in her heart lay the memory of being whole, of laughing with abandon. For that joy, she would walk any wilderness, hand in hand with the one who had awakened her spirit. At a crossroads on the outskirts of town, Elizabeth paused, gathering her courage. She had burned all bridges behind her. There could be no return from this point onward. Her family, her reputation, her home - all were lost to her now. All for the faith she clung to, that Peter still waited somewhere ahead. The morning breeze tousled her loose hair, carrying sounds of distant church bells chiming the hour. George would be standing at that altar alone, wondering what fate had befallen his bride-to-be. Elizabeth's heart twisted painfully, knowing the distress her disappearance must be causing. She wished she could explain it was not from lack of care or gratitude for George's good heart. Only that she must follow the cry of her own soul, wherever it led. Drawing a deep breath, Elizabeth turned her face from the pealing bells toward the open road. "Forgive me," she whispered to the girl who had walked hopefully to the chapel just yesterday. Then she gathered her skirts and struck out toward the rising sun. The deserted landscape unfurled endlessly ahead through forest and field. Alone but unbowed, Elizabeth moved onwards, Peter's letter tucked safely against her heart. She did not know what their future held, or when they would find each other again. But she held fast to her faith that Providence would someday guide their paths to cross once more. Until then, she would wander unfettered, her spirit answerable only to the four winds. Come what may, she would greet it boldly, with her eyes wide open. The branches swayed above her like outstretched arms, beckoning her onward. Forward, they seemed to whisper, into the great unknown. And Elizabeth followed unafraid, ready to live and love freely beneath the open sky. Ready to become the unfettered version of herself she was meant to be.

Chapter 17

Elizabeth walked until the steeple of the village chapel disappeared behind hills and trees. Only then did she collapse on a stone wall to catch her breath, the day's events crashing over her. Mere hours ago she had been dressed in finery, resigned to become George Wilson's bride. An ordinary existence of comfort and privilege stretching blandly ahead. Now here she sat bedraggled in a dusty gown meant for a wedding that would never take place, the warm metal of Peter's locket pressed over her racing heart. She had thrown respectability to the wind on the strength of his mysterious letter alone. There could be no turning back now. Looking down at the crumpled parchment smoothed flat across her lap, Elizabeth read over his hastily scrawled words again, parsing for any clue where Peter had disappeared to after being "forcibly prevented" from rescuing her. But the letter gave no direction, only fervent conviction he still held her dear and hoped to reunite someday. She must trust the rest to fate and her own determination. Tucking away the precious page, Elizabeth straightened resolutely. She had made her choice, for better or worse. Now survival and finding Peter were all that mattered. With no idea where to begin, she set off in the direction his farm lay. But that road led nowhere except a vacant house and barn, no signs of life or clues for months. Questioning his friends and former neighbors yielded sympathy but no useful knowledge. A week of fruitless searching left Elizabeth dispirited and at a loss. With no family or acquaintances to turn to, she took up residence in an abandoned crofter's cottage and found work sewing piecemeal. The villagers still whispered of her jilting poor George, but pity overcame scandal when they saw her circumstances. She kept to herself, all energy focused on saving enough to eventually leave for cities Peter might have gone to. But months passed with no breakthroughs in her quest. With winter setting in, Elizabeth weighed whether she should accept this isolated village as her home. Perhaps she should marry the blacksmith widower interested in a mother for his young sons, make some sort of life for herself here. Her dreams of reuniting with Peter were starting to fray and fade. Then late one snowy night, a faint knock stirred her from anxious dreams. Opening the weathered door with surprise, Elizabeth found herself staring up at a mountain of a man obscured by a thick muffler. When he unwound this covering, the scraggly beard and stern visage struck an uneasy chord of familiarity. "You are Elizabeth, the lass Peter Maxwell planned to run off with? I was told you had been left behind." His tone held more curiosity than malice. At her mute nod, he exhaled heavily. "Thought as much. Woman troubles stick on a man's conscience. Can't say I expected to cross paths with you here." Dazed, Elizabeth found her voice at last. "I beg your pardon, sir...but who are you, exactly?" The man shifted awkwardly. "No one of consequence. We crewed together some years back before Peter left the seafaring life. But we parted on good terms." He smiled sadly. "I miss the rascal still. Never laughed so hard nor got in such mischief as we did in those days." Heart quickening, Elizabeth clasped his sleeve. "You were his friend! Then please, if you know anything of where Peter went..." She swayed in sudden lightheaded desperation and hope. The old sailor gently grasped her shoulders, frowning now. "Easy lass. Losing a man can turn any woman's wits, but don't go getting wild ideas. I've heard no rumors of Peter's whereabouts in years now. Only passing through brought me the gossip." Seeing her crestfallen face, regret filled his craggy features. "Wish I could say more to help, for your loyalty if nothing else. I can tell you Peter always spoke of going west to seek his fortune if he ever left here. Beyond that..." He lifted his big hands helplessly. West. The word seemed to echo in Elizabeth's mind. She had exhausted all options here scouring the countryside and seaports. But new frontiers called to those running from something or seeking fresh starts. If Peter meant to vanish fully, the expanding west was surely where he would go. Impulsively she grasped the old sailor's rough hand in both of hers. "You have helped more than you know. Thank you." Standing on tiptoes, she boldly kissed his weathered cheek. "Take care, friend." Before he could respond, Elizabeth had spun inside, heart racing with sudden purpose. She threw her few possessions into a rucksack and donned her warmest cloak. Possibly it was foolish to set off into the snowy night on such vague direction. But she could sail for America on the next ship, lose herself in chaotic growing cities like New York and Boston in her search. Just knowing Peter might be somewhere out there kindled new fire in her belly. Pausing at the threshold, Elizabeth whispered a prayer into the silent flakes. "Wait for me, my love." Then she stepped resolutely forward into the night, towards the distant harbor and the future.

The creaking of wagon wheels stirred Elizabeth from fitful slumber. Rubbing her aching neck from sleeping sitting up, she blinked against the harsh sunlight. An endless rugged landscape stretched out around the convoy, but something on the horizon caught her eye - clusters of buildings and tents pitched haphazardly amidst half-finished structures. Sitting up fully, she tapped the shoulder of the weatherbeaten man driving their wagon. "Is that our destination then? The frontier township of Fort Cooper that the signs spoke of?" He nodded, cracking a gap-toothed smile. "Aye ma'am, we've arrived. Not much more than some dusty cattle pens and saloons, but folks are flocking to it. Any of these little hamlets could become the next St. Louis or Chicago someday." Spitting a stream of tobacco juice, he flicked the reins to hasten the oxen. Elizabeth nodded, a new tension creeping into her bones as the ramshackle town drew closer. When she had booked passage to America, she had not thought much beyond reaching its shores. Now here she was, truly alone amid the lawless chaos of the frontier with no clue where even to begin her search. The dismal prospect was forgotten momentarily as the wagons rolled down the dusty main street, people of all stripes mingling in front of clapboard buildings and open storefronts. Though rough around the edges, the scene burst with energy and optimism she had not felt in her sleepy village. Elizabeth sensed anything could happen here. Collecting her carpetbag, she paid the driver his final fare before he moved off. But then she found herself standing lost in the bustle of strangers. Each face held no familiarity, and she had no local acquaintances or lodgings secured. Hesitantly, she approached a solliderly built woman directing crates onto a store porch. "Beg pardon, are you Mistress Miller, the boardinghouse owner?" Elizabeth inquired politely. When the woman nodded, she extended a gloved hand. "Elizabeth Harlowe recently arrived from Massachusetts. The driver indicated you may have rooms to let?" The woman gave her a curious once-over but seemed to approve. "You're clearly no trollop off the stagecoach. Come inside out of this heat and we can square away a rate." Relief broke across Elizabeth's face. She had not been run off immediately at least. "Bless you, ma'am." Hoisting her bag, she followed the woman into the blessed shade of the clapboard building, ready to begin her life here, however temporary. Over the subsequent weeks, she settled into the community, keeping eyes and ears open for any mention of Peter. When not asking round as discreetly as she could manage, she passed time assisting neighbors with odd jobs or reading to the boardinghouse owner's young niece and nephew. They warmed to her quickly, keeping her loneliness at bay. She even received a few calls from local men drawn to the lovely, cultured newcomer in their midst. But Elizabeth gently refused all suitors without revealing much of her past or purpose here. Fortunately most were wanderers themselves, accepting rejection philosophically before moving on. She came to appreciate the isolation and anonymity the frontier offered. Back home her circumstances would still mark her a scandal, but here she could simply be Elizabeth. Nights, however, when the demons of doubt emerged, were the greatest test. Had this wild cross-continent pursuit been madness? Peter might well have forgotten her or perished somewhere remote. Perhaps she should accept the smitten young pastor's offer and make some sort of life here rather than chasing phantoms. Yet inevitably the next day would rekindle her stubborn spark of hope. She would stay just a little longer, follow just one more whisper or rumor. As long as any chance of finding Peter remained, she could not abandon the quest. He had won her heart and she would trust him with its keeping, however long it took to reunite. So her days fell into a simple routine, occasionally brightened by the kindness of strangers or new sights like visiting natives. Spring came and went

Chapter 18

Elizabeth paused to catch her breath, looking out over the bustling seaport. It had been nearly a year since she left everything familiar behind to chase rumors and whispers across an ocean and half a continent. So many frontier outposts blurring together - El Paso, Santa Fe, Carson City. Endless miles traversed on dusty mail coaches, creaky wagons, and even on foot when necessary. But today her determination had finally brought her here, to the lawless Pacific Coast port of San Diego. Word in a mining camp brought rumors of a ship called the Cassandra maintaining a regular northern route up the coast. A vessel vaguely matching the one Peter had crewed on when they first met. It felt like her first real lead, though she dared not let hope take flight just yet. Too often such trails had led nowhere. Hitching her threadbare skirts, Elizabeth picked her way down the dock peering at the names emblazoned on sterns and wheelhouses. She ignored the catcalls and propositions shouted by rough, sunburnt men going about their loading and unloading. Their vulgarity was tiresome but harmless; she had endured far worse dangers alone out here thus far. As long as she located the Cassandra, nothing else mattered. At long last near the end of the pier she spotted it - the brisk three-masted clipper looking a bit worse for wear but seaworthy. The name was painted in faded white letters along her side. Heart suddenly racing, Elizabeth quickened her steps toward the gangway. "You there, miss! This be private berth, not some public house!" She froze at the sharp hail and turned to see a brawny, brown-skinned man regarding her suspiciously from the deck above. His headscarf and gold earring marked him as one of the foreign sailors commonly found crewing such ships. Dipping her head respectfully, Elizabeth approached the base of the ramp. "My deepest apologies, sir. I did not mean to intrude." She offered her most genteel smile. "I merely hoped to inquire with the captain regarding someone who may have served under him in former days. A brief audience is all

I ask." The sailor frowned, looking her over critically. Elizabeth fancied she made a rather odd picture in her dust-coated dress with wild hair escaping its braid. But she stood calmly under the scrutiny. At length he nodded but did not move from blocking the way onboard. "Wait here. I will ask if captain has time to indulge questions from strange females." He turned away dismissively, leaving Elizabeth to wring her hands. So close, yet still tantalizingly out of reach! After an agonizing wait, heavy footsteps sounded on the gangway boards. She lifted her head expectantly as a barrel-chested white man in a navy coat emerged, thumbs hooked into his belt as he looked her over with an imperious scowl. "I'm Captain Josiah Hornbeck. What business have you with me or my ship, Miss...?" Elizabeth dipped swiftly into a curtsy, lowering her eyes demurely. Proper manners were her only currency here if she wished to win him over. "Harlowe, sir. Elizabeth Harlowe. I have traveled long in hopes you may be able to aid me." Straightening, she met his gaze directly. "I search for a man I believe may have sailed with you some years past. Peter Maxwell." The captain's heavy black brows shot up in surprise at the name before his expression clouded warily. "Ol' Maxwell, eh? What stake do you have in chasing down ghosts from his past, lass? Last I heard he'd abandoned the seafaring life for the Americas." He eyed her shrewdly. "How'd you come by word of our acquaintanceship?" His caginess pricked her own curiosity, but she merely smiled. "I knew Peter before he departed England for this continent. We were..." She faltered, a flood of emotions rising. "Close. I only wish to find what became of him, or any clue where he journeyed. I left my whole life behind on the faith he would want me to follow." The audacious admission seemed to soften the crusty captain slightly. He tugged thoughtfully at his whiskers for long moments. "Suppose I did know something of Maxwell and his whereabouts," he said at last, slow and careful. "A pretty young lass like yourself turning up alone - might be just the kind of trouble I'd prefer not to invite." Frustration flared hotly in Elizabeth's chest. She had not endured endless hardship to be so maddeningly close to answers only for this pompous man to deny her now! Drawing herself upright, she fixed him with her most piercing gaze. "With all due respect, Captain, any troubles loom larger for a woman alone in the world. I have crossed oceans and continents in faith, lost everything in hope." She blazed, throwing propriety to the wind. "I shall not be deterred when Peter may be just within reach. Now either assist me, or stand aside." For an electric moment she thought Hornbeck might bellow at her audacity. But instead he threw his head back and laughed uproariously. "Quite the firecracker! Very well, Miss Harlowe, I can see why Maxwell might find you worth pursuing. Come aboard and I'll tell you what I know." He turned and strode up the gangplank without looking to see if she followed. With a shaky exhale of relief, Elizabeth gathered her skirts and scrambled after him. She was near delirious with promise of finally having her tenacity rewarded. The captain lead her to his Great Cabin, mercifully shooing out the other loitering crewmen. "Take a seat, lass. Care for a brandy to settle those nerves?" At her nod, he splashed two glasses before settling heavily behind the desk. "Now then, about your Mr. Maxwell." Hornbeck swirled the liquor pensively. "Fine seaman in his day, but too much fire in his belly and wildness in his heart. Promising officer material but chafed at taking orders." He eyed Elizabeth curiously. "Fancied himself quite the ladies man too, though tended to leave broken hearts scattered about." Elizabeth shifted under his scrutiny. "Peter and I were...close, as I said. But he left unexpectedly. I only wish to learn what became of him." The captain nodded thoughtfully and took another swig before continuing. "Like I told you, Maxwell eventually tired of the seafaring life. Last I heard he'd set off alone for the frontier some years back. Talk of opportunities out West in trapping, prospecting, timber." He shrugged. "Can't say more beyond that. Man always did prefer his own counsel." Disappointment curdled in Elizabeth's chest. She had half hoped Hornbeck could provide Peter's exact location, or at least narrowed the scope of places to seek him. But the uncharted wilderness still stretched vast and daunting before her. Draining his glass decisively, the captain pushed to his feet. "I wish you fair winds in your chase, Miss Harlowe. Ol' Pete may be elusive quarry, but you've got grit enough to run him to ground. Upon my honor." He clasped her hand in his weathered grip. "Now if you've no other questions, I've a tight schedule to keep." Elizabeth knew dismissal when it was handed down. "You have given me new hope, Captain, however faint. I am in your debt." Rising, she offered him her most gracious curtsy before seeing herself out the cabin door. She had one foot on the gangplank to disembark when a thought struck her. Turning back, she called up to the swarthy first mate coiling ropes on the deck, "Pardon me, sir! What port are you next bound for?" He eyed her warily. "San Francisco, with a cargo of cotton and coffee. We sail on evening's tide." Nodding her thanks, Elizabeth descended to the bustling dock, mind churning. She had exhausted all clues pointing east. Perhaps her instincts had been right that Peter would continue ever-westward. And the mining boom towns of northern California seemed as likely a destination as any untamed place. Stopping short beneath a shop awning, Elizabeth made swift calculations. The meager coins in her purse would just be enough for a berth as cook's assistant or maid if the captain allowed it. She would wire the pastor back in Carson City that she must sadly decline his proposal. Tonight these docks would recede behind her, but ahead lay new possibility. Resolved, she marched back up the gangplank where the first mate still coiled ropes. "Excuse me again sir, but might you have need of an extra cook's maid for your journey? I work hard and require only modest lodgings." The grizzled sailor looked her over speculatively before jerking his chin toward the crew quarters. "We set sail near dusk. Present yourself then ready to work." Relief broke across Elizabeth's face even as her pulse leapt in anticipation. "Bless you sir! I will prove myself an able seafarer." She turned and made her way back down the dock, clutching her worn skirts to keep them clear of the planks. The sea breeze tousled her unkempt hair like an old friend welcoming her return. Soon she would be underway again, sailing ever closer she prayed to the missing piece of her heart. Reaching solid ground, Elizabeth hesitated, suddenly overcome with emotion. She had come so far, endured so much hardship alone. But she had not faltered, even when the trail went cold for months. And now the horizon shone bright with promise once more. Someday when she and Peter were finally reunited, she would look back on this cross-continental pursuit as their own grand odyssey. The memories of dusty coach rides crowded with colorful pioneers, nights spent curled in threadbare blankets beneath the stars, faces weathered by frontier living would stay vividly etched within her. For now, she need only take that next step closer, and the one after, for as long as it took reach his side again. Their story stretched before her, coaxed onward by the wildness of hope. Raising her face to the setting sun, Elizabeth smiled fearlessly. Tonight a ship awaited to launch the next leg of her journey. But the true voyage was that of her intrepid heart, which she would follow faithfully wherever it led. Gripping her worn satchel, she turned her steps briskly back toward the bustling docks. The future shone bright on the horizon, calling her home.

Chapter 19

Elizabeth leaned against the railing, salt spray kissing her cheeks as the clipper ship sliced through blue swells. In the crow's nest overhead the lookout gave a shout spying the first distant smudge of land after weeks at sea. The West Indies at last. She had to shield her eyes against the dazzling sunlight bouncing off the waves to even glimpse the low hills growing steadily clearer on the horizon. It looked hardly more than a stain on the vast seascape yet, but her spirits soared. After so many dreary months crisscrossing the frontier chasing rumors, this azure escape beckoned like a dream. When Captain Hornbeck had denied any knowledge of Peter's whereabouts, despair threatened to swallow Elizabeth again. Perhaps she should accept defeat and try to build some semblance of a life amid the rough-hewn settlements springing up. But the thought of wandering those harsh dusty streets, ever vigilant for dangers, held little appeal. Especially when the alternative was securing passage back out to sea, towards lands exotic and new. Though her search here seemed a hopeless cause, the prospect revived her restless heart. And so Elizabeth had cultivated her most winning smile and talked her way into a job assisting the cook and keeping the crew's quarters tidy. To her relief, once the clipper left California's coast behind, the gruff sailors seemed to forget any impropriety of a lone young woman living amongst them. She kept politely aloof but did not fear them. The days fell into simple routine - helping prepare meals in the cramped galley, scrubbing decks and laundry on hands and knees, retiring modestly to her berth while the men caroused above deck. At night she would curl atop her thin pallet and read tattered books borrowed from the captain's shelf, transported by tales of far-flung places and people. This existence was far humbler than her upbringing, but Elizabeth reveled in the anonymity and freedom. Here she was beholden to no one, bound only by the horizon and her own whims. As those exotic lands drew closer now, she tingled with anticipation. What mysteries lay waiting to be discovered ashore? Though she still held out a faded hope of crossing Peter's path, suddenly the future stretched wide open for her to claim however she wished. The realization left her giddy. The crewman at her elbow must have noticed her thrilled expression. He chuckled and nodded toward the now visible green hills fringed with white sand. "Quite the sight, eh lass? You'll find the islands every bit as wild and beautiful up close. The makings of many a young lad's fantasies, though mind the dangers too." Elizabeth smiled politely, but her gaze remained fixed longingly on the horizon. "I am sure your warnings are wise, sir. But I confess it all looks quite magical to me now." Turning her face to the wind, she added softly. "I shall be glad to step ashore after so long at sea, that is certain." The sailor merely laughed knowingly again before moving off to help ready the ship for port. Elizabeth gripped the worn railing, willing the island's secrets to reveal themselves faster. What exotic fruits and birds awaited her? What intrepid ladies had ventured here through the centuries, and what wisdom might they share? What forgotten parts of herself might emerge beneath the swaying palms? The thrill of discovery overtook any lingering seasickness as the clipper glided smoothly into the glittering harbor. Elizabeth craned her neck at the cane fields and plantation manors dotting the hillsides. Much was still wild and untouched, but signs of civilization had crept in. While the crew made ready to disembark for drinking and carousing, Elizabeth lingered aboard, loathe to miss any spectacle. Bronze-skinned dockworkers and merchants mingled with European sailors and less savory characters beneath rows of bright stucco buildings and towering palms. Snatches of unfamiliar melodic languages danced on the breeze between shouted greetings in English and French. Elizabeth clasped her hands, overwhelmed with possibility. Here she was an utter stranger in a new world unlike any she knew. The thought thrilled as much as it daunted. Abruptly excited voices floated up from the quay as all eyes turned toward a sleek schooner anchored at the far end slipping into port. Though smaller than their own clipper, the vessel had a lethal grace that drew the eye - every line built for speed. A ripple of uneasy deference passed through the crowds as the gangplank lowered. Elizabeth felt the sailor at her elbow stiffen as he muttered under his breath, "Black Henry come to port. Best we both keep our noses down and attend to our affairs, lass." Nudging her firmly toward the ladder, he glanced warily over his shoulder at the mysterious schooner as if it spelled trouble. Brow furrowing in puzzlement, Elizabeth nevertheless let herself be herded below deck without protest. She would have time enough later to inquire discreetly about this Black Henry who seemed so infamous. For now, she had a cargo manifest of supplies to tally and help unload before the men flocked ashore. There were still adventures to be found crewing a ship, humble as her role was. But over the next weeks as the clipper plied a trading route through the islands, Elizabeth felt herself chafing at the restrictions. She had glimpsed just enough of vibrant island life to hunger for more - the dancing at ramshackle taverns open to the sultry night air, raucous card games played on the piers late into the evening, the faded grandeur of old sugar plantations clinging to their glory days. She longed to explore beyond just the seedy wharfside haunts the sailors frequented. Her chance came during an unscheduled liberty port at one of the smaller Dutch islands after a major storm. Repairs would take nearly a fortnight, leaving the crew free to roam. When the others set off carousing, Elizabeth quietly disembarked into the cobbled streets lining the harbor. She had no fixed destination in mind, only a longing to discover the isle's secrets. Wandering aimlessly through narrow alleyways, Elizabeth found herself in a shabbier quarter far from the gaily-painted facades nearer the docks. Pausing to get her bearings, she realized with unease that the sun hung low in the sky. The streets had mostly emptied around her, and she heard raucous laughter echoing from some nearby tavern. Frowning, Elizabeth retraced her steps, trying to find a familiar landmark, but only seemed to get more tangled in crooked side lanes.

As twilight deepened, she quickened her pace, fighting back panic. Then a rough hand suddenly seized her arm from the shadows. Elizabeth cried out as she was yanked forcibly against a body reeking of spirits and stale sweat. Twisting in his grip, she glowered up at the leering drunkard sailor who had clearly mistaken her for some docksider. "Unhand me this instant!" she spat, stamping on his foot viciously for emphasis. Caught off guard by her defiance, he slackened his hold just enough for Elizabeth to break free. Abandoning dignity, she hitched up her skirts and fled headlong through the now deserted streets. Dashing heedlessly around corners and down alleys, she outpaced her pursuer but soon lost all sense of direction. Gnarled tree roots threatened to trip her in the deepening gloom beneath the dense canopy. At last, winded and hopelessly lost, she slumped against a mossy stone wall to catch her breath. The jungle around her was eerily still and shadowed as sunset faded to twilight. Strange cries echoed in the distance, sending prickles of unease down her spine. She was dangerously far from town with no means to retrace her steps through this maze in the darkness. A nearby rustle in the undergrowth made her jump. But it was only a bedraggled yellow dog watching her with curious eyes. On impulse Elizabeth slowly held out a hand. "Here boy, come here. That's a good lad." She kept her tone gentle and soothing. The dog's ears perked up as it slowly crept forward to sniff her fingers. After a moment it began wagging its thin tail uncertainly. Emboldened, Elizabeth carefully stroked behind its mangy ears, cooing reassurances until the creature leaned into her touch. "There's a good boy. You'll be my trusty guide out of this pickle, won't you?" she murmured playfully, giving the dog's belly a good scratch for emphasis. Its steady panting almost resembled an affirmative reply. Chuckling in spite of her nerves, Elizabeth straightened and gestured coaxingly for the animal to lead onward. With the clever mongrel trotting dutifully ahead through the overgrown path, she followed deeper into the jungle with renewed courage. The dog glanced back periodically as if to ensure she still trailed close behind. Its loyalty stirred her heart after so much time adrift alone. At long last, the trees opened up to reveal a grassy lane leading toward the harbor's distant torches. Weak with relief, Elizabeth ruffled her faithful rescuer's scruffy head in gratitude. It butted affectionately against her skirts, tail wagging at full force. "What a good and loyal friend you are. I wish you could join me to see the islands, but you likely have a home to return to." Crouching down, Elizabeth stroked the dog's dusty fur and peered into its eyes. "I shall not forget your kindness. Perhaps when I am settled someday, I shall find a stout hound like you for companionship." The dog licked her hand amiably before turning and trotting back the way they had come. Elizabeth watched its shaggy form disappear into the jungle with a smile and lingering wistfulness. But her path led in the other direction now. Dusting off her rumpled skirts, she set off toward the harbor with refreshed resolve. This misadventure had taught her to temper her restless spirit with wisdom so she might continue roaming free. With courage and an open heart, the whole horizon lay before her to explore at her own pace. The lantern lights of waterfront taverns guided her until she found the familiar pier where the clipper remained docked for repairs. The jovial voices of her crewmates rose up from a nearby establishment, but Elizabeth bypassed them for the gangplank. Tonight her narrow bunk seemed more welcoming than any boisterous company. Collapsing onto the creaking pallet, she felt the day's tensions ease as the familiar rocking of the ship lulled her. Though she had known fear and confusion in the jungle's shadowy reaches, the memories of her loyal guide and the beauty glimpsed along the forest paths lingered sweetly. She need only learn to balance her thirst for independence with wisdom. Her future course was hers to chart, unhurried. Smiling drowsily, Elizabeth drifted off to dreams filled with sun-dappled grass and a shaggy yellow hound faithfully at her heels. Wherever she roamed in days to come, she would carry the island's last gift - hope of a companionable solitude.

Chapter 20

Thunder rumbled menacingly as Elizabeth hurried to secure the shutters on the small seaside hut she had taken shelter in. Outside, rain poured in drenching sheets, reducing the sandy path and lush jungle to a blur. It had all happened so quickly - the dark clouds appearing on the horizon that morning as the clipper anchored off this remote island to take on fresh water. Most of the crew had gone ashore briefly to stretch their legs, Elizabeth included after weeks confined onboard. But with barely a whisper of warning, the storm had blown in fast and fierce. Attempting to row back out to the ship in churning waves would mean certain death. The islanders who lived in the tiny village had taken pity and given the stranded sailors refuge in huts and sheds. Now Elizabeth could only huddle against the wood plank walls and anxiously watch through cracks as the storm raged outside. She sent another silent prayer skyward that her crewmates had found safety somewhere amidst the downpour. At least she was high enough to avoid the crashing surf, though the hut still shook and creaked alarmingly under the buffeting wind. Curling on the single pallet, she wrapped her arms around herself and tried not to imagine what might become of her if the ship could not return for them. Gradually the deafening roar faded as the storm moved on, leaving only steady cascading rain. The hut had held fast, but Elizabeth felt anything but relief. However long they were stranded here, she had only the clothes on her back and a few coins in her purse. What little provisions the islanders had would likely be scarce after such tumult. She was utterly alone and at the mercy of strangers. When a scratching sound came at the door sometime later, Elizabeth jolted in alarm. But it was only a rain-soaked native girl proffering a pathetic looking hunk of bread and shaking water from her black braids. Elizabeth accepted the meager gift with effusive thanks, relieved they did not seem inclined to cast her out. Over the next week, she fell in with the other crewmembers and did what she could to make herself useful to the villagers - mending damaged thatch roofs and fishing nets, minding small children, preparing what humble meals their supplies allowed. They were simple people but welcoming in their own shy way. During her time spent combing the now debris-strewn beach, Elizabeth occasionally spotted the mast of the clipper far out in the bay. But the islanders warned the waters remained too treacherous for small boats so far. With each passing day, the hope that the ship would return dwindled. So she reluctantly settled into her new lonely existence on the remote isle - keeping busy as she could manage, smiling through the crew's ribald jokes to ward off despair. At night she lay awake listening to the breakers pounding the shore just yards away, wondering if she would die here forgotten. Perhaps this isolated paradise would become her entire world now. Nearly a month after the storm, Elizabeth was making her way back from the rocky tidal pools with an apron full of oysters when a skeletal figure staggered out of the treeline toward her - torn ruffled shirtsleeves, matted hair and beard. Shock rooted her to the spot. "Miss Elizabeth..." the stranger croaked, looking near collapse. Recognition jolted through her. "Captain Hornbeck!" Elizabeth rushed forward to support the swaying man. "We had feared you lost when the storm blew us off course." The blustery captain she recalled was reduced to clinging weakly to her shoulder as she led him to the largest hut serving as their communal quarters. Laying him gently on a pallet, she trickled fresh water into his cracked lips while barrage of questions filled her mind. After he had drunk his fill, the captain gripped her wrist with surprising urgency despite his haggard state. "Listen close, lass...I haven't much time." He broke into ragged coughing but pushed on resolutely. "I ran the Bonny Pearl aground trying to ride out the tempest, but she broke up quick. Most of the men made shore same as you." His rheumy eyes held hers fiercely. "We got separated marching inland seeking help. But before we did...I retrieved something from my cabin I swore to keep safe." Fumbling in his vest, he drew out a folded, weathered page and pressed it weakly into Elizabeth's hands. "It's the map to Maxwell's lost treasure - the bounty he and the boys amassed during our privateering days." Elizabeth's head spun. She recalled the cagey captain's tales of Peter's time as a cunning scoundrel of the high seas. But she had not realized literal treasure was involved. Captain Hornbeck was speaking urgently again. "This island is where we buried the haul before the authorities caught wind. Only Pete and I remained who knew its location." He broke down coughing again momentarily. "I've failed you in this chase, lass. Consider this a token for your trouble." He nodded at the map with grim finality. "Just promise me you'll use that gold as Peter would've wanted - to live free. Now leave me to my rest." Exhausted by this last effort, he sagged back against the pallet before Elizabeth could press further. Questions rioted in her mind, but clearly the ailing captain could say no more. All that mattered now was the cryptic parchment in her hands. Slipping quietly from the hut, Elizabeth found a sunny rock facing the sea and carefully unfolded the page. It was stained and frayed but showed a rudimentary outline of the island with landmarks - two peaks, a cove, river fork. And tucked within a hidden inlet, a solitary X marked the spot. Elizabeth's pulse quickened, imagining what such a pirate's buried riches could mean for her nomadic future. The prospect of security beckoned, a chance for stability and comfort she had all but relinquished. And yet...how long had she yearned for freedom above all else? Unease trickled in as she studied the mysterious map. However pressing her needs, did she have any right to Peter's hard-won spoils? He had left this life behind without claiming the treasure. Was it not best left to the past? But the tiny island offered few prospects once the crew eventually departed. She had no means to buy passage from here or sway her future. The temptation simmered as she traced the mark at journey's end. All that wealth, there for the taking... Folding the map hastily, Elizabeth squeezed her eyes shut as if to banish such dangerous thoughts. She would safeguard the captain's gift but make no move to seek it out.

The choice must come from wisdom, not desperation. There was time enough to weigh it fully. Tucking the parchment securely into her dress pocket, she rose and made her way up the beach to help the crewmen repairing damaged huts. She would speak nothing of maps or buried treasure to them. For now it would remain her secret alone - and hopefully her conscience could guide whatever course she chose. The reprieve was short-lived. A few days later Elizabeth went to bring Captain Hornbeck some fish stew only to find him dead in the hut, finally claimed by his frailties. The shock left her reeling. Then dread seized her throat as she realized - the crew would surely ransack his belongings, seeking anything of value. The map could easily be discovered and lost. Moving swiftly, she rolled the captain's body in a woven mat, murmuring prayers for his spirit. She would ask the villagers to prepare him for burial. But first there was something she must do. Within minutes she was racing along the rocky shoreline to a secluded cove tucked beneath the headlands. The place marked on the map as concealment for Peter's lost treasure. If its wealth must be claimed by someone before others seized it, better her who understood its troubled origins, she reasoned breathlessly. Reaching the hidden cove, Elizabeth scanned the towering cliff face for the landmarks - twin peaks shaped like cat's ears near a freshwater stream. She knew she was in the right spot. Now to locate the precise place to dig. The sun climbed higher as she combed the white sand obsessively, seeking any disturbance. But the cove remained still and pristine, with no signs of excavation. Doubts crept in as sweat beaded Elizabeth's brow. Perhaps she had interpreted the crude map incorrectly. The treasure might be mere fantasy, like the rest of Peter's scattered past still eluding her. Finally as shadows stretched across the inlet, her toe struck something - a wooden plank half buried in sand. Kneeling swiftly, Elizabeth clawed the area clear until the unmistakable outline of a trap door was revealed. Heart pounding, she grasped the iron handle and pulled. Rusted hinges screeched in protest after years sealed against the elements. But slowly the door carved from driftwood gave way. The musty darkness below made Elizabeth hesitate only a moment before descending the carved rock steps until her feet touched solid ground again. Flint and tinder from her apron pocket sparked a makeshift torch to light her way. All around her, golden glow reflected back from chalices, lamps, platters and more. Elizabeth staggered, overcome. She had found the treasure cave at last. The fortune Peter had plundered from merchant ships lay before her now, hers for the taking. Running her fingers reverently over the heaping mounds of coins and gilded relics, she marveled at the spoils these pirates had amassed through cunning and daring. It would ensure her security and independence, just as Captain Hornbeck promised. She need never depend on anyone's mercy again. Temptation warred with unease as Elizabeth lingered amidst the glittering bounty. This wealth was tainted by violence and loss, its origins murky. Yet she had sacrificed everything in pursuit of freedom. What was left now but to seize it boldly with both hands? Taking a ragged breath, she reached for a jeweled goblet to begin filling her satchel. But an ornate mirror in the treasure pile caught her eye, halting her mid-motion. Her own hollow-eyed reflection stared back accusingly, a stranger. Elizabeth recoiled, the treasure's allure shattered. These were not her spoils to plunder or profit by. They would only shackle her to past crimes, not liberate her spirit. Her destiny still awaited elsewhere. Resolute again, she grabbed an empty sack and hurriedly swept as many glittering pieces as she could into its depths. The crew must not discover this cache and squander it on drink or worse. Back up the stone steps she lugged it, then dumped the entire load into the sea till nothing remained but harmless sand. The tide would reclaim the rest in time. Tonight she would rest easy, knowing she had honored the brave girl who once tended wounded soldiers, who loved poetry and beauty and truth. Her course was still her own to chart. Drenched and spent but with a lightened heart, Elizabeth made her way back along the cliffs as the sun dipped low. Perhaps soon a ship would return for them. But for now, she had this island's small comforts, honest labor, and the whispering sea. It was enough.

Chapter 21

Elizabeth paused to wipe sweat from her brow and surveyed the cleared field with satisfaction. It had taken weeks, but the debris from the enormous storm was finally cleaned away. Palms swayed gently once more, with no signs of the devastation that had nearly swept her life away. Leaning on her hoe, she turned her face to the breeze coming off the turquoise bay. This place was becoming almost comfortable and familiar, she mused - the rhythms of village life, the kindly but shy people, the hut nestled amid waving flowers that she had come to think of as home. Part of her still longed to escape this isolated outpost and find passage back to civilization. But the ship remained delayed for repairs, and the patient generosity of the villagers had softened her restlessness. Perhaps she could yet be happy here embracing a simpler existence, even if it meant relinquishing her old dreams. Since burying the captain's treasure map with his remains, Elizabeth had felt oddly at peace with her choice. She wanted no part of plundered wealth, however pressing her needs. Better to rely on common decency and her own perseverance to forge her path, as wildly impractical as that often proved. Lost in thought, Elizabeth began the trek back to the village center. But raised voices down a side lane gave her pause. Curious, she followed the angry tones to a small thatched hut. Inside, she could just glimpse a wizened woman on her knees pleading in the local tongue with a burly man shouting and pointing harshly to a sack of sad root vegetables. Anger kindled in Elizabeth's chest. She knew this woman - Akela, the village's elderly medicine woman who often stopped to share kind smiles or bits of fruit on her walks past. Clearly the man was some greedy creditor trying to take her last possessions. Striding through the curtained doorway, Elizabeth fixed him with her most imperious stare. "Pardon me, but I believe you have some business with this woman? As her guest, I must ask you to leave at once. She owes you nothing." Whether intimidated by her commanding presence or unable to understand her words, the man scowled but backed away reluctantly. With a final grunt that may have been a threat, he turned and pushed out into the lane. Akela had watched and listened to the exchange silently from her spot on the packed dirt floor. Now her eyes shone with tears as she grasped Elizabeth's hands, effusively thanking her in the local dialect. Feeling self-conscious over the woman's heartfelt gratitude for such a small service, Elizabeth gently helped her to stand again. "Hush dear woman, all is well. We ladies must support one another, no?" She hoped her warm tone conveyed that she asked nothing in return. But Akela was already shuffling around her single cramped room, babbling excitedly. With gestures she seemed to insist Elizabeth stay. Understanding the offer of hospitality, she finally accepted a seat on the woven mat and share of sweet potato stew. Thus began a routine of stopping to check on the widow daily as she walked to and from the fields. Though they could barely manage two words in the other's language, a tender friendship blossomed. Akela would brush and plait her hair and listen to Elizabeth's meandering stories as if enraptured. In turn, her gentle aura gave comfort when old griefs stirred. The weeks wore on without the ship's return, but Elizabeth's restless anxiety had largely faded. She found purpose in helping Akela around her hut, listening to her sing haunting folk songs, and trying to bridge their language gap piece by piece. Isolated together, both blossomed liked flowers starved of sunlight before. But at night, Elizabeth still dreamed of the sea - gliding over waves towards the horizon's promise, sails billowing like wings. No matter how she tried to accept her new then one evening, after they had eaten, Akela brought out a handful of aged maps, pointing excitedly. Peering closer, Elizabeth saw they were navigation charts of the islands and seas beyond. Her throat tightened with longing as she traced the exotic names. Akela smiled and mimed a ship sailing away over her heart, then pointed encouragingly to Elizabeth. "You believe I should sail again to find my destiny?" Elizabeth whispered in wonder. The old woman simply patted her hand with a knowing look. In her wise eyes, the past was anchor, not prison. The future's horizon stretched endless. That night, Elizabeth walked slowly down to the shore as moonlight dappled the inky waves. The sea's murmur filled her ears, calling her name. The loyal sailor's heart within still trued ever seaward, however she had tried to deny it. Smiling bittersweetly, she gazed up at the stars' patient light. "Soon," she whispered to them. Within her once more beat the pulse of wanderlust. She need only have courage to unmoor. The next morning she woke before dawn and walked to Akela's hut. The old woman met her in the doorway, gently placing a woven bag in her hands - simple food and drink for the journey ahead. Though tears shone in her eyes, she smiled proudly and pressed something else into Elizabeth's palm - a crudely carved wooden charm to protect her. Overcome, Elizabeth embraced her surrogate grandmother tightly. No words could convey her gratitude for restoring courage and purpose when she had lost her compass. Together they had navigated by the stars in their souls. Pulling back, she cradled Akela's lined face in her hands and kissed her forehead in farewell. But their spirits would ever steer the same course. Turning reluctantly but without looking back, Elizabeth walked away down the shore as the sun crested the waves. The wind caught her sails once more.

Chapter 22

Elizabeth hacked at the jungle undergrowth with her machete, sweat beading on her brow. All around, towering palms and vines formed an endless verdant maze under the dense canopy. Strange birdsong and insects provided the only signs of life. She was utterly alone. Glancing again at the crude map sketched from the ship captain's dying memories, Elizabeth oriented herself. The distinct twin peaks should be visible over the treetops if she continued heading north. That would place her closer to the remote valley Peter had supposedly gone to prospect. Folding the parchment carefully, she slipped it back into her dress pocket and pushed on through the muggy green gloom. Mosquitoes and unseen animals rustled just out of sight, but she tried to maintain courage. Peter had survived out here for months alone. Surely she could manage a few days' journey. Hacking stubbornly through the suffocating underbrush, Elizabeth tried not to dwell on just how long and lonely her own isolated months on this island had become. With the ship delayed for repairs indefinitely, she had little human company save occasional brief encounters with the shy villagers when trading fruit for fish. She often thought of simply asking passage on one of the small local sloops that came infrequently to port. But legends of pirates still haunted these waters, making such journeys risky for a woman alone. And some stubborn ember of hope still smoldered that her own missing crew might yet return for her, if she just had faith a little longer. Tramping doggedly up a forested ridge, Elizabeth paused to gulp gratefully from her canteen. As desperate as her circumstances seemed, she refused to fully relinquish the wild dreams that had brought her half-way across the globe and through countless trials to this place. Even if she must spend her remaining days here exiled from society, it would be on her terms, chasing freedom. Peter and his elusive secrets had brought her to this island - perhaps somewhere in its wilds, answers still waited. She would traverse every inch if she must to unravel the enigma of their past and her own future. The faint gurgle of running water met her ears suddenly. New energy propelled Elizabeth forward through dense ferns until she parted a final curtain of vines and stumbled abruptly into a sun-dappled glade. A thin stream tumbled over stones through the grassy meadow before disappearing again into the jungle's shadows. Ensnared by the idyllic spot, Elizabeth sank down on a fallen log to soak in its perfection - warm dappled light, riotous tropical blooms, the water's melodic murmur. Some benevolent spirit had led her to this refuge. Here time itself seemed to pause, all cares receding, if only fleetingly. When she finally continued on refreshed, Elizabeth marveled that such unspoiled beauty could persist virtually untouched while humanity battled and conquered the natural world back home. Would that more appreciated the sacred wonders still layered all around them, if only they had eyes to see. The sun had climbed past its zenith when Elizabeth finally glimpsed the twin peaked mountains framed through a break in the trees ahead. Consulting her makeshift map against the landscape, she corrected her course towards the western foothills. By nightfall, she hoped to reach the valley and make camp. Then tomorrow's search for Peter's old prospector camp could begin in earnest. The tantalizing proximity to possible answers revived Elizabeth's spirit and quickened her stride. But the path grew more treacherous the higher she climbed. Loose stones sent her feet sliding back down the steep incline. Thorny vines clutched hungrily at her clothes and skin. Still she pressed doggedly upward, refusing to be bested. Peter had survived this crucible alone and so would she. Reaching the valley floor at last as the sun dipped low, Elizabeth wanted to collapse in exhaustion. But she forced leaden limbs to gather fallen branches and clear space for a fire-pit first. Soon cheerful flames crackled, holding the thickening jungle shadows at bay. Lifting the first paltry sip of broth to her cracked lips, Elizabeth sighed, eyes drooping closed. This place seemed impossibly remote from humanity or comfort. What had driven Peter here alone to seek his fortune? And what end had he met beneath the stifling green canopy? She prayed this desperate gambit might yet reveal the truth. Bone-weary, she curled on the hard ground, using her pack for a pillow. The fire's soft crackling soothed her fears of prowling predators. Sheltered by the ancient forest, Elizabeth slept dreamlessly until birdsong roused her at first light. The morning dawned muggy and grey, but she wasted no time breaking camp to continue her search. Peter's crude map indicated a freshwater spring and large outcropping of rocks where he had encamped nearby. She need only maintain faith despite each fruitless day. He had carved a life somewhere in this wilderness. She would find it. For the next several days Elizabeth settled into routine of methodically combing the valley and hills - peering into caves, scanning trees for markings, searching for any signs someone had passed before her. But Peter's presence remained ever elusive as tropical storms rolled in, forcing her to take meager shelter. Undaunted, she battled through denseets of stifling heat that sapped her energy and landscapes that all looked eerily similar, making her feel turned round for hours. The challenges only seemed to strengthen her stubborn resolve. She would wring whatever answers she could from this island. Until late one afternoon when she stumbled through the trees into yet another rocky clearing and froze, scarcely daring to believe her eyes. For there beneath a makeshift lean-to of fraying oilskin stood the dilapidated remains of a workman's camp. Heart pounding, Elizabeth rushed forward, hands skimming reverently over the scattered belongings - pickaxe and shovel, a rough-hewn table still set with tin plate and mug... Here in this remote wild spot, someone had survived and toiled beneath the shelter of palms. Frantically she began searching for anything to prove the missing prospector had been Peter. But the camp appeared long abandoned, with few identifiable traces remaining. Just when frustrated tears pricked her eyes, Elizabeth spotted a rusty pistol wedged beneath a supply crate. Drawn by instinct, she picked it up and turned it over carefully. Etched into the handle so worn it was nearly invisible, two initials - P and M. Peter Maxwell. Joy and sadness crashed over her at this tiny proof of his presence. The ghost she had chased halfway across the world had walked this very spot, touched these same items. He had been real. Clutching the engraved pistol to her chest, Elizabeth's legs buckled as she sank to the dusty ground and wept. She had found him at last, but their paths still had not crossed. Now she might never unravel why they had been drawn together only to be pulled apart by fate. He remained a beautiful enigma. Wiping her eyes resolutely, she tucked away the precious artifact Peter had left behind. She could not dwell on missed chances or might-have-beens. Somewhere ahead their story still waited to unfold. She need only proceed bravely, one step at a time. With renewed conviction, Elizabeth spent several more days searching the hills but found no further traces. Whatever secrets the island still guarded, this abandoned camp was her sole evidence that Peter had walked this same difficult road. It was enough. She had completed her pilgrimage. The trek back to the coast passed swiftly, terrain she had memorized. But Elizabeth paused often to absorb the island's savage beauty in case she never passed this way again - exotic birds sweeping beneath the canopy, orchids vibrant as spilled paint, vines that fell in sinuous ribbons. Life here pulsed fierce and unbound. Reaching the dusty village by week's end, she was greeted as one returned from the dead. The old medicine woman Akela hobbled forward to clutch Elizabeth's hands, eyes brimming with joy that she had survived the perilous jungle. Despite the long lonely days, she had never felt more alive. That night, Elizabeth walked down to the starlit shore alone. Standing gazing out at the moon's rippling reflection on the waves, she finally slipped the pistol from her dress pocket. Gripping it tightly like an anchor to Peter's memory, she drew back her arm and threw it with all her strength into the sea's waiting embrace. There it could rest among the Bones of the island they had both traversed separately. Now her course led outward once more. But the days roaming beneath the brilliant birds and towering palms would forever dwell bright in her spirit. She had been baptized anew. Turning calmly from the murmuring tide, Elizabeth went to pack her few belongings. At first light, her feet would again follow the sun.

Chapter 23

Elizabeth hacked through the dense underbrush, swatting angrily at the swarm of insects that seemed determined to torment her. The jungle pressed stiflingly close on all sides, with no paths in sight, only endless suffocating green. Pausing to wipe the sweat from her eyes, she consulted the crude map sketched from the ailing captain's memories one final time before letting it drop in disgust. Clearly she was well off course now, if the twin peaks to the north were any indication. She should have reached the freshwater lagoon and Peter's old camp by midday. With a sigh, Elizabeth leaned against a mossy boulder to regain her bearings. Probably she had strayed downhill rather than climbing. Perhaps if she backtracked up the ridge she had just descended and tried circling around... A faint humming sound in the canopy above gave her only a split second of warning before strong hands seized her arms and a sack was thrown over her head, plunging her into darkness. Elizabeth shrieked and thrashed wildly, but she was lifted bodily into the air. More hands grasped her legs to hold her immobile. Blinded and gagging on burlap fibers, she felt herself carried swiftly through the muggy jungle, branches and leaves whipping against her muffled screams. When her captors finally halted, she was lowered roughly to the ground, ankles and wrists swiftly bound with coarse fiber. Then the hood was yanked off unceremoniously. Blinking against the sudden sunlight, Elizabeth found herself surrounded by a circle of nearly naked tribesmen pointing crude spears in her direction. Beyond them towered an enormous carved idol draped in garlands of flowers and feathers. Some primal place of worship then. Heart pounding, she shrank back as far as her bindings allowed, eyes darting for any means of escape. But the fierce painted faces around her remained impassive. None stepped forward to do her harm, merely watched and waited. Unsure whether she would be cooked in a pot or sacrificed to their gods, Elizabeth lifted her chin and addressed the nearest warrior priest boldly. "I mean no harm or insult to your ways. I am merely lost in this jungle and wish safe passage." He stared back uncomprehending but calm, flanked by his equally stony brethren. Trying again slowly in what little she knew of their dialect, Elizabeth implored, "Please. I...seek...friend." She attempted a weak smile. "We...understand...one another?" At this, the man tilted his head thoughtfully before murmuring something to the warrior at his side, who slipped silently away into the dense foliage. The rest stood rooted like statues around her. Left with little choice, Elizabeth waited anxiously for whatever fate would unfold. Perhaps they meant to summon their chieftain to decide her punishment. But surprisingly, it was a young woman the warrior reemerged with a few minutes later - likely some priestess or shaman given her colorful feathered headdress. She moved gracefully to kneel before Elizabeth, studying her with sharp but not unkind eyes. "You...lost?" she asked haltingly in the common tongue. Elizabeth nearly sobbed in relief at being addressed in her own language. "Yes! Lost in jungle. Seeking friend." She struggled to present her case while the woman listened intently. "His name...Peter. He lived...these mountains. Do you know him?" At the name Peter, a ripple of recognition passed through the warriors. The woman asked a question over her shoulder in their language, to which the men nodded and grunted affirmatively, pointing to the peaks overhead. "Peter...gone long time." The priestess turned back to Elizabeth with a regretful frown. "Our tribe help him...he sick. But he leave...not return." Elizabeth's heart sank even as she clung to this new glimmer about Peter's time on the island. At least he had been cared for when ill rather than perishing alone. Sensing her disappointment, the woman patted her shoulder kindly. "I Aiyana. We take you...village. Eat...rest." She gestured to the waiting warriors who moved to cut Elizabeth's bindings and help her stand on shaky legs. Though wary, she allowed them to lead her deeper into the lush jungle, having little other choice. The terrain soon opened up into neatly cultivated fields and orchards ringing a settlement of thatched huts and cook-fires. Children peered from behind their mothers' skirts then dashed off yelling excitedly at the strange sight of Elizabeth and her escort. She was brought to the largest dwelling and gently urged to sit before a low table. Moments later Aiyana appeared with a clay jug and cups, then proceeded to pour a sweetly tart juice, chattering away in her own tongue. Though Elizabeth grasped little except occasional references to "Peter", she smiled and nodded gratefully. Clearly these people meant her no immediate harm. For now she was content to rest and build what trust she could. Perhaps they might yet help guide her search. Over the next several days, she was welcomed cautiously into daily life in the small village - breaking bread with the family who gave her lodging, trying to pick up words of their language as the children laughed at her bungled phrases. During festivals, Elizabeth marveled at the elaborate painted masks and communal dances around the fire. Her curiosity seemed to endear her to most, though some elders continued watching her warily. If she could only stay long enough to prove she came in friendship, that Peter had been more than a passing fancy. Then surely they would understand she shared their spirit, if not their tongue. Growing bolder, she ventured to ask Aiyana again about Peter's time here. The shaman frowned thoughtfully before presenting Elizabeth with a rough bundle that night at dinner. Unwrapping it, she gasped to find Peter's pistol and a worn leather satchel of crude charts and journal pages. "Peter's things," Aiyana explained gently. "He ask we keep if friend come seek him. Now we give to you." Eyes shining with gratitude, Elizabeth clutched the precious artifacts. Here was the proof she needed. Peter had wished her to follow, known in his heart they would find one another again. Moved beyond words, Elizabeth haltingly hummed a few notes of song instead - a folk tune Peter had taught her in days gone by. The wistful melody captivated her audience as she allowed her voice to rise on the chorus, weaving in the island's own rhythms. Music bridged all distance. When the last notes faded, she gazed around at the hushed faces. "My song...say..." She placed a palm over her heart. "Peter...and you...my friends." Impulsively she sang again, inviting them to join in clapping or swaying. Aiyana watched this exchange thoughtfully before turning to address the elders in quiet council. At last she beckoned Elizabeth forward and tied a woven bracelet around her wrist in what seemed a gesture of acceptance. Greatly relieved, she bowed in thanks. Their hearts had heard her song. The next morning as she prepared to depart, Elizabeth was surprised to find Aiyana and a small band of hunters waiting to accompany her. They explained simply, "We go...help find Peter." Deeply moved by their generosity, Elizabeth could only nod and set off into the jungle with her new companions. Wherever Peter's spirit had fled, she and this unlikely fellowship now shared a bond beyond words. They would uncover the truth together. Over the ensuing weeks, they combed valley and mountaintop for any other traces beyond the scant ones in his abandoned camp. During rests, Elizabeth pored through his journals and charts, treasuring these small insights into his inner landscape. But of his ultimate fate, no clues emerged. When the day arrived for the tribesmen to return home, Elizabeth was saddened but knew she could not keep them from their families and duties forever. This remote place held no more answers for her. She must look outward again. At the village edge, she clasped each person's hands warmly in parting. For Aiyana, she removed the bracelet from her own wrist and knotted it around the woman's with humble thanks. Though their time together had been brief, they had forged a bond beyond words. Wherever the winds carried her, she would remember. Alone again on the jungle path leading to the sea, Elizabeth felt the pull anew in her soul - the instinct that always drove her onward when she had been still too long. Peter remained elusive, but her true quest was for self-knowledge. And for that she must sail bravely forth. Pausing once to look back at the lush green horizon that had been her whole existence for months, she blew a silent kiss toward the mountains. Somewhere beneath those peaks, she and Peter had passed like two ships in the night, never knowing how closely fate had brought them together. One day perhaps the currents would steer them to a safe harbor where their voyages could finally converge. Until then...onward. With a rustle of leaves, Elizabeth turned resolutely away and continued down the winding trail, into the future's bright unknown.

Chapter 24

Elizabeth paused to catch her breath as the narrow jungle trail crested a ridge overlooking the native village nestled in the valley below. It still seemed incredible that these isolated people had welcomed her into their midst after discovering her lost and bedraggled in the rainforest. In the weeks since, they had met her curiosity about their customs and stories with patience and even pride at sharing their heritage. In turn, her willingness to join in daily chores and learn fragments of their lyrical language had earned acceptance, if not yet complete trust. Picking her way back down the slippery path, Elizabeth felt her spirits lift. Ragged clothes and deeper tanned skin aside, this place had become more home to her than the so-called civilized world across the ocean now. Here she was judged only by her willingness to embrace each day's small joys and challenges, nothing more. Reaching the outskirts, Elizabeth wove through the orderly crop fields towards the central cooking fires. But a commotion near the headman's longhouse caught her attention. A group had gathered anxiously around one man gesturing wildly as he shared some news. Curious, she drifted closer but hesitated to intrude until old Shando, one of the elders she had befriended, waved her over urgently. The gathered villagers made space for her with encouraging smiles. Her heart swelled at this simple acceptance. Turning to Shando, she asked quietly, "What has happened, Wise One? Good tidings I hope?" The old man nodded enthusiastically, continuing to point toward the agitated man who had arrived with some message. Elizabeth listened closely as Shando spoke to the assembly in broken but clear enough common tongue, seemingly for her benefit. "Moki come from far north. Say pale man found in old trapper camp...hurt leg, half dead. He nurse the man there." Murmurs rippled through the crowd. Heart suddenly racing, Elizabeth moved forward and grasped Shando's arm urgently. "This pale man...did he say his name? Or leave belongings?" She pulled Peter's worn leather journal from her satchel. "Please, I must know who he is!" Shando studied her distraught face for a long moment before turning to confer with the newcomer. After an exchange in their native tongue, he spoke to Elizabeth gently. "The man fevered and weak still when Moki find him. But we go see if he your friend. I send warriors to carry you swiftly." Nearly dizzy with anxious hope, Elizabeth squeezed Shando's weathered hand in gratitude. If even a chance existed that somehow fate had finally guided her across Peter's path, she must seize it before life ripped the opportunity away once more. Time blurred to a crawl as she hastily gathered meager supplies for the journey north and waited amongst the buzzing villagers for the departure party to assemble. Had Peter been here all along she wondered frantically, so close but always one step ahead? She prayed this was not some cruel illusion about to shatter like all the rest. At last with Shando and a handful of guides, Elizabeth set off into the lush jungle. The warriors moved smoothly along narrow trails with long loping strides, and she struggled to match their tireless pace. She would have gladly crawled on hands and knees through thorn bushes if it brought her to Peter's side sooner. When they finally reached the secluded valley after nearly two days of relentless travel, Elizabeth thought her heart might burst from suspense. She was beyond exhausted, filthy, ravaged by insects - none of it mattered. They were close, so agonizingly close. Moki, the young hunter who had found the wounded stranger, greeted them eagerly outside a small thatched hut. He spoke rapidly with Shando before turning to Elizabeth, miming someone sleeping and pointing inside. She made to rush forward, but Shando gently held her back. "Wait, child. Let Moki tend him best he can first." Seeing her crestfallen face, the old man smiled kindly. "Suffered long to find your friend. Have faith a little longer." Releasing her arm, he gestured encouragement. Forcing impatient limbs to stillness, Elizabeth sank down against a broad tree to keep watch. She focused on steadying her breathing and tracing patterns in the dirt to ignore the tempting proximity. Peter had been delivered back to her against all odds. She would give him space to heal now. When Moki finally emerged and inclined his head affirmatively to her, Elizabeth jumped up, heart hammering wildly. This was the moment she had chased across continents and endless lonely miles. Struggling to contain her shock and joy, she stepped through the low doorway. A gaunt figure lay sweating and mumbling fretfully on a woven mat, his back to her. But the tousled auburn hair was unmistakable. "Peter..." she whispered hoarsely, tears springing to her eyes. It was him, flesh and blood, not a specter. Rushing forward, she fell to her knees and grasped his hand, pressing fervent kisses to fever-hot skin. At her touch, his eyes blinked open, bloodshot and confused, searching her tear-stained face hovering over him. "Lizzy?" Peter croaked weakly through dry, cracked lips. "Can't be...you're a dream..." He grimaced as if the effort of speaking pained him terribly. Pressing her palm to his stubbled cheek, Elizabeth shook her head, emotion threatening to choke her utterly. "I am here, my love. I am real." She placed his limp hand over her racing heart. "I have crossed the world to find you again. Stay with me now." Eyes shining with wonder and tears, Peter managed the ghost of his old roguish grin. "Ever my siren...calling me home." He sagged back onto the pallet, exhausted but clinging fiercely to her hand in his. At long last, their twin stars had aligned. Time blurred as Elizabeth tended Peter day and night, gently washing fevered sweat from his brow, trickling medicine broth and precious fresh water down his throat. Though still terribly weak, the fire slowly returned to his eyes as he regained strength. Her heart could burst from profound joy. On the third morning when she woke, he was sitting up watching her sleep, wretched illness finally passed. A myriad words crowded her heart, but she simply laid her head in his lap like the old days under the willow tree, tears slipping down. His body was thin and battered by harsh years, hair streaked with silver now. But it was Peter - the man who had imprinted himself on her very soul. Fate had mercifully steered them through the wilderness back to one another's arms. When his gnarled fingers began softly stroking her hair just like memory, Elizabeth thought she might die from sheer bliss. No greater balm existed after endless lonely exile. Here she was whole at last - known, held, understood. Nothing else signified. The details of loss and heartache could wait. This moment was too precious, like a dream neither dared wake from. The outside world with its snares and lies would still be there tomorrow. But not even empires could touch them here. At some point, words must pass between them, explanations be shared. What currents of chance had separately borne them over years and continents to arrive in this remote corner? For now, only the shelter of Peter's arms mattered. They had found their compass home.

Chapter 25

Elizabeth traced her fingers reverently over the faded lines on the parchment map, disbelief and hope swirling within her like the tides. Scant days ago she had been lost in grief when Peter's mysterious fever claimed his life before they could even fully reconnect. Now this cryptic map uncovered among his few belongings promised she might yet find answers. According to the tribal shaman, Peter had regained lucidity only once after Elizabeth had vigilantly tended him back to health following the snakebite. In a moment of startling clarity before the fever returned, he had pressed this paper urgently into the healer's hands. "For Lizzy," he had rasped. "Give her this when I am gone. She will know." Then the fire had consumed him again, and by morning he was gone. Two grief-stricken days later when the shaman presented her with Peter's final gift, the mysterious chart initially meant nothing to Elizabeth. She recognized none of the landmarks or script in his hurried scrawl. But Peter had believed she would decipher its meaning in time. She must trust this last act of faith. Carefully folding the fragile map, she tucked it into her satchel with Peter's few other recovered belongings - his lucky sailor's amulet, a compass, the leather-bound journal she had not yet been able to open since it seemed the last sacred remnant of his innermost thoughts. Looking out at the mist-shrouded jungle, she blinked back fresh tears. Somewhere within its feral beauty still waited discoveries and answers, perhaps even peace, if she had courage to seek them. With Peter gone, this map was her only tether - to the past and to herself. She must follow without hesitation. The elders had graciously allowed her time to grieve before urging Elizabeth gently to continue her sojourn. They knew her spirit's home was not with their tribe. She belonged to the wild open horizon, chasing dreams - the very same spark that had drawn her and Peter together across worlds. So she had set off into the forest three days later, turning her feet where the map dictated, trusting that Peter had created some trail for her to follow. She owed him this faith after how far she had already journeyed led only by the compass of her untamed heart. Several loyal tribesmen accompanied to help track and forage, though they clearly knew little of where Peter meant for her path to wend. Each night around the fire, Elizabeth pored over the cryptic chart, willing it to yield some epiphany. What had Peter wished her to find out here? She could not fail him now when they had come so close. Gradually her escorts turned back as the terrain grew too difficult, until only she remained trekking doggedly onward. She did not fear being alone here anymore, not with the map as her guide and talisman. Peter's spirit seemed to whisper encouragingly through the dappled light - just a little farther. The day she stumbled unexpectedly into the rocky clearing at what appeared the journey's end, Elizabeth sank to her knees in disbelief. A small cave veiled by hanging vines matching the distinctive shape on Peter's map. She had found it somehow despite the impossible odds. Fate yet guided their entwined story. On shaky legs, she parted the cascade of leaves and entered the cool quiet gloom. Etched symbols and drawings covered the walls, evidence of the cave's sanctity to past tribes. Peter would have revered such a refuge. Perhaps his soul had wished to rest here too. Calming her racing heart, she lifted the makeshift torch aloft and scanned for anything resembling the crude 'X' on Peter's map. In the flickering light, a smudge of color caught her eye and she hurried over to a small stone cairn topped with a carved wooden chest. Hardly daring to breathe, Elizabeth carefully lifted the lid. Inside, a journal and bundle of cloth nestled atop a worn leather satchel. Clasping them gently to her chest in disbelief, she sank down, tears slipping silently down her cheeks. These were Peter's deepest secrets, left in trust that only she would uncover them. However bitterly destiny had parted them in flesh, some immutable bond between their spirits had persevered. Setting aside the cloth and satchel for now, she reverently opened the small leather journal. Pages crowded with sketches, verses, pressed flowers, and Peter's untidy scrawl bared the landscape of his soul that she had only glimpsed fleetingly in their stolen nights together. She traced each line hungrily, hearing his voice emerge at last from the silence. When she came to the final entry weeks before his death, Elizabeth's throat tightened, seeing her own name appear amidst fevered delirium... My Lizzy, Truest North of my compass, how I have failed you. Our time was cut too short by my cowardice. All I can leave you now are these scattered fragments of a life lived half ashore, half at sea without ballast. Forgive what small amends I tried to make. Know that you ever guided me right in spirit, if not deed. Let my last gift be the freedom to seek your destiny unburdened. With deepest love, your Peter With hands now shaking, she slowly folded the letter away and sat staring into the light until her vision cleared. Even at the end he had thought of her, left a trail so she might find this last piece of himself. Her own grief seemed suddenly selfish. Wiping her eyes, she reached for the satchel and parcel of fabric. Inside the worn bag, Elizabeth drew a startled breath to find a small fortune in gold and jewels - likely pirate plunder from Peter's seafaring days. In the cloth wrappings lay an exquisite emerald necklace that could only have been meant as a bridal gift for her. Overwhelmed, she sank back down to the earthen floor. This treasure could have granted them a life together anywhere in the world - leisure, comfort, joy. But Peter had chosen to leave it, wanting her free to chart her own course beyond material constraints...or perhaps ashamed of its tainted origin. Carefully she placed the necklace atop the gold and gems before wrapping them again. This cave would continue guarding its secrets. She had faith now that Peter walked at her side in spirit. That mattered far more than earthly fortune. Let this remain hidden for those who sought such wealth, like the Pulitzer family. Taking a last moment to soak in the solace of the grotto Peter had wished her to find, Elizabeth pressed a farewell kiss to the wooden chest. Some things were beyond price. "Be at peace, my love." Emerging from the cave's cocoon felt like being reborn. The jungle breeze caressed her tear-stained cheeks. Brave new hope and purpose kindled in her breast. Just as Peter had gifted her freedom one last time, she must now summon courage to walk on alone. Trailing her hand along the sun-warmed rocks like an old friend, she turned to follow the light filtering through swaying leaves. So much lay ahead to discover and fill with meaning. This map had been but the first threshold. Now her own vision must guide the way. On she pressed through lush verdant beauty, the future unfolding one step after another. Someday they would meet again at journey's end under a sky with no compass but their souls. Until then...onward.

Chapter 26

Elizabeth traced her fingers over the weathered leather cover of the journal, hesitant to open it. This was Peter's inner world laid bare on the pages within - his past, dreams, deepest thoughts. Part of her felt she was intruding on something profoundly intimate. And yet he had left this book for her to one day uncover, along with directions to find his hidden jungle grotto. He wanted her to know him fully at last. Taking a deep breath, she slowly opened the first page. Peter's untidy scrawl covered the paper edge to edge. Some entries were mere snippets, while others ran on for multiple pages, his emotions pouring out like the tide. Some passages were scribbled over or scratched out entirely in frustration. She ached imagining him alone here struggling to reconcile his turmoil. May 17, 1781 This forsaken island both heaven and hell. I have not glimpsed another soul in weeks it seems, yet never have I felt less alone. It is solitude as I have long needed - space for the soul to stir and take wing after being locked in irons so long by past deeds. My only companions are memories, regrets, and the spirits speaking through the land itself. Each day I wander deeper, learning its secrets and testing my limits against its indifference. If I am humble, this place may yet cure what has long festered in my spirit... July 25, 1781 She plagues my thoughts ceaselessly though I have no right. Our boyish tryst seems another lifetime ago, when the world still shone with dew-kissed promise. How could I have dreamed a soul like Elizabeth's would linger to light my darkness? Even now I see her watching each sunset with those eyes clear as truth itself, feel her hand slip into mine unafraid as we raced under stars. A undeserved gift of grace I left cold in the dust without explanation. My penance now is waking each dawn choked with longings and old shame... October 14, 1781 This morning I woke drenched in sweat from the same nightmare that has haunted me since youth - chains dragging me down into fathomless black depths while a shadowed form looks on pitilessly. I know whose face the phantom wears. My failures trail behind like iron ghosts. This island was to be my refuge, but it seems one cannot outrun the past. If salvation exists, it will only be through reckoning honestly. I have scratched these walls with pretty words and verses, but avoided etching truth in my heart. It is time now to lay down arms, prepare amends, and pray Lizzy's capacity for forgiveness is not also wasted... Elizabeth set down the journal, eyes blurring with tears. Even out here in solitary exile, she had been woven through his days - a guiding light he neither felt worthy of nor able to fully extinguish. These weathered pages held years of unsent letters from his soul to hers. Wiping her cheeks, she lifted the book again. She would honor Peter's courage in baring his shadows by reading every line without judgment. He had been more than just a wild, charming rogue - he was a man stretched taut between honor and darkness, always reaching for the light. November 3, 1781 What a small, pathetic thing this hunt for gold seems now. When I first set off oozing bravado, I thought only of how such wealth might win Elizabeth's hand. But her spirit seeks finer ore than can be weighed in scales or stamped as coins. She awoke that truth in me as well before we parted - that I am more than base metal, beat and weathered as I am. I wish I had been wise enough then to cling to her vision... January 17, 1782 This morning I woke suddenly gripped by longing to see England's green shores again, walk the cobblestone lane to Lizzy's cottage thick with honeysuckle. Do our childhood secret places remain undisturbed? Does she also reminisce by that moonlit pond, or have more worthy memories overwritten me? I pray she is well and blooming still. When she comes to mind, I see only the bright girl untainted by how I later darkened her joy. Would that I could send these letters I compose to explain all and beg her grace. But I relinquished any claim on her heart long ago and can only pray she is happy now... February 14, 1782 I sat watching the thunderstorm rage over the sea today, feeling my own restless spirit reflected in nature's fury. If only there existed such a cathartic outlet for old regrets and passions. At times I consider casting everything to the waves - journal, past, identity - stripping myself to essence alone. Yet I fear what would remain in that silence. There are still words unspoken my soul needs to birth before it can be reborn. I long for an end to this aimless wandering exile, but the way back remains unclear. So I persist here adrift between worlds, belonging to neither. Storm within and without. Elizabeth set down the journal again, throat tight. Her heart ached for the Peter here so full of longing and uncertainty. If she had known the internal conflicts tormenting him then, she would have crossed any distance to listen, offer acceptance. They had both been just young wanderers seeking their place. Perhaps she could still grant him some measure of the hard-won wisdom time had etched on her own soul since. He had left this chronicle as a bridge between their journeys. She would finish reading it as a sacred rite to bless all they had been and might yet become. March 5, 1782 By chance today I discovered a hidden grotto that struck me as singularly beautiful and serene, washed in streams of light despite its sunless depths. I sat for hours tracing my fingers over etchings left by others who had taken refuge there through time. Seldom have I felt such a sense of solace and containment within stone walls, as if the earth itself could absorb all tribulations. I wish someday to share such a place with Lizzy, see joy light her face at its wonder. For now I commit the grotto's location to this journal should time and fate allow us paths to converge once more. My compass ever points to her, no matter how far I roam. Our spirits yet trace lines across the sand longing to intersect. The day they finally do I can set my battered vessel to rest forever.... April 16, 1782 Each dawn now I wake surprised to be alive still. It is not that I seek an end by my own hand. But I feel my flame guttering low, the inexorable tide tugging me away grain by grain from all moorings. Perhaps this solitary existence has served its purpose in stripping me down to essence and truth. But the soul needs roots and sun to thrive, not just storms scouring it raw. I am so very weary of wrestling these demons alone. Faith, absolution, most of all a caring touch - I have denied myself too long. Pride insists on maintaining this futile exile, but the heart knows you cannot outpace what haunts... Elizabeth closed the journal gently as the last pages ended. Tears slipped down her cheeks for the Peter here so desperately seeking solace amidst inner demons, still holding fast to the redemptive vision of their entwined futures. If she had come to this island sooner, could she have eased his struggles? Or would fate always have torn them apart as it did in the end? What mattered now, she decided, was the love and understanding she could yet grant his memory by truly absorbing his unsent words to her. Peter had committed his innermost dreams and regrets to this journal, a message in a bottle meant for her alone. She would honor its sanctity and all it signified of their enduring bond. Running a finger over the weathered cover, Elizabeth smiled through her tears. The man she had thought just a reckless rogue had possessed a poet's soul, weathered by life but still seeking truth and connection. She could give no greater gift than embracing the totality of him, shadows and light alike. Their souls had recognized the call of kinship, whatever paths divided them after. Carefully she wrapped the precious book in its protective leather and stowed it in her pack. Though their time together had been fleeting, Peter's spirit would walk beside hers now through every step of the unknown road ahead. And someday they would meet again in a place beyond maps or words, where two journeys finally intertwined into one. With peaceful hope settling in her chest, Elizabeth rose and set her face towards the gently beckoning light. The landscape of their entwined story stretched onward, and she would continue writing its poetry in footsteps.

Chapter 27

Elizabeth shuddered beneath the thin blanket, sweat beading on her brow despite the chills racking her body. The hut spun and tilted sickeningly whenever she tried opening her eyes, sounds and light blurring together in a disorienting haze. Somewhere through the agonizing fog, she heard a woman's soothing voice speaking words she could not decipher. A mercifully cool cloth bathed her fiery skin. Hands lifted her head to trickle water and bitter medicine broth down her throat. She clung to the comfort of a human presence anchoring her when it felt she might float away entirely into darkness. Time ceased to hold meaning as the fever ravaged her without relent. Elizabeth was only dimly aware of days and nights passing in a hellish monotony of bone-deep pain and delirium. In lucid moments, she knew death hovered at the bedside awaiting its chance to claim her. But somehow she found strength to hold on when shadows beckoned. Giving up felt like a betrayal to life and its promise still. Gradually the death-grip of fever loosened by imperceptible degrees. When at last Elizabeth woke clear-eyed beneath the thatched roof instead of thrashing in nightmares, she marveled at the precious feel of crisp linen on skin, birdsong drifting through the open window. She breathed in the blessing of simple sensation that almost slipped away forever. Turning her head weakly, she saw the village widow Akela sleeping upright in a chair beside the bed, face creased in exhaustion even at rest. Deep gratitude welled up at the realization this devoted woman had single-handedly shepherded her back from the brink through long days and nights. In all her life Elizabeth could not recall anyone caring for her so selflessly. The woman's faith in her survival went beyond obligation - it betrayed a steadfast love beyond words. Elizabeth was suddenly overcome by how much she had needed that grace. Stirring quietly, Akela blinked herself awake and broke into a joyful toothless grin to find Elizabeth conscious and coherent again. With the island dialect they had slowly constructed between them, she effused praise to the spirits for the miracle of her recovery when so many succumbed to such jungle fevers. Too weak for more than a few rasping words in return, Elizabeth simply covered the old woman's hand with her own, blinking back tears. Whatever this illness had been, she knew she would not have survived its ravages without this faithful soul. She vowed silently to spend her remaining days trying to repay that devotion. As her strength gradually returned over the following weeks, Elizabeth found Akela had become far more than a healer. She was mentor, confessor, mother - the steadying anchor her adrift spirit had unknowingly needed. Every small kindness revealed new depths of compassion beneath the woman's outwardly stern bearing. They developed their own routines - long walks collecting herbs at sunrise, preparing meals together and telling stories late into the evening by firelight. Akela's sly wit and wisdom deeply impressed Elizabeth. She taught her which jungle plants cured sickness, which brought visions, where the spirits spoke. Elizabeth taught her writing and numbers in the dirt. Both blossomed. One quiet afternoon as they sat weaving baskets in the shade, Akela spoke gently, sensing the old melancholy in her young friend's spirit. "My son, many summers gone now...your age. Bright light too soon darkened. But helps me see." She lifted Elizabeth's chin tenderly. "All life precious. Future still open." Elizabeth's eyes misted at this insight from one who had suffered deeply yet chose kindness. She still clung to the ghosts of her naïve past dreams so tightly. Akela was right - the present held gifts enough for those who embraced it. She laid her head in the old woman's lap then as she had her own mother's long ago. With comforting fingers stroking her hair, the knot of grief in Elizabeth's chest finally loosened and tears fell. Amidst so much loss and uncertainty, she had found unanticipated home. For this she was humbly grateful. By unspoken agreement they never mentioned Elizabeth's eventual departure, though they knew separation must come. Word had spread that her ship had safely limped into port after the storm finally passed. Plans for mapping the island's coast were resuming now that conditions allowed. They would need to take on fresh crew. Each evening as they stirred the cookfire, Elizabeth wrestled with anticipating that bittersweet day's arrival - torn between longing to see familiar faces and share tales of all she had experienced...and reluctance to leave this cherished new life behind forever. She could not deny part of her spirit had taken root here when she least expected it. Goodbyes would be painful. But late at night when she lay restless, staring into the dark, Elizabeth would feel the sea's distant murmur calling her name persistently. Circumstance had swept her here, but destiny yet beckoned her onward however she tried ignoring its pull. She could not simply hide away in isolation forever, however comforting. Out there somewhere, her course lay still unfolding. She need only find courage to hoist anchor one more time. So the morning the captain himself hiked up through the jungle to implore Elizabeth and any able crew members to return so they might depart with the tides, she knew in her soul the time had come, ready or not. Swiftly she gathered her few belongings, the gifts from Akela, and weathered pages that were Peter's only legacy. She had all she needed. When they stood at last on the misty shore to say farewell, Elizabeth saw the old widow's eyes were dry - sad but proud. Taking both her hands, Elizabeth spoke fervently the words she had rehearsed all morning. "You gave me life itself when fate washed me astray here. I have no gifts or words to repay such kindness. If ever you need me, I will cross oceans and more." Akela squeezed her hands tightly, eyes sparkling with love and understanding. But she glanced over Elizabeth's shoulder to where the captain waited respectfully up the beach before answering gently, "Your path leads onward, though you forget sometimes. But I will be here if you need haven." With a final fierce embrace, Elizabeth surrendered her heart's desire to cling to nostalgia and forced her feet to turn away down the glistening sand. The old woman's wisdom had set her free once more. Though the horizon's uncertainty called, the coming tides seemed less daunting with Akela's spirit lighting her way. She set her sails pointed resolutely forward.

Chapter 28

Elizabeth stood on the craggy cliffs overlooking the island's wild eastern shore as the morning mist burned away, revealing towering breakers crashing against jagged rocks far below. Somewhere out there beyond the foam lay the opposite coast she had spent weeks journeying towards - where Peter's hand-drawn map indicated he had explored in his years here. Consulting his weathered journal, she found the passage describing his crossing to that uncharted side of the island: "I have caught glimpses of a fabled ridgeline across the bay when conditions allow. There are tales among the villagers of a hidden paradise valley over there, untouched since the first people landed generations ago. I confess the allure of being the first modern man to lay eyes on such unspoiled Eden calls to my restless spirit. Perhaps answers I seek reside not in wandering endless circles here but in striking out boldly across the divide..." The account ended abruptly, with no further mention of whether he had attempted the dangerous voyage. But the lure of answers - about Peter and herself - had become overpowering as Elizabeth recovered her strength after the fever. She knew now she would never be content on this side where they had walked the same sands separately. Her destiny awaited on the far shore. The tribal elders had solemnly given permission when she beseeched them, movable by her determination. They had bestowed their blessing along with provisions, warnings, and three sturdy canoes for the crossing. Strong youths had volunteered as oarsmen too, though their faces betrayed more apprehension than courage in the face of the notoriously turbulent channel. Now as the sun climbed higher, burnishing the sea gold, Elizabeth turned to her small crew already crowded into the boats. "Remember, we must time our crossing carefully, staying tight together. The island will guide us through if we show courage and respect." The men nodded silently, gripping their oars with white knuckles. Elizabeth gave a small reassuring smile though her own stomach churned anxiously imagining the miles of open water ahead. "Let us be off then while the day is still young!" With that she climbed into the lead canoe, clutching Peter's journal like a talisman. At her signal, the men dipped oars and powered steadily away from shore into the crystalline cove. For now the waters remained calm and shallow, lulling the boats gently. But she knew the real test awaited beyond the headlands. As the high bluffs fell away behind them, vaster swells began to lift and drop the hulls ominously. Elizabeth kept her eyes fixed staunchly ahead, though the shore had faded to a thin green line behind. "Keep forward momentum!" she called encouragingly above the building wind. "We have come too far to falter." Impossibly, the men bent their backs harder, voices chanting in rhythmic time with each punishing stroke as the sea swelled ever higher. The canoes became tiny corks bobbing at the troughs' mercy as endless walls of water crashed perilously close, drenching them in foam. Elizabeth tasted salt on her lips, hair flying damply across her face. Exhilaration vied with raw fear now at the ocean's ferocious power. They were utterly at its mercy. But still she gripped the canoe sides and shouted herself hoarse urging the flagging men onward. They had passed the point of returning. Ferrying Peter's journal safely across this barrier had become her sole purpose. Without warning, a colossal wave stove the stern of the last canoe, sending its occupants spilling out. Crying out in horror, Elizabeth nearly dove in after them before the awful truth stopped her - injured and floundering in these deadly swells, they were as good as dead. With anguished resolve, she turned away, screaming at the remaining boat to pull ahead out of reach of the capsized men's desperate grasps. This sacrifice was necessary, however it shredded her soul. Long torturous hours later, the clouds parted to reveal the island's far shore at last, impossibly close. With a choked sob, Elizabeth urged her one remaining crew on faster through the crashing surf onto blessed sand. They had survived crossing into the unknown. But at what cost, she shuddered, remembering the lost faces swallowed by those merciless waves. There could be no turning back now. After dragging the canoe higher to avoid the tide, they collapsed in exhausted silence on the pristine cove. Elizabeth's eyes stung with salt and tears - for the men taken by the sea's wrath, for precious pages of Peter's journal ruined by seawater in her pack, for their own fates now so uncertain. But she steadied her voice to speak calmly to the wind-scoured crew. "We have reached this sacred place through gravest trial and loss. Let us honor those sacrificed by embracing the gift of days still granted us. Tomorrow we will restock supplies and then press on to find whatever awaits here." She met each man's eyes, seeing her own bone-weariness reflected. "You have my deepest thanks and loyalty. Now try to sleep." As the men slumped gratefully into slumber around the driftwood fire, Elizabeth wandered the edge of surf alone, taking melancholy comfort in the heaving swells that seemed to echo her own roiling emotions. She had gained so much wisdom since leaving her sheltered upbringing what felt lifetimes ago. But this stark reminder of her own limits against nature's might left her humbled to the core. She prayed such wisdom was not gained too late nor at too steep a cost. With the morning sun, optimism gradually displaced grief and doubt once more. Raking the glowing embers to life again, Elizabeth managed a brave smile for the men roused by the warmth. "I believe some rich fishing grounds lie not far offshore. Let us break fast and then you shall teach me to properly bait a hook and line!" The mundane task salved spirits and replenished energy. Bellies full, pack reprovisioned, and courage restored, they left the quiet cove to follow the shore inland. Scrambling up the densely forested slopes, they came across a winding waterfall spilling down ancient stones into idyllic pools, too perfect to be anything but sacred. Had Peter sat here watching those same silvery cascades in awe? She traced the mossy rocks, sensing his ghost. As the days passed hiking rivers and winding tracks through majestic peaks and valleys, Elizabeth often paused, feeling they drew closer to answers still veiled. Tribesmen spoke in awed voices of a high hidden plateau beyond the next crest, pristine and rarely glimpsed by outsiders. If Peter had journeyed here seeking refuge, surely that remote paradise would have called to his weary soul. When at last the dense jungle canopy broke to reveal a meadow roamed by exotic plumed beasts, Elizabeth gasped in awe. This was the fabled valley from tribal lore and likely Peter's journal. They had discovered a glimpse of unspoiled Eden. With reverence, they made camp at the far edge, leaving the plateau's beauty untouched. That night around the fire, Elizabeth's voice rang clear and steady recounting their long and perilous quest to reach this rare place. "Tomorrow, once we have rested and paid homage, I will continue on alone to find what we lost." The men looked uncertain about abandoning her, but she silenced their protests kindly but firmly. "You have fulfilled your promised duty beyond expectation. Live and keep our story if I do not return." At their solemn nods, she smiled bravely and turned in, Peter's water-warped journal tucked under her head. Whatever came next, she would face with faith. His spirit guided hers now. At first light, Elizabeth shouldered her pack alone and strode purposefully towards the plateau shimmering in the distance. Her strides steadied with each step closer to accepting destiny's mysterious course. Peter's journal crinkled comfortingly inside her tunic, pressed over her heart. Its remaining pages must yet hold clues if she was worthy to uncover them. The life she had known and the woman she dreamt of becoming had merged somewhere along the long road here. She glanced back only once at the shadowed coast behind, then stepped resolutely forward into sunlight. Whatever answers awaited on this undiscovered shore, she was ready.

Chapter 29

Elizabeth jolted awake to a mouthful of wet sand and waves lapping at her ankles. Coughing violently, she pushed up onto her elbows and squinted against the harsh sunlight. Her head throbbed as she struggled to recall how she'd ended up sprawled alone on this unfamiliar shore. Wisps of memory flitted just out of reach - a violent storm...pounding surf swamping the canoes...yelling in panic as the world became a blur of darkness. And now this. Blinking slowly, she took in her surroundings. No sign of the canoes or crew who had braved the crossing with her. She was utterly alone on this remote coast with only her water-logged rucksack. At least Peter's journal was safe against her chest, shielded by oilskin. She had fulfilled her oath to bring it here, though little else remained of their expedition. Rising unsteadily on still wobbling legs, Elizabeth shaded her eyes to scan for some landmark to get her bearings. But the beach curved empty for miles in either direction. Steep jungle shrouded the shoreline, with no paths or breaks visible. Clearly this was an untamed corner of the island far from any villages. Unease flickered through her at the ominous isolation, but she steadied herself against despair. Her crew might yet wash ashore somewhere. She need only choose a direction and search for life. Surely she could forage sufficient food and shelter day by day. Gritting her teeth, Elizabeth shouldered the heavy bag and turned north along the tideline. Wherever this place was, it became her path now. Several days passed in grueling but uneventful march as she skirted tangled mangroves and rocky cliffs. The sea remained her constant murky companion, though she began to worry about fresh water with none found yet inland. Strange bird calls echoed eerily at dusk. But she was grateful to encounter no further souls in this desolate country. Solitude among wild beauty remained far preferable to the violence of men. Until the morning distant shouts jolted her from sleep curled on wet sand. Peering cautiously through palm fronds, Elizabeth felt her empty stomach lurch. Several hundred yards up the beach, shadowy figures emerged from the treeline - even at this distance clearly European convicts from their ragged prison uniforms. Desperados likely escaped into the island's uncharted interior to evade capture. Fear surged through her. Clearly these men had been loose and growing increasingly feral for some time. And a lone female castaway would be helpless against their lusts. Keeping low, Elizabeth slipped back into the camouflaging jungle fringe with breath held. The heavy footfalls and guttural laughter eventually faded up the shore. Once it seemed safe, she crept from hiding on shaky legs. Cold reason warned her to turn back south and flee this stretch of coast now clearly prowled by murderers and miscreants. But hunger, exhaustion, and stubbornness rooted her to the spot. She had sacrificed too much to simply surrender and cower from evil men. This was her island as much as theirs. Still, caution seemed wise at least until she learned just what darkness lurked here. Glancing around the secluded inlet, Elizabeth's eyes alighted on a rocky cliff face draped in vines that concealed a deep cleft. If the passage went deep enough into the hillside, it would provide cover. Gripping her knife, she began slowly working her way up the crude path. The narrow gully twisted deep into the rocks until it abruptly opened onto a hidden sheltered cavern near the top of the bluff - large enough for several people and stocked with basic provisions left by past castaways. Elizabeth nearly wept in relief. This would shelter her indefinitely while she gained strength and planned her next move. Fate had provided reprieve. Over the ensuing days, Elizabeth settled into cautious rhythm in the cave hideaway. She crept down by night under moonlight to fish and forage, evading the escaped prisoners who she now realized roamed this whole frontier coast. Their numbers seemed to grow daily, judging by distant laughter echoing off the water. They were masters here now, savagery replacing humanity. Part of Elizabeth still recoiled at being driven into hiding like quarry. This was her island as much as theirs! But she knew confronting evil directly would gain her nothing but a shallow grave here. If she was patient, some opportunity for escape might yet arise. She need only endure and not abandon hope. The thought of Peter kept her fighting despair. Nights were the hardest, listening to raucous male voices and wild shouting carrying on the offshore breeze. They sounded increasingly drunk and unhinged as their exile dragged on. She wondered fearfully how long before madness drove them inland to root out any prey. The day Elizabeth returned from fishing to find bootprints in the cave's muddy floor, she knew her brief sanctuary was ending. They had discovered her haven, likely following some careless tracks. Nowhere remained safe from their predations. Fleeing with only her bag of precious journals and clothes, she did not stop running until she reached a tiny hidden cove she had scouted before as possible emergency retreat. But the sheer rock walls allowed no escape except back into the waiting jungle. She was cornered finally. Footsteps echoed on the cove's rock walls by mid afternoon, followed by jeering voices calling crude taunts. Elizabeth stared defiantly as filthy faces ringed the rim above, leering down at her. So this was how her defiant journey ended - prey for vultures. She clenched her fists and stood tall, determined not to cower or begging before these brutes. A brawny red-haired man with wild beard seemed to be their leader. He leered down at Elizabeth's slight form pacing angrily below. "Look here lads, catch of the day!" Raucous laughter followed. "Don't worry poppet, we aim to treat you real hospitable-like. Won't last long out here alone anyhow." Ignoring his crude threats, Elizabeth fixed him with her most imperious stare. "I belong to no man, least of all pathetic criminals. Do your worst, I shall never submit." She kept her chin high, sounding braver than her quaking heart. But she would cling to pride and agency until the end. The men roared laughter, clearly enjoying her fiery defiance. "Ooooh lads, this kitty has claws! We'll tame her right enough. Who's first for a tussle?" They began shoving each other bawdily. Elizabeth scrubbed furious tears away, refusing to show fear. But she could not stave them off forever.

These brutes meant to ravage and enslave her until she lost even the memory of who she had been. The thought made the cove walls spin sickeningly. She bent double fighting panic, breaths coming in ragged gasps. Strong arms gripped her shoulders suddenly from behind as a gruff voice hissed, "Get hold of yourself! We haven't a chance unless you keep your wits. I'm here to help you but we must move quickly." Twisting round in shock, she met the weathered face of a tall bearded man in sailor's garb, scarred and wind-tanned beneath a fraying hat. Despite his rough exterior, his grey eyes shone with unexpected warmth and wisdom. An ally had impossibly arrived in this blackest hour. Too stunned to speak, she nodded mutely. Taking her hand, he peered quickly up at the unsuspecting men still arguing and laughing raucously above before pulling her toward a thin crevice along the rear wall. "Stay close by me and match my footsteps exactly, miss. Our only hope is slipping free before they notice." Hardly daring to breathe, she followed him sideways into the narrow crack, the damp walls squeezing tight as darkness enveloped them. He edged them deftly along nowhere as fast as the voices faded above. Her faith in this mysterious protector was absolute now. She clung to his calloused hand like a lifeline. After long torturous minutes, squinting eyes made out a distant pinprick of light. A root-tangled opening lay just ahead. With a final heave, they burst from the stale blackness into open sunlit air again, home free. Her rescuer gentled her to sit atop a mossy boulder and pressed his canteen into her mud-caked hand. "Drink first, then we'll talk more." He studied her solemnly as she managed grateful sips. This faded fatherly sailor had saved her from a wretched fate. But she sensed their meeting here was more than mere chance. A deeper knowing tugged at her heart, something in his eyes... Wiping her mouth with the back of one filthy hand, she found her voice at last, still hoarse. "However can I thank you enough sir? I am in your debt beyond words. You arrived just when... I thought I would..." Sobs cut short her stumbling gratitude. He waved her tears away gently. "Hush now, lass. Let's not dwell on what evil may have been, else we hand it power." He tilted her chin up. "But if thanks are owed, might I know my damsel's name?" She swiped at her cheeks, embarrassment rushing in to replace stark terror. "Forgive me, sir. I am Elizabeth." She extended a muddy hand hesitantly. "And you are?" The sailor grasped her small hand in his broad calloused one. "Name's Edmund. And think nothing of it, Miss Elizabeth. Couldn't leave a lady to those brutes in good conscience." His eyes darkened. "Seen their fiendish work before." Elizabeth shuddered. "I was nearly overcome until the Lord sent you. However did you find me in that cursed place?" Edmund looked out over the endless jungle pensively. "I know this island better than most, its secrets and such. Heard tales of escaped convicts roaming wild up the coast, so thought to investigate..." He caught her gaze. "But that's a story for another day when you've rested." Too exhausted to press further, Elizabeth simply nodded. "You are right, of course. We should find shelter and sustenance." She gestured to the daunting jungle. "Lead on as you think best. I shall follow." With a reassuring smile, Edmund headed uphill through the dense trees. Elizabeth trailed behind her rugged savior, blinking back grateful tears. By grace alone she had been spared a wretched fate. Now redemption lay along the trail ahead - obscured but drawing closer she felt with each step beside this kindly sailor who seemed heaven-sent. She would not surrender her quest again to darkness.

Chapter 30

Elizabeth huddled beneath the rocky overhang, shivering as the cold night wind knifed through her tattered dress. Nearly two weeks had passed since she fled the convicts' vile clutches, only to become hopelessly lost in this trackless jungle. With no shelter or human contact, she was growing dangerously weak from hunger and exposure. But she refused to surrender her spirit. Burying her face against her knees, she sent up another silent prayer to the heavens for deliverance. She still believed the crooked path held purpose, though hope flickered dimmer each passing day. Somewhere ahead her story waited to unfold. There must yet be meaning in the suffering. Voices suddenly jolted Elizabeth from restless slumber. Heart lurching, she pressed back against the damp rocks as tramping boots and coarse laughter drew closer through the trees. More escaped prisoners come to ravage her anew. But she would not go quietly this time. Gripping her knife, she steeled herself as the shadows took shape in the gloom. The filthy, bearded faces leering down at her were unfamiliar, but they clearly knew her identity. "There's the mad girl causes such trouble!" one chortled, kicking at her feet. "Boss be glad we drug you back. He's got plans to tame that temper." Raucous laughter followed. Fury scalded away icy fear as Elizabeth sprang up, slashing wildly with the knife, forcing the men back. "I'll die before letting brutes touch me again!" She spat at the nearest man's boots. "Do your worst, I will never break." Though her ragged voice shook, defiance blazed in her eyes. She would die proud and untamed. The circle of prisoners shifted uneasily, faces no longer so sure. Their leader grimaced at the blood now dripping from his arm where her blade had found its mark. With a growl, he backhanded Elizabeth savagely, sending pain exploding through her skull. Stars filled her vision as she crumpled to the dirt, knife falling from limp fingers. "Search her bag and be quick about it." The leader grunted orders as he nursed his wound. "Boss wants the crazy wench alive, but won't miss a few pieces." Their rough hands pawed through Elizabeth's precious satchel, discarding anything deemed worthless, until only Peter's weathered journal remained tucked in her bodice. As they yanked her to her feet, the convict called Jack lingered, eyeing her thoughtfully. She returned his searching gaze, refusing to be cowed. His stare held less cruelty than his fellow brutes and something haunted that made her wonder if humanity yet lingered beneath his grime and tattoos. But perhaps it was only illusion born of desperation. The men marched Elizabeth at knifepoint back down the twisting jungle trail as she struggled to maintain composure. But despair gnawed at the edges, warning that whatever cruel fate awaited her now, she was utterly at their mercy. Her defiant soul could only withstand so much. Without warning Jack moved up close behind her as the path narrowed. "Got no quarrel with you, missy. No sport hunting females." His whisper was so quiet she barely caught the words breathed against her ear. "Watch fer a chance tonight, then run. I'll create distraction once camp's asleep." Elizabeth whipped her head round, searching his downturned face for deception. But his eyes remained fixed ahead, jaw clenched. She dared not believe this offer, yet dared not ignore any hope. Wordlessly turning forward again, she continued marching - buoyed by this possible ally in the most unimaginable place. Holding fast to her courage was the greatest defiance left. The convict camp was an even more squalid den of depravity than Elizabeth recalled. She kept her head high and lips sealed against jeering taunts and lewd threats, following Jack toward a crude lean-to clearly meant as her holding cell. But she would not be caged quietly. As the brutes eventually succumbed to liquor and exhaustion, she watched Jack slip into the surrounding jungle gloom, just another shadow. Only the rhythmic wheeze of sleeping men disturbed the silence as moonlight illuminated her makeshift prison. Each passing minute stretched agony. Was her aide's promise just a cruel ruse? Without warning a thunderous crash resounded through camp, followed by enraged shouts. In the commotion Elizabeth glimpsed Jack silhouetted across the clearing, hacking at tents with wild abandon before disappearing into the dark. Now was her only chance. Bolting from the lean-to, she hitched up her skirts and plunged recklessly into the dense trees. Sounds of pursuit echoed behind but she did not slow, following what paths she could by moonlight. Her lungs screamed for air and muscles cramped, but she staggered on until the camp's distant glow faded. Only then did she sink to her knees sobbing, each gasp laced with disbelief at having slipped their grasp again. By dawn, Elizabeth had hobbled an impossible distance, fear and desperation fueling her long past the point of collapse. When the ground swayed sickeningly beneath her, she crawled hands and knees toward the sound of rushing water. Gulping frigid mouthfuls revived her enough to shove herself under an eroded bank, finally surrendering to oblivion. She floated half conscious for untold days, vague snatches filtering through fevered dreams - unfamiliar voices, a swaying hammock, bitter liquid poured down her throat. Each time she surfaced she was weaker, memories fraying further until only Peter's blurred face lingered before the dark claimed her again. She clung to his ghostly image desperately amidst the void. When Elizabeth finally came fully awake, it was to coarse wool covering her, the earthy scent of thatch overhead, and a wizened woman bent intently over a steaming pot in the corner, humming tunelessly. She blinked slowly, trying to grasp the impossible reality of her rescue from death's door yet again. The crone turned with a toothless grin, muttering in singsong local dialect as she hobbled to the mat with a clay cup. "Drink. Mend bones." Her expression was stern but caring as she lifted Elizabeth's head to help her swallow the rich sweet elixir. Strength seeped back into her battered body with each sip. Over the following days she learned her name was Kalinda, medicine woman and seer. The old woman tended Elizabeth tirelessly, coaxing her back to health with rejuvenating jungle cures. In halting language they traded stories - Kalinda of island spirits and rituals; Elizabeth of her lost love and desperate search that drove her here. Though frail, the crone's dark eyes flashed when she spoke of independence and wandering destinies that would not be denied. They were kindred spirits. It was Kalinda who eventually revealed that a young man had carried Elizabeth's fevered body from the jungle, begging the healer to save this defiant soul. Though she never saw him again, Elizabeth knew in her heart it could only be Jack, convict-turned-redeemer. Her desperate faith in him had proven true after all. Not all humanity was forfeit here. The day she embraced the old woman at her hut door, thanking her in broken words for restoring life and hope, Elizabeth felt reconciliation finally quiet her restless spirit. The past could remain buried. This chance to begin again was all that mattered, wherever the future led. She turned to follow the beckoning sunlight without regret.

Chapter 31

Elizabeth gripped the weathered ship's rail, salt spray tingling on her skin as the island receded to a dark line on the horizon. Part of her heart would forever remain there in that remote sanctuary that had proven trial, refuge, and redemption. But the sea called her onward. Glancing at the motley crew of escaped convicts turned sailors now manning the stolen sloop, she marveled again at the improbable turn of events. Barely a week ago she had still been Lost in the jungle resigned to exile or death after the native village was destroyed in a vicious raid. Then Jack had appeared like a specter in her palm frond shelter, risking everything to spirit her away to the secret cove where he and a handful of others were building their unlikely escape vessel. "Got no right to ask more of you, missy," he had implored. "But we aim to be shut of this cursed place and could use an extra hand." Part of her recoiled at casting her fortune again with criminals, however desperate. But something in Jack's weathered face gave her faith. "I will grant you the same mercy I was shown," she had sworn, gripping his rough hands in tenuous trust. "Now let us be gone from here forever." They had merged their ragged band of runaways into a crew bound by shared purpose - slipping anchors at midnight on the highest spring tide, eluding patrol ships, standing watch and bail while Elizabeth navigated by the stars and lodestone. Though often tossed brutally off course, they had impossibly stayed afloat through storms and skirmishes, each day putting more distance between themselves and the island that had nearly claimed them. Now they aimed for the seedy pirate haven of Tortuga, where they might scatter anonymous. Elizabeth wanted only secure passage home to begin life anew. The map she had so fervently chased was ash in her heart after everything - the missing pieces of Peter's past mattered less than the whole flawed man she had come to know in her soul. Whatever lay ahead, she would embrace without reservation or retreat. She sensed Jack approach from behind before he spoke, gravelly voice low. "Quite the navigator you be, lass. Got us this far somehow." He rested calloused hands on the rail beside hers, squinting toward the craggy cove emerging ahead. "Why'd a lady like you ever sail halfway across the world alone anyhow if you don't mind my asking?" Elizabeth smiled softly, keeping her eyes on the waves. "Seeking my destiny I suppose. And I found it - just not how I envisioned." She turned to face him fully for the first time. "But what of you Jack? You risked everything for a stranger. Why?" Shadows flickered across his weathered face at the memory. "Knew men like me once good and honest...before the drink took hold." His fingers worried at a fraying rope absently. "Helped me remember maybe I weren't too far gone, if I got shut of that place." He grimaced. "We all just beasts in cages there." Moved by this confession, Elizabeth touched his wrist. "Well I owe you my life, kind sir. Whatever awaits back home, I shall begin again wiser for having known you." Impulsively she reached up to brush her lips to his stubbled cheek. Jack looked startled by the tender gesture, eyes glistening. But he quickly masked any emotion and nodded toward the approaching shoreline. "No need for thanks, missy. Let's just never glimpse that cursed isle again." With that he turned briskly back to the rigging, leathered face shining with more than seaspray. In the bustling lawless port town, Elizabeth slept easier her first night on solid ground knowing the former inmates she had sailed with would soon melt away into the populace. At dawn, she made her way through the brawling streets to the harbormaster's office. Folding her tattered map of the journey here, she committed it to the sea at last. That chapter was closed. The portly clerk peered skeptically down his hooked nose at her worn ladylike boots and faded dress. But her imperious stare dared him to question her business. "I require swift passage back to England if you would be so kind. Cost is no object." She slid a small pouch across the desk and raised one eyebrow. Clearly eager to rid his office of this strange female castaway, the man quickly secured her a cramped berth as ship's cook aboard a merchant trader departing that week for

Southampton. Elizabeth clutched the ticket tight, pulse racing. It was finally ending - the years of disillusionment and heartache, fevered quests and despair since she had first lost Peter. She was going home to start anew. Of course bittersweet nostalgia swept over her that last evening as she stood alone watching the sun sink into the crimson sea. So much of her wild youth had been left scattered across this side of the world - dashed dreams and foolish hopes buried beneath those swaying palms forever now. But the wide horizon ahead still beckoned. A gruff voice spoke just over her shoulder. "Come to see you off proper, Lady Elizabeth." She turned to see Jack shifting hesitantly, cap twisted in his weathered hands. His ruddy face broke into a crooked grin. "Who'd have thought we'd both get free of that devil's snare?" Elizabeth could not help returning his infectious smile, eyes pricking with tears. Wordlessly she clasped this unwitting guardian of her soul in a fierce embrace under the fading stars they had navigated by. When she pulled back, palming moisture from her cheeks, Jack nodded solemnly. "We all got our stories still left to tell." With a final squeeze of her shoulder, he turned and limped off whistling down the lamplit quay, disappearing into the crowd forever. The next morning, sails billowed for home on the morning tide. Taking a last long breath of the sultry tradewinds that had borne her here, Elizabeth left behind all she had been or expected to become. Turning her face East, she stared resolutely toward the rising sun. Her time on that wild and broken shore was done. Whatever lay ahead now, she would continue onward unflinching - older, wiser, unfettered. And though part of her whispered Peter's name to the ocean spray, she let it fall away like the wind. He would remain enshrined in her heart untouched. That youthful dream was ended; she had been reborn through fire. All that mattered now was the blank page before her and her pen reshaped by wisdom. She would write fearlessly.

Chapter 32

Elizabeth gripped the rail of the clipper ship, salt spray stinging her face as she watched the dark smudge of island growing smaller in their wake. Nearly a year had passed since fate first swept her to that remote tropical shore where she endured endless trials. Now it faded into memory and horizon at last. Part of her soul would forever remain tangled in the lush jungle folds where she was stripped bare and reshaped by suffering into someone both stronger and kinder. She had grown beyond measure there. But it was time to release the ghosts and turn her eyes back toward unknown horizons ahead. With a bittersweet sigh, she turned away from the stern, making her way to the bow. They would dock on the colonial mainland by morning if winds held steady. She could barter passage home to England from there somehow. It still seemed a miracle that any opportunity for escape had presented itself, let alone success. Leaning against the railing, Elizabeth peered down to the lower deck where sailors and ragged convicts like herself seized their chance for freedom mingled uneasily. For a lawless bunch, they had proved reasonably civilized so far, eager for redemption. But she kept her distance just the same. Old instincts remained. One lanky man with tied-back dreadlocks looked up just then, meeting her gaze. Elizabeth managed a small grateful wave to Jack, unable to forget how she owed her place here to his daring risks twice over. His returning somber nod held neither cockiness nor warning. A worthy man, for all his flaws, she judged. Perhaps they all deserved second chances. Reflecting on her own unlikely transformation stirred up thoughts of Peter once again. Throughout all her trials on the island, imagining they still might find each other somehow, somewhere had sustained her darkest hours. But imagining was not enough anymore. She needed truth, completion. Until she knew their full story, ghosts would haunt, keeping her from moving forward unfettered. Once back on familiar ground, Elizabeth resolved to finally commit to uncovering Peter's real fate, no matter how difficult. For all she knew, he could be long dead or wed to another. But she must know for certain. Then perhaps this restless seeking spirit could finally discover peace. The creak of boards nearby drew her from bittersweet musings. Jack leaned casually on the railing, keeping respectful distance. "Quite the tableau we make, is it not Miss Elizabeth? Rogues and lost souls desperate for second chances." His smile held sadness. "Makes a man believe grace might not be just fairy stories." Elizabeth studied him thoughtfully. "I have learned here that no soul is beyond redemption, whatever its depths. We need only accept mercy and change course." She extended her hand hesitantly. "Thank you again for the gift of possibility when I had lost all hope." Jack clasped her small hand gently in his large rough one. "You saved me too that day, showing courage I thought'd been whipped outta me forever." His face was pensive now. "Never met a woman like you, willing to fight for her freedom with such fire." The admiration in his tired eyes warmed Elizabeth's spirit. "Then let us both embrace lives worthy of the suffering that birthed them." She smiled up at him brightly, this unlikely comrade. "Fair winds carry you, Jack wherever you voyage next. Remember you are braver than you believe." With a rakish wink, he kissed her hand before sauntering away. But Elizabeth saw him swipe a sleeve roughly across his weathered face. Her words had found their mark. She prayed he would remember the man glimpsed behind the convict's brand and cling to hope of grace. The best anyone could do was move forward and try to balance the scales. The next weeks passed in a blur of uncertainty as Elizabeth took berth on the first ship returning to London she could. The voyage dragged out agonizingly as storms swept the North Atlantic, pushing their landfall further and further past the horizon. But she endured impatiently, knowing each league carried her closer to the truths that haunted her still. Walking the weathered London docks like a ghost, she made her way numbly back through the winding streets that had once been home. But much felt foreign after years roaming distant shores across oceans. She was changed, belonging nowhere and yet still tethered by bonds of memory and longing. Elizabeth paused outside the scuffed door of the narrow brick row house she had left so eagerly once. The tiny rented room within waited just as bare and lonely as the day she had shut it firmly, imagining never looking back. How foolish her younger self had been, so certain of grasping destiny boldly. The path proved far less direct. Yet standing here again now, Elizabeth felt only wistfulness, no pull to remain. This place held no answers, only nostalgia's hollow comfort. True north lay elsewhere, wherever Peter's story wove into her own. She need only discover the clues to guide her. Over the ensuing weeks she slowly tried piecing together fragments of information from old sailors' haunts and shipping logs. But facts remained sparse, shrouded by years and hearsay. Most assumed Peter Maxwell had simply perished at sea in a storm as such rogues often did. But she clung fiercely to faith that he had survived out there somewhere. Until one dim afternoon Elizabeth's steps wandered near their childhood fountain where Peter had gifted her the compass rose pendant. Still she wore it now, under layers of loss and maturity. Some memories yet glowed steady to light the way, when all other stars failed. Settling wearily on the stone bench worn smooth by years, she let her eyes drift shut, seeking that bright hopeful girl for a moment. When a gnarled hand gently grasped hers sometime later, she opened her eyes with a grateful sigh, imagining Peter had somehow heard her longing. But the elderly face meeting her gaze was kindly yet unknown. His eyes crinkled with quiet wisdom as he spoke. "Forgive an old man his intrusion, miss. But I see you are troubled, and these aged ears yet work." His voice was rich with compassion. "Might I lend them?" Stirred by his gentle aura, Elizabeth found herself pouring out her jumbled story to this grandfatherly stranger - all her hopes and trials in pursuing Peter over endless miles and years. The old sailor listened silently aside from occasional murmurs until she finally ran dry of words. Dusk was falling. When she finished, he patted her hand softly. "Quite a journey you have made, my dear. Few would dare so much to follow their heart's purpose." He studied her solemnly. "But the man you seek is no longer in this world. I regret to tell you Peter Maxwell was lost in a gale off Cape Horn three years back. I saw the wreckage myself." Though Elizabeth had steeled herself against this truth, still the words pierced like a bullet to her core. She could only sit staring at him numbly as he recounted kindly the details of the hurricane that had claimed Peter's ship and crew. There was no doubt. After so many endless miles and trials still hoping, he was truly gone. The old sailor left her there cradling her churning grief as full darkness fell. But somehow she found footing to stumble onward through the winding streets until she stood again before the vacant room that had once held her dreams so tightly. Now there was nowhere left. She was untethered, unmoored, adrift. With a mirthless huff that might have become a sob, Elizabeth shouldered the creaky door open anyway. She had no destination anymore but could not bear the streets' pitying eyes. Perhaps here in this dusty familiar tomb, her soul might finally accept the truth - Peter and her old self were gone. All opportunity had slipped through her fingers after all. The story was tragically done.

Here are a few ways I could imagine the story continuing from here:

Elizabeth embarks on a journey of self-discovery, realizing she needs time alone to heal and figure out who she is now after all her experiences abroad. She travels, meets interesting people, and starts to rebuild her confidence and sense of purpose.

Needing money to support herself, Elizabeth leverages her knowledge of foreign cultures and lands to become an explorer, translator, or author. She embraces her independence and enters intellectual circles where her adventurous spirit is valued.

Though society shuns her for leaving her husband, Elizabeth remains resolute, refusing to be chained in a life that is not hers. She finds meaning championing other women oppressed by convention through writing, activism, or opening a shelter.

One day Elizabeth receives a mysterious letter that hints Peter may actually still be alive out there somewhere. Unable to resist this ghost from her past, she begins following clues to track him down again, reigniting her old hopes and restless longings.

On her travels Elizabeth meets an unconventional man who appreciates her free spirit. Though she swore off love and marriage, she is drawn to him, and they encourage each other to live life fully. Slowly she opens her guarded heart again.

There are many possibilities for how Elizabeth could reclaim her agency and identity now that she has refused to be caged by societal expectations. I'm happy to continue brainstorming plot ideas if any of these appeal to you! Let me know if you had something specific in mind for the next part of her tale.

Chapter 33

Elizabeth stared at her reflection critically in the ornate mirror, smoothing the lace and satin over her narrow hips. The wedding gown was exquisite, though still felt more like exquisite armor binding her to duty and respectable propriety. In just over an hour, she would walk down the aisle to unite her life with kind, devoted George. Their union made perfect practical sense and would safely secure her future, restoring her family's good name. She should have felt only excitement and joyful anticipation. Yet looking past the finery to the wan face beneath, Elizabeth saw none of the radiant sparkling bride of society's ideals - only a wildhearted spirit staring back mournfully, swearing she glimpsed the shadow of prison bars closing in behind the veil's gauzy fiction. Was this truly her destiny after defiantly chasing dreams halfway across the world - to accept cage and key willingly at twenty merely because convention demanded? How quickly she had surrendered bold conviction in exchange for comforting refuge. A soft knock interrupted her brooding, followed by her mother bustling in, already dabbing at happy tears. "Oh Lizzy, you make such a vision! I can hardly believe my little girl is a bride..." She paused, taking in Elizabeth's conflicted expression and reaching to squeeze her hand. "Just nerves I'm sure. All will be well." Elizabeth managed a faint smile. "Of course. I only wish..." Traitorous longings clogged in her throat. She could not voice how Peter's ghost haunted her still or how desperately she craved a life lived freely on her own terms - passions spent, risks taken, horizons chased rather than politely curtailed. Not today. Kissing her forehead gently, her mother tucked the veil into place. "Hush now dear. This is your fresh beginning. The past is gone." With an approving pat, she glided out, oblivious to the silent tears now slipping down beneath the lace. Gathering herself with deep breaths, Elizabeth turned from the mirror deliberately before doubts could take root. The ornate carriage and beaming bridesmaids awaited. She had chosen this course and must play her part convincingly, however profound the sacrifice. Forward lay only one path now. Yet when the driver halted to pick up several girls from the village en route, their girlish laughter and gossip drifting through the window, Elizabeth felt her stomach drop at the words she overheard: "Thought I glimpsed that handsome sailor Peter Maxwell last week down the pub. Remember him from school days? Looks a right rough sea captain now though. Tried getting passage to London apparently but skipped out before the ship sailed." Heart thundering, Elizabeth leaned forward praying she had imagined it. But the girls chattered on casually, recounting details that perfectly described Peter and speculating where the scoundrel had disappeared to yet again. He was alive and had returned here within the last week seeking her. But soon he would find only news of her marrying another. Slumping back in despair, Elizabeth pressed shaking hands over her mouth as a thousand desperate thoughts collided. She had vowed at the altar to forsake all others barely an hour ago. Any path diverging from that sacred commitment would bring only scorn and ruin. Such wild impulses belonged to a naive girl she had outgrown. Yet the prospect of Peter waiting somewhere just down the coast, expecting her to appear, refusing to believe she would break faith until the last moment... Something primal in her cried out that she must reach him somehow before it was too late - that together at last they might build a life bold and free as once she had dreamed. Perhaps it was only mad fanciful hope. But she could not silence that inner voice or harden her heart so fully yet. There were words they must speak. As the carriage rattled down the village lane toward the flower-decked church, Elizabeth felt decision crystallize. At the last cross street, she would leap down and race on foot to the docks. It was rash, impossible - and her only chance to see the story's ending before she sealed her fate. She held no illusion of futures now. But for her soul's peace she must look Peter in the eye this one time. Peering out at the passing shops and cottages, she tensed, watching her chance approach. The driver slowed slightly rounding the bend. As they drew parallel with the narrow side road, Elizabeth gathered her skirts and slipped noiselessly from the carriage to hit the ground running. She did not look back. Scandalized shouts echoed behind her but soon faded as she darted down alleys and wove through trees, half-blind with desperation. She dashed on heedless, unacceptable as she must appear in her billowing satin gown and veil. Let them gawk - she was past fear of gossip or even lost hope. Only the docks ahead mattered now. Bursting from the trees onto the bustling waterfront, Elizabeth paused only to drag in ragged gasps. The familiar taproom sat just steps away where the girls had spotted Peter. Forcing quaking limbs into motion, she covered the short distance and pushed inside before she could lose courage. The raucous noise and gloom enveloped her. Rough sailors and dock men drinking away morning's wages stared openly as she stood wild-eyed just inside the door, fruitlessly scanning the shadowed faces. He was nowhere to be seen. She was too late after all. Then she glimpsed through the back windows a lone figure standing at the end of the weathered pier, hat pulled low and hands in pockets, gazing out to sea. Without hesitation she hitched up her skirts again and broke into a run, ignoring the scandalized hoots trailing her out the door. She was sobbing fully now from panic, desperation, elation as her feet pounded the creaking dock boards. She had no idea what muddled words might pour out when she reached him. But as he turned slowly at the commotion, beloved face creasing into amazement when his eyes met hers, Elizabeth knew somehow through tears that language hardly mattered anymore. Then she was in Peter's arms, years and propriety and every scrap of dignity forgotten. The past broke over them like a wave. He was murmuring her name again and again as he cradled her close. She clung to him equally tight, vowing silently never to loose her grip on this moment or the unmanageable joy of their impossible reunion. When her sobs finally eased, Elizabeth pulled back just enough to trace shaking fingers over every familiar weathered line and grey-flecked burnish of his wind-rough cheeks. "How can you be real, my love...?" she managed hoarsely. "I was told you had died." Peter smiled down at her with wonder unclouded by the intervening years. "And you are now a vision in white satin with no time for scoundrels." He brushed a thumb gently over her tear-stained cheek. "What matters is we have this moment again beyond hope. Our compass needles crossed once more." As Elizabeth gazed up at him, the twin weights of longing and regret settled around her neck. She had found him against all odds just when fate seemed determined to sunder them forever. Yet still their paths led irreconcilably apart once more. It could only be a brief stolen moment here on the pier before she turned back to the church bells calling her name. Peter seemed to read the anguish in her eyes, for he cradled her face in his hands firmly. "Listen to me, Lizzy. This life you did not choose holds nothing but slow death for your wild spirit. I know it." His own voice held deep sadness. "We each must sail the course set before us alone it seems. But promise you will keep fighting for the freedom you were born to. Promise me, Lizzy." Unable to speak past the ache rising in her throat, she conveyed with her eyes every buried hope and regret laid bare, along with the silent vow she would heed his plea. Then she stretched up to press her tear-salted lips to his one last time under the muted sun. Innocence and possibilty lived again for a heartbeat before she pulled away with quiet resolve, footsteps echoing hollow on the pier as she walked from the quay without looking back. The carriage had paused down the lane packed with relieved friends and family. As Elizabeth numbly allowed herself to be helped back inside, she met her mother's concerned gaze unflinching while smoothing her disheveled gown. What waited at the altar now was a specter of herself she could no longer pretend to be. She would sail uncharted waters alone from here.

Chapter 34

Elizabeth stepped through the carved oak doors into the hushed sanctuary, bouquet clutched in trembling hands. The pipe organ swelled triumphantly as all eyes turned to watch the bride's long-awaited walk down the aisle. She kept her steps measured and chin high, avoiding the curious stares burning into her. No doubt rumors were already swirling after her dramatic disappearance and disheveled return. Let them wonder. She was focused only on maintaining composure before duty's final crushing weight fell upon her young defiant shoulders. Reaching the front, she took George's extended hand, bypassing his relieved smile to stare fixedly at some indistinct point along the far wall. The minister's sonorous voice rang out, solemn words reduced to mere echoes as she willed her raging heart to quiet its stubborn protest one last time. It was too late for anything but surrender now. Only distantly aware of George repeating vows beside her, Elizabeth fought to steady her breathing and blink back brine that blurred the watching faces into a mute accusing crowd. But she could not halt the single tear that slipped free, leaving a scorching trail down her cheek. Hastily she dashed it away while fixing a stoic mask back in place. Anticipating locked shackles, even her courage faltered. "...to join this man and woman in holy matrimony. If any object, speak now or forever hold peace." The minister paused, glancing expectantly around the breathless room. Time crystallized as Elizabeth felt long-sought words swell up in her chest unbidden, words to finally reject this smothering future so at odds with her soul's soaring cry for freedom. She nearly swayed beneath their weight. But the watching crowd pinned her mute, stealing voice and volition equally. Then before the silence could seal her fate, the heavy wooden doors groaned open, drawing all shocked eyes to the back of the church. Framed there in the sudden spill of sunlight stood Peter, weathered face set with quiet resolution. Gasps fluttered through the pews at this impossible interloper. As he strode purposefully down the aisle without a glance to either side, Peter's steady grey eyes locked on Elizabeth burning into her very core. Pacing slowly up the steps until he stood before her, he reached for her limp hands, cradling them tenderly between his own rough and steady grasp. The years fell away between them. She was whole in his presence. When Peter's voice rang out clear and strong over the gathering furor, he spoke only to her unflinching gaze. "Forgive this intrusion, Elizabeth. But I have been a coward too long, caring too much for convention when souls like ours were fashioned to soar unfettered." He stepped closer, radiating certainty and care. "Marrying another out of duty would be slow death for your defiant spirit. I know because my own has been half-lived without you. We deserve joy and honesty, Lizzy. Take my hand now, and say you will walk a new path with me wherever it leads." Stunned murmurs erupted through the church, but Elizabeth reacted only by slowly lacing her fingers between Peter's, wonder-struck gaze never leaving his. The decision was already etching itself on her lungs with each breath. She had been drowning in tepid shallows too long. At his side lay fathomless waters that at least promised adventure and discovery before she drowned. With their hands entwined, Peter gently guided Elizabeth down the steps again away from the scorning crowd and duties closing in. As they reached the heavy doors thrown open, joyful sunlight and possibility flooding through, she felt her soul stir awake beyond words at the promise of an unfettered life still ahead. Turning at the threshold to face the gawking wedding guests one final time, Elizabeth spoke with calm certainty, her voice carrying clear to the rafters. "I have honored you all as family and looked to you for refuge when my spirit was weary. But the woman you wish me to become is not who fate shaped me to be. I must seek my path elsewhere now, even if alone." With that, she set her satin-slippered foot over the boundary into the unknown without hesitation as church bells pealed wildly overhead. Gripping Peter's hand tightly, they raced laughing down the steps into the street thronged with stunned onlookers. The crowds parted mutely to let them pass. Reaching the wharf at last, the clipper ship Atlas stretched majestically out to sea, waiting on the evening tide. Turning to Peter with eyes shining bright, she proclaimed, "She is our destiny now. Let us sail her together with no more regretted years apart!" And so they boarded to cheers and rice from the motley crew, both former rogues now respectable outcasts embarking on new lives. As the sails unfurled to catch the freshening breeze, the tiny chapel and all within receded to memory astern. No script but their united longings guided them forward now. It was terrifying and perfect. Adventure unfettered lay ahead across the vast beckoning sea so long as they charted it together boldly. The Atlas leaped forward over surging swells through sunset's colorful farewell to the known world behind. Tonight a new story stretched before them to craft hand in hand. Salt spray stung their smiling faces as England faded beyond the horizon. Turning to Peter at the prow, Elizabeth let shy hopes and passion surge free from long confinement in her breast. What landscapes remained to explore in each other's company at long last! This freedom was everything. Standing on tiptoe, she clasped her hands around his neck, inviting his arms to encircle her tightly as their lips met. The kiss held relief and longing, tremulous joy and promises still unspoken between these unlikely voyagers joined in defiance of the world's chains. Here in the gathering twilight, bound only by the waves and sky, they clung to this moment where fates finally converged unhindered. Ahead lay undiscovered country, and they would sail to meet it together, come what storms may.

Chapter 35

Elizabeth leaned against the ship's railing, salt spray kissing her cheeks as the coastline faded to a thin green line behind them. Somewhere amid those receding hills and trees were all the people she had known - family, friends, her jilted fiancé. But she did not regret turning her back on that world of expectations and polite society. Beside her, Peter slid an arm around her waist, gesturing towards the open horizon. "No limits out there now, love. We're off to live the adventures we always dreamed of, you and I." His eyes shone with optimism and vigor that matched her own. She covered his hand with hers, heart swelling. "I'd sail to the world's end and beyond if it meant being together and free. You've given me back my spirit's fire, Peter." Stretching up on tiptoes, she kissed him soundly, heedless of the crew's hoots and whistles. "Well I aim to keep that fire lit, missy. Can't promise smooth sailing always, but we'll weather storms side by side." With a roguish wink, he peeled himself away to confer with the first mate, leaving Elizabeth glowing with anticipation of the life awaiting. They spent the next days blithely - talking, singing, planning their future between stolen moments of passion below deck. It was an idyllic fantasy, liberation from the chains of propriety. Each morning the sun rose on possibility pure and boundless as the sea itself. Until one morning Elizabeth woke to find Peter's customary place empty and cold. Wrapping a blanket around herself, she climbed up into icy wind and slate grey skies that seemed to leach the color from the world. The crew moved about silently, refusing to meet her gaze. Dread crept upon her. She found Peter hunched in the bow, staring out at the churning swells. At her approach, he reluctantly lifted a piece of paper clutched in one hand - a telegram received from the last outbound ship. With growing unease, she accepted the crumpled page and read: Elopement inexcusable and humiliating. Cease this foolishness immediately and return to fulfill your duty. Until then, you are no longer any daughter of ours. M. The brisk words blurred as Elizabeth's throat constricted. She had expected anger from her parents, but this outright renunciation stabbed deeply. They truly saw her choice as a selfish betrayal with no chance of reconciliation. Hot tears escaped down her cheeks as she braced herself against the icy railing. She had been their beloved only child, and now they were lost to her forever. The weight of it was crushing. Two strong arms wrapped around her from behind before she could spiral down into despair. Peter's gruff voice murmured against her hair. "I'm so sorry, Lizzy. But don't despair - you still have family right here who loves you dearly for exactly who you are." Turning in his arms, she clung tightly and let sorrow drain away into the frigid sea air. However much it hurt, she did not regret choosing the freedom to steer her own course over convention. She had gained so much more than just Peter's love - she had found her true self again. Pulling back, she gazed up at him with resolve. "Thank you, my love. Our life is ahead together, come what storms may." Then, taking his hand, she led him wordlessly back down into the warm cabin that was now their haven against the world's cruelty. Sheltered in each other's arms through the endless swaying nights ahead, they had all they needed. The next weeks saw Elizabeth settle into shipboard life, finding purpose in small ways - assisting the cook, mending sails, singing sea shanties during long watches. The crew's initial wariness faded as they accepted her as one of their own, admiring her pluck and willingness to work. She was thankful for their camaraderie amidst the isolation. Peter seemed energized by it all, in his element guiding them onward through fair weather and foul. In the misty evenings when the sea was gentle, he spun glorious tales of the adventures awaiting at journey's end that were sure to earn them fame and fortune. His enthusiasm and passion made her believe anything was possible so long as they clung together. The steel bands around Elizabeth's heart loosened with each knot logged farther from the old world's constraints. Out here chasing the horizon, she was free to chart her own bold course forward as fate intended. Wind, stars and ever-changing seas would redefine her, not strictures. Whatever unknown shores awaited, she and Peter would discover them joyfully side by side, untrammeled spirits. On the day the ragged sails of Tortuga island peeked over the tossing swells, she stood at the prow as they surged ahead, Peter's arms encircling her. The past was sunk beneath the waves, and their true future about to break over the bow in all its wild possibility. Elizabeth smiled into the wind-stung sunlight, savoring the word that thrummed in time with her pounding heart: Home.

Chapter 36

Elizabeth awoke to creaking boards and morning sun slanting through the porthole. For a blissful moment she forgot where she was, expecting her canopied bedchamber back home. Then she felt the gentle roll of swells beneath her and Peter's warm body pressed against her back. Home was now simply wherever they were together. Turning to study his relaxed features bathed in dawn's glow, she marveled again at the improbable turns of fate that had reunited them after fearing him lost forever. So many mysteries still remained of where he had journeyed between their parted ways years ago and finding each other once more against the odds. She traced a finger down his bearded cheek. "Wherever you roamed, you are here now beloved. That is all that matters." His grey eyes blinked open, crinkling into a smile. "Trying to determine if I'm just a roguish figment of your dreams still?" Rolling to face her, Peter gently tucked back a stray hair. "I know well how impossible this seems, my Lizzy. I have feared waking myself these past weeks in case you disappeared." Propping herself up on one elbow, Elizabeth gave a wry smile. "Well I am no phantom as you can attest, sir." Sobering, she squeezed his hand. "But I do wish to know everything of your lost years apart. I realize painful memories lie there, yet they are pieces of you." With a pensive nod, Peter sat up and pulled her close. "You deserve those stories. I have been a coward avoiding them, but can hide no part of myself from you now." He lifted her hand to his lips before beginning hesitantly. "After we parted, shame drove me onto a dark destructive path..." As morning light shifted across the cramped cabin, Elizabeth listened silently - only occasionally interjecting questions as Peter narrated his directionless years of drinking, brawling, mercenary sailing after losing all compass but bitterness. He spared none of the ugly truth, watching her closely for recrimination. But she only gently urged him onward. Finally he arrived at the violent gale that had marooned him across the very island

where Elizabeth later landed. Recounting those lonely seasons
wrestling inner demons in the remote jungle, Peter's voice grew fervent
describing the transformation of spirit she had unknowingly still
guided. "Your memory was a beacon lighting my blackest times, Lizzy.
I clung to impossible hope we would meet again, though I deserved
it not after my cowardice." He shook his head ruefully. "Even when I
finally found passage back, every leads went cold and fortune conspired
against us." Taking both her hands in his, Peter gazed at her earnestly.
"But now that I have been gifted this second chance, I swear to lay
down old ghosts for good and dedicate myself to you alone." He slid
off the berth to kneel solemnly before her. "Elizabeth, would you do
me the honor of - " A thunderous knock interrupted his proposal,
followed by the first mate shouting urgently for Elizabeth. Exchanging
anxious glances, they hurried above deck into chaos - sails being hastily
furled, oars manned, faces grim. The captain beckoned her over grimly,
spyglass in hand. "Apologies m'lady, but we've a royal naval frigate on
our tail keen to escort you back to England it seems." Cold dread
washed over Elizabeth as she saw the distant warship bearing down on
them, closing the miles steadily. "But how did they find us out here?"
She looked at Peter desperately. "We have to outrun them! I won't go
back to that life now." Jaw clenched, he squeezed her shoulder. "Aye lass,
we'll losing them yet and buy time to plan more permanent solutions
after." Raising his voice, he bellowed, "Man your stations lads! We've
a race to win today!" The deck exploded into activity as Elizabeth
was ushered below for safety. She spent the next hours pacing the
confines of the cabin restlessly, ears straining for any indication of
dread pursuers boarding. But only occasional distant shouts and thuds
reached her. They seemed to be maintaining distance, though the
frigate continued hounding their tail. When Peter finally slipped down
to her, his face was grim. "We're faster with the wind but they've ten
guns to our two and will catch us eventually once close enough." Taking
her rigid hands in his, he softened. "But don't fret Lizzy. We've

maneuvered out of worse scrapes than this many times over." Despite his reassurance, stark options weighed oppressively as the day waned. Elizabeth knew with cold certainty that if the navy captured them now, she would be returned to society's shackles and scorn with no say. Her only bargaining power lay in the family name her parents had renounced. But she would do whatever sacrifice required to safeguard the freedom finally within reach. As the first mate's knuckles rapped at the cabin door again late that night, Elizabeth rose to meet him resolved. Wordlessly she let him escort her topside where moonlight limned the pursuing warship's silhouette tauntingly closer now. She stood with lifted chin, ready to concede surrender if only they guaranteed Peter's safety and her willing return. But instead of a boarding party she found the scruffy crew assembled expectantly around where Peter waited before the mast, face tender as he extended his hands to draw her near. Her breath caught as she realized his intent. "There is one unbreakable vow that will ensure we remain together free across all oceans, my love." In hushed tones coloured by creaking boards and swells, he spoke the private ritual words that bound their fates eternally as man and wife. The sounds of pursuit receded until only the two of them existed under the stars now alone. When Peter finally tilted her chin up to seal the vows with a kiss, Elizabeth knew she was home. The next days were a blur of evasive course changes, postponing the inevitable confrontation looming ever closer on the horizon behind them. But Elizabeth's spirit remained unshaken. Come what may, they belonged only to each other now. She would go peacefully and appeal to her parents' mercy rather than sacrifice Peter's safety. Their love was not fragile. Late one night as she kept her moonlit vigil on deck hoping for inspiration to strike, Elizabeth noticed the pursing frigate had fallen suspiciously far back on the horizon. At her alert, the crew manned the oars and lanterns, ready to slip away under cover of darkness if fortune allowed. Peter appeared beside her silently, following her gaze astern. "Could be they've given up the chase as fruitless, or..." His jaw clenched. "More likely it's a trap to corner us. But either way, we'll use this chance." He turned to embrace her fiercely, eyes blazing. "I swear to you Lizzy, they'll not part us again." Together they watched the last flickering lights of the warship disappear astern with bated breath. When even the lookout could make out no sign on the moon-silvered sea, Peter squeezed her shoulder and turned to the men, voice ringing with command. "Right lads, make sail and oars both! We've a voyage ahead to freedom yet!" Despite their stealthy flight, apprehension still gnawed at Elizabeth in the days that followed. The navy could reappear at any time, and they were vastly overmatched. But Peter's tireless optimism bolstered her courage. One stormy evening he drew her into the rhythm of the dances they had loved as youths together. As laughter overtook her anxieties, she let herself trust they might outrun threats just a little farther against the odds. They sailed night and day, stopping only when exhaustion overcame them. And miraculously, the seas remained clear but for merchantmen. After two weeks with no signs of pursuit, relief finally replaced vigilance. Perhaps lady fortune had spared them somehow after all. The morning the olive groves and terracotta rooftops of Mediterranean lands peeked over the horizon, Elizabeth dared hope again that a new anonymous life awaited ashore. With Peter's hand warm in hers, she watched the ancient port swell closer. Out there somewhere beyond aristocratic chains and familiar shores, their next chapter awaited. Together they would turn the page without hesitation now.

Chapter 37

Elizabeth leaned contentedly into Peter's shoulder as the carriage rattled down the dusty coastal road. Behind them the crowded port city of Marsailles faded into the distance, replaced by rolling hills dotted with seaside villas and sleepy hamlets. A new tranquil life awaited just ahead now if they were bold enough to claim it. When she had nervously suggested making a home somewhere obscure and remote to avoid her family's grasp, Peter's face had lit up with that familiar adventurous gleam. "Of course, darling! We'll find a quiet piece of paradise to call our own. Anywhere is home so long as we're together." With a grateful kiss, she had let him take the reins planning their future unfettered. Now as the driver called out that they were approaching the village ahead, Elizabeth squeezed Peter's hand, joy and anticipation welling up inside her. The outlines of colorful stucco buildings came into view, nestled in a cove with fishing vessels bobbing nearby. It was a scene from the idyllic paintings she had admired but never imagined inhabiting herself. Yet here that dream was coming to life. The carriage bumped to a halt before an aged stone cottage with vines twining up the weathered walls and a blooming garden spilling color. Shyly Elizabeth peeked at Peter. "It's perfect. I can hardly believe we'll live here untouched by the world." He grinned back reassuringly as he helped her down. Home. The inside of the cottage proved just as enchanting, modest but brimming with character. Elizabeth trailed her hand over the scarred oak table as she crossed to unlatch the windows overlooking the glittering sea, inhaling the salt air deeply. Peace encompassed her. After so many lost years, she and Peter would build a sanctuary here together. They settled blissfully into unhurried routine - strolling hand in hand along the shore gathering shells or through the village market to hear chatter in soft rolling dialects. Nights they nestled beneath the eaves like two birds sheltered, murmuring hopes and stories and promises until sleep claimed them entwined. Elizabeth let the tranquility wash away past scars and fears. When dark dreams came, she would wake to Peter's kisses, reminding her all was well. They were bound now for life and beyond. Each dawn seemed a gift. As she tended the garden or mended fishing nets on the porch alongside the local wives, joy welled up that she had found contentment so profound. Until one crystalline morning when she woke feeling unsettled without knowing why as Peter slept soundly beside her still. The room tilted dizzily as she stood, and she only just made the window to empty the previous night's supper into the bushes outside. Feeling clammy but relieved, she rinsed her mouth and blamed the fish stew. Yet unease lingered. By week's end, her body's changes could no longer be ignored or dismissed. Headaches, tender breasts, sleepless nights, a pervasive weariness. As Elizabeth sat staring vacantly at her cooling tea, absent hands resting over her still-flat stomach, understanding settled over her at long last. She was with child. Hers and Peter's. Here was the next chapter's start unfurling already. The realization carried wonder but also disquiet. They had been careful, envisioning children someday still over the horizon. How would Peter react to arrival of this little life unplanned? Dizzy with the implications, she longed desperately to share the revelation burning inside her, yet hesitation held her back. She would wait until the perfect private moment presented itself rather than lay surprises at his feet this night. Patience had served them this long after all. But fate often laughs at mortal intentions. And so it transpired that on a mild evening as they strolled the moonlit shore and spoke lightly of trivial matters, Peter suddenly paused to face Elizabeth, expression heartrendingly tender as he took both her hands between his own. "My Love, there is something I have been wishing to discuss with you." Gripping her palms tightly, he knelt before her in the wet sand. "Never have I known a happiness so profound as at your side this past year. And now I dream of our family growing. Would you..." His eyes met hers expectantly, words hovering. With joyful incredulity, Elizabeth sank to her own knees, releasing one hand to press his palm against the slight swell of her belly tentatively. "A new life already flourishes here, my heart. We are to be parents." A radiant laugh escaped her at the wonder overtaking Peter's face. "Your wishes and mine are aligned it seems." Whooping for joy, Peter seized her up into a crushing embrace before setting her gently down to cradle her abdomen in awestruck reverence. "We have created new life, Lizzy!" His eyes shone wetly in the moonlight before he pressed an ear to her stomach. "Greetings little one, your parents eagerly await your arrival. What a wondrous family we three shall be." Enveloped in contentment, Elizabeth stroked Peter's hair as he continued murmuring to their child, voicing hopes and dreams. The future felt over-brimming suddenly with possibility where before she had still half-braced for their hard-won joy to shatter again. But with this new blossoming life, hope had taken root for good, binding their fates and hearts eternally now. The next weeks passed quickly as they prepared the cottage for the baby - whitewashing the nursery, sewing blankets, stockpiling provisions. Peter was consumed with gathering supplies to build a cradle himself as she protested amusement that it was too early for such things. He only winked roguishly. "No child of mine will want for anything. I'll fashion the finest cradle the village has beheld!" His enthusiasm was contagious, pushing back the encroaching fears of impending motherhood as her petite frame swelled and strained to nurture new life within. When they lay together at night gently cradling her changing body, the future no longer seemed uncertain but rich with promise. She was ready to embrace it joyfully, if only to see Peter's eager smile each morning. On a golden afternoon strolling the market stalls, Elizabeth paused to admire knit caps and infant gowns, imagining a tiny head and hands they might soon clothe. The merchant woman chuckled knowingly, patting her growing belly. "Any day now, no?" With a wink, she tucked an extra cap in Elizabeth's basket. "For when your babe arrives." That night after Peter had planted a tender kiss and drifted to sleep, Elizabeth lay watching shadows play across the rafters as anticipation and trepidation mingled within her. Any day now their lives would be reborn alongside their child's - was she truly ready for that transformation? Silently she prayed for the wisdom and patience motherhood would require. If love alone sufficed, their baby would never want. The summer waned, the days following one after another measured now by their child's steady growth and kicks that kept her awake long past Peter's snores. Their world was this haven by the sea and the unfolding miracle within. Elizabeth marked the passing months with shells on the windowsill, waiting as her body changed and the great mystery beckoned closer. Until finally one dark night heralded by howling wind, the promise turned to piercing waves of agony radiating through her core. As Peter clasped her hand eyes full of tender awe and fear, the cottage filled with her cries chasing away the ghosts of the past year by year. All was stripped to primal focus and drive now - bringing forth new life through her own sweat and tears. She sailed alone through agony to emerge wiser. And when thin mewling cries finally joined hers, the sound was sweeter than any siren's song. They had navigated the passage together, crossed from one shore to another, been stitched together in bonds eternally by a squalling infant. Their beautiful son. Joy and purpose flooded Elizabeth's heart to the brim as she cradled him close. A new adventure begun.

Chapter 38

Elizabeth smiled softly, watching the children's small figures race ahead along the sandy path - her son Elias' gangly legs churning as he called encouragement back to his little sister. At eight and six, they were a spirited handful, keeping life brimming with mischief and adventure. Settling the basket of fresh fish more securely over her arm, she followed their fading voices around the grassy cliffside bend to the cottage door. How improbable those early days of motherhood now seemed, consumed with worry over each skinned knee and sleepless night. Now she knew the secret was simply to cherish each moment fleeting by. Pushing the weathered door open with her hip, she called, "Do wash up for lunch now. And fetch your father from the garden." The answering groans and thumps brought a wry chuckle. Some things never changed. Humming tunelessly, Elizabeth swiftly scaled and gutted the glistening trout on the scarred table before rinsing her hands. Outside the window she could glimpse Peter's broad shoulders among the bean vines, elbow-deep in soil as he did each time he wrestled some new dilemma. The crops and his family's wellbeing, so long uncertain, now anchored him. Wiping her brow with the back of one earthy wrist, she watched the children scramble up to wrap their father in eager hugs until he laughed aloud, the somber set of his face smoothing away. Her heart swelled at the image. For all the humble simplicity of this life, she was grateful beyond words for it. Later as they sat down to mealtime chatter about fishing trips and seashells, Elizabeth caught Peter's eye over Elias' dramatically reenacted mishaps. His warm crinkled smile, echoing her own contentment, needed no words. The years had only honed their love and partnership to a steady glow, whispering that they had found what truly mattered. So on a mild autumn evening as she prepared for bed, loosening her hair from its practical braid with a sigh, the knock below jolted Elizabeth from nostalgic musing abruptly. Visitors after nightfall were unknown here

– and unwelcome, she suspected from the prickling dread down her neck. Slipping a robe over her nightdress, she padded cautiously downstairs in the dark. The quavering voice from the front step was unfamiliar. "Please, I must speak with Elizabeth. I mean her no harm." Quiet authority belied the polite entreaty. Elizabeth hesitated, nerves fraying as her family's peace was disrupted unexpectedly yet again. Before she could reply, heavy footfalls sounded as Peter appeared at her back, pushing her protectively behind him. Rarely did she glimpse the ghost of his dangerous past now, but it surfaced as he flung the door wide, rigid and towering. "State your business. My wife is unavailable at this hour to one without appointment." The stranger's face in the dimness was proud and vaguely familiar – a mature well-bred woman, Elizabeth realized with surprise, dressed for travel. But her polite veneer faltered into supplication before Peter's intimidating stance. "Please sir, I intend only to talk. There are matters to be resolved between us, events you must remember..." She peered past him beseechingly at Elizabeth. "I was once known as Mary to you both." Peter's sharp intake of breath echoed Elizabeth's own muted shock. Mary Worthington...her family's former housemaid who had nearly come between them when young and foolish. Her reputation left in ruins by Peter's careless dalliances. Another lifetime, yet here she stood years later, composed and refined, turning their existence upside down with her spectral presence. Before Peter could reply harshly, Elizabeth dared crack open the door further. "You are not welcome in our home after the damage wrought. But I will grant you this - speak your mind plainly. No more lies or games." Her voice did not waver, bolstered by the dear life she protected here. The past could not haunt them unless she allowed its talons to rend fragile peace. The woman paled, clearly surprised to be addressed so bluntly by one she still saw as a sheltered young lady. But she inclined her head graciously. "You are quite direct now, I see. Very well, my errand is simple." Her voice turned icy. "I want remuneration for my years of suffering and public shame at the hands of your husband and yourself. I wish to negotiate reasonable compensation for my silence." "Extortion!" Peter surged forward, temples throbbing. "Not one damned penny. How dare you disrupt innocent lives with threats long buried! Begone before I..." "Husband, please." Elizabeth's grip on his shoulder softened his fury. Turning to Mary, she considered the strained figure sadly. "I understand you want amends for old pains. And perhaps we owe you that, though we too acted in innocence. But what good comes of exhuming the past if we only perpetuate it with resentment?" Her sigh was weary now. "Stay or go freely. Either way I wish you peace." Mary stared at her uncertainly for a long moment, bitterness seeming to recede in the creases of her face. But the damage was too deep for hasty healing. With a final silent nod, she gathered her cloak and disappeared into the night as mysteriously as she had arrived. The words lingered echoing between husband and wife heavily after the door latch clicked to. What other ghosts lingered outside their sheltered lives? In the painful weeks after, Peter brooded ceaselessly, reduced to monosyllables and subtle coldness when before she had known only tenderness. Their world was upended by something that should have remained buried securely. But roots had been unearthed, and the foundation no longer felt so certain. Trust, once rock-solid, became fog. Until finally, after the children were abed, Elizabeth could bear the strangling silence no longer. She knelt between Peter's knees as he glowered into the cold hearth, gently cradling his bearded face until their eyes met wearily. "Let the past go, my love. Do not retreat from your family now over sins long absolved." Her voice dropped to a fervent whisper. "Stay with me, Peter." Those simple words seemed to exorcise the worst ghosts. He pulled her fiercely into his lap, shoulders heaving with choked apologies until she whispered soothingly and let her kisses reaffirm that they yet had all that truly mattered. Together they would face unraveling pasts with courage, reminding each other it was not who they had been but who they were now that counted. The quiet days would return in time, unfractured. They yet had life and faith and each other. Gradually laughter and light filtered back into the cottage as they all determinedly stepped forward beyond old shadows. But Elizabeth began noticing odd lapses in Peter's memory. Small concerning incidents accumulated until denial was impossible. Her stalwart protector, once sharp and vigorous was losing pieces – misplacing tools or garbling words frequently. His decline was gradual but certain. The morning she awoke to find Peter huddled by the cold hearth, unaware how to spark a flame or even feed himself, despair pressed down. Their haven was crumbling all too quickly. Yet still love's light remained, however dimmed. She could only cherish each lucid moment left as the precious gift it was. They would navigate this unknown passage too, day by day, forgiving when names eluded or confusion frustrated, remembering sunnier seasons together. So evenings when he rested peaceful with his grey head in her lap asking for old tales while their grown children looked on sorrowful yet supportive from the doorway, Elizabeth held back tears. Their time was ending, but they would walk on gently until the end hand in hand. The life they had built together was a gift, however fleeting. Its memories would guide her forward when left to carry the torch alone. Leaning down to brush her lips across his wrinkled brow, she whispered, "I will tell our story to all who will listen." When the end came some months later with family ringed around their bed, Elizabeth cradled his weathered face through labored breaths growing ever shallower, murmuring promises between kisses that though their paths diverged now, she would find him waiting across the years. As dawn broke softly through the shutters, his breathing slowed to silence. Their long voyage was ended. She held him close and grieved sweetly for this stoic noble man fate had once drowned but who had emerged to give her life its deepest purpose. A final gift remained. She would craft from their shared story's threads a rich tapestry honoring how love had quietly transformed them both.

Chapter 39

Elizabeth stared at Peter in stunned silence, his shocking revelation still sinking in. The mysterious woman who had appeared was not the Mary from their past at all, but her twin sister seeking vengeance by impersonating her. "I can scarcely believe it," she finally managed, sinking onto the bed beside him. "I was so certain Mary had returned to haunt us. But why would her sister construct such an elaborate ruse?" Peter rubbed his face wearily, guilt creasing his brow. "Because I wronged them both deeply, though I did not fully realize it at the time. I was reckless with Mary's affections, not understanding the damage I caused." His eyes pleaded for understanding. "We were young, and I naively believed our liaison harmless. But for her, the betrayal went soul-deep." He gazed out the darkened window, lost in the past. "When she learned I planned to end it, Mary grew distraught beyond reason, speaking wildly of disappearing and how her sister would avenge her." Peter's voice dropped. "I confess I did not consider her hysteria seriously then. But a week later, she was dead from suspicious causes." Taking Elizabeth's hands in his, he continued hoarsely. "I should have prevented such tragedy. My callousness sealed poor Mary's fate. Her twin has rightly despised me ever since, though we never met." He shook his head bitterly. "Now Clara seeks justice at long last as I deserve." Despite the painful revelations, Elizabeth squeezed his hands, heart aching for his remorse. "You cannot carry the weight of this forever, my love. We were all young and reckless once. What matters is who you are now." She touched his cheek gently. "This Clara knows only the misguided boy you were, not the honorable man before me." Peter covered her hand with his own, eyes glistening. "You have always seen light within me I could not. I shall try to be worthy of that faith." Pulling her close, he rested his cheek against her hair. "Whatever comes, we will face it together." Elizabeth nodded silently into his chest, clinging to hope their steadfast bond could withstand this ghostly trial.

Over the ensuing days, an uneasy pall hovered between them despite attempts to regain normalcy. Peter wrestled with past demons, while Elizabeth reeled from the knowledge that their visitor Clara yet watched the cottage from afar, biding her time. Her motives remained inscrutable, yet clearly a reckoning was at hand. Until late one foggy evening, a rap at the door shattered their uneasy peace once more. Exchanging grim glances, they rose together to confront the inevitable. Clara stood haloed in mist on the threshold, face coolly composed. "I have made arrangements in town. If you wish to discuss the matter sensibly, I shall expect you tomorrow - both of you." With that, she disappeared into the gloom again. "We cannot ignore this summons," Elizabeth declared after sleepless hours debating their narrowing options. "The threat will only worsen otherwise." She squeezed Peter's hand. "We must try to make her understand how you have changed, that you too have suffered." Though uncertainty gnawed beneath her bold words, she knew they could not evade Clara's righteous anger forever. The only path led forward. The next morning found them seated stiffly across from Clara at a dockside inn, while patrons gave them a wide berth. If the stern woman was surprised by Elizabeth's presence, she did not show it. "So, you have come. I wish to hear you confess your wrongs plainly against my sister. Do not attempt denying culpability." Her voice was iron. Peter nodded heavily. "I offer no excuses or justification. I treated your sister callously and intensified her distress. My actions contributed to her death, and I bear that remorse always." His grey eyes shone with sorrow. "If my apologies and regrets can ease your family's pain, I submit them freely and humbly." Clara's icy facade flickered briefly at this abject humility. Clearly she had expected defiant avoidance. Elizabeth leaned forward entreatingly. "Mistakes made in blind youth need not destroy lives forever. I know Peter is not blameless, yet nor is he the same man you judge him as. Is there no room left for grace?" She willed Clara to see past old wounds to healing. For long moments, Clara only surveyed them both stonily while the inn's din seemed muted. But finally she relented with a slow sigh. "Your words ring sincere, however inconvenient. I had prepared only for denial, not contrition." She glanced away, turmoil plain on her face. "Perhaps in time forgiveness may grow. But I require space from ghosts long haunting. Do not seek me out again." Rising abruptly, she hesitated, seeming to wrestle some internal battle before adding quietly, "Your life together is your own now. I shall not interfere with matters long beyond changing." And then she was gone, leaving Elizabeth and Peter empty in her wake. There was no triumph or closure, only weary relief that the reckoning's fury had passed them by this time. Their paired devotion had weathered the storm. In the days that followed, an air of convalescence settled over the cottage. Peter's melancholy and restless shame eased slowly with coaxing. Together they walked the familiar seaside paths, speaking of the future again not the past. The nightmares would fade eventually if they did not feed them. What mattered most was each new dawn side by side, not ghosts. And so it was that several weeks later on a crystalline autumn evening, Elizabeth greeted Peter at the door with a basket of blackberries and smile untroubled. Taking his hand fondly, she led him out to wander their small kingdom contentedly. They paused atop the cliffs where wind and wheeling gulls reconnected them to life's essence, checking old fears loose from their hearts. Here on the brink, they opened themselves to only this moment and each other. As the last molten colors seeped from the sky, Peter pulled Elizabeth down to rest against his chest near the cliff's edge. His voice held quiet awe. "This view never grows commonplace to me. Each time, I understand how blessed we are." Strong arms enfolded her. "Thank you for the life we have built from ashes, my love. Let us keep cherishing each day together as the gift it is." Nuzzling closer as the first stars glimmered overhead, Elizabeth let peaceful joy well up and spill over. The past with its regret and grievances had fallen away for good she sensed. Their enduring devotion shone as a beacon cutting through the lingering fog of the day's uncertainties. Whatever unknown lay ahead, they would face it heartened by a love that fear could not diminish or time fade. Nestled here together, they were home.

Chapter 40

Elizabeth hummed softly as she kneaded the dough, thoughts drifting fondly to Peter off tending their fishing nets. Though weeks had passed since "Mary's" disruptive visit, the sense it could reoccur hung over them both, eroding the trust so painstakingly built. But she refused to relinquish their hard-won happiness. Whatever this stranger tried, their devotion would weather it united. A sharp rap at the cottage door startled her from brooding. Wiping floured hands, Elizabeth peered cautiously through the front window. Her breath caught at the sight of that severe, hauntingly familiar profile waiting on the step. What fresh torment was coming now? Steeling herself, Elizabeth unlatched the door, spine straight. "You are not welcome here. Please leave us be." The stern woman's mouth thinned impatiently. "You judge rashly. I have come only to share information in your best interest." Her sharp eyes darted about before leaning in. "Peter keeps sinister secrets that endanger you both. But I can prove the truth if you will permit it." Elizabeth bristled, fighting to remain composed against this assault on all she held dear. "I do not know what mischief you scheme by smearing my husband's name, but I will hear none of it. His heart is true." She moved to shut the door firmly. "Now go and do not return." A surprisingly strong hand caught the wooden frame, wrenching it open again. The woman's gaze burned with zeal. "You are willfully blind, but I swear he deceives you! Why do you suppose we never crossed paths before? He hid his old life for nefarious reasons." Her voice dropped. "I can reveal all if you follow where I lead." Temptation flickered briefly. This stranger clearly believed her own claims, however deranged. But the quiet voice of trust in Elizabeth's heart drowned it out. "I do not pretend my husband flawless, but his heart is true. We protect each other from ghosts." Drawing herself tall, she met the piercing eyes unflinching. "Now go and haunt us no more. You will never shake what we have built." With that, she forced the door shut and slid the bolt home, breath coming in shaky gasps. The venomous words had awakened old doubts and hurts. But the love surrounding her was armor. She would not relinquish all they had forged together to malice. Let the forces try to unravel it - they would only strengthen its threads. When Peter returned in the fading light, she let the comfort of his arms soothe away the encounter's lingering unease. Some threats came from without, but the greatest from within. She would not betray the vows binding their hearts by indulging suspicion sown by strangers. Nestled close as darkness deepened, she whispered promises to withstand wicked seeds of distrust. The life they had built would stand firm. But over subsequent days, Elizabeth found poison tendrils creeping in despite her resistance. Peter's distracted silences seemed ominous, his past a shadowed jungle where anything lurked. Her faith felt fragile against ceaseless wondering what he yet withheld that she was blind to. The wary distance opening between them was agony, especially knowing the cause. Elizabeth steeled herself relentlessly to cling to hard-earned trust. But doubts proliferated like weeds until she found herself studying his beloved face for some dark stranger hidden beneath. Much was eroded by even entertaining such thoughts. Still she could not evict them fully, however she tried. Until one evening as they sat together before the hearth, she found accusatory words slipping out unbidden, questioning secrets kept and fidelity worn thin. Each doubtful lash seemed to age Peter further, his eyes two sadder reminders of how fragile even deepest love proved. When had she transformed into this suspicious stranger? Finally he silenced her embittered barrage by taking both her hands gently in his. "Lizzy, enough now. This bile does not become you." His voice held untold sadness. "If you believe I have deceived you, we have far greater troubles than mystery women's tales." Looking into the grey earnest eyes that had been her refuge so long, Elizabeth felt poison doubts start to dissolve. The man before her was the same flawed mortal who had won her heart through devotion proven over and over. They had built towering love from ruins. Whatever sinister secrets the past held, she chose to cling to what she knew beyond doubt in this moment. Leaning forward, she cradled Peter's weathered face in both hands, gaze pleading for forgiveness. "You are right, my love. Mistrust solves nothing." She touched her forehead to his. "I choose faith in what we have made together. Forgive my doubts." His whispered absolution against her hair was balm. They had found their way through shadowed wood back to steadfast love. The rest was just ghosts that held no power unless she ceded it. They would face whatever came linked arm in arm. In the tranquil days that followed, Elizabeth let the peace of routines replace restless unease - kneading dough, tending the garden, laughing with Peter over small joys. The stranger's cryptic warnings seemed meaningless murmurs now against love's steady heartbeat rhythms. Her faith had wavered briefly, but emerged renewed and deeper-rooted. No malice could separate them unless she allowed it. Their devotion was armor and refuge. So when the dour woman appeared yet again at week's end, patrician features constricting in frustration, Elizabeth simply smiled wearily and blocked the door's gap. "We have nothing to discuss. I care not what you believe you know." Gazing calmly into the seething eyes, she spoke with slow precision. "No truth you reveal could outweigh what lies between us. Our life is our own. Now let ghosts rest." When Peter's strong hands grasped her shoulders in silent unity, the intruder shrank back, muttering bitterly before turning away. As her faded figure disappeared down the cliff path, Elizabeth released the breath caught in her lungs. The ripples would persist awhile, but she knew now their love would weather whatever swelling storms came. They stood rooted firm together, seesawing doubts calmed Her place was here beside him till time's end; their story safe in each other's hands.

Chapter 41

Elizabeth wiped her brow, squinting against the afternoon sun beating down as she hurried back from the village well. The air was stifling, matching the unease coiling in her stomach. Several weeks had passed since Peter had turned the false Mary away from their home, but a shadow still lingered. Pushing open the cottage door, she called a cheerful greeting, hoping to rouse her husband from the gloom he had sunk into since that day. But only silence answered. The stillness within made her pulse quicken anxiously. Setting down the water bucket with a thump, she rushed through the small rooms until she found Peter sitting motionless in the bedroom, staring at nothing. At her gentle touch on his shoulder, he blinked up at her dully before turning his face away. "Leave me be, Lizzy. I am poor company." His voice was flat and defeated. Her heart ached to see him so diminished by the ghosts they thought banished. Kneeling beside him, Elizabeth took his limp hands in hers. "What is it, my love? You have been distant for days. How can I help ease this burden?" She searched his downcast face worriedly. With a heavy sigh, Peter met her gaze, his own eyes haunted. "Her accusations stir up memories I have tried keeping buried. I was not always an honorable man, and you deserve better than one so tainted." His expression grew tormented. "I do not know how to make amends for my past sins." Cupping his bearded cheek, Elizabeth willed him to feel the sincerity of her words. "The man before me now is who I love and trust. Whatever shadows haunt you, they cannot change that truth." Leaning closer, she added firmly, "You owe no debt to the past or to me. Our life is ahead, not behind." She cradled his head to her chest then, trying to lend him strength to wrestle free of remorse's grasp as he had done for her so many times before. They stayed locked together for some time, until Peter's taut frame finally eased and his breathing slowed. Gently helping him to bed, Elizabeth resolved not to leave his side until the dark mood had passed. Their devotion would light the way back, however long it took. She would shelter and strengthen him now. But over the following weeks, Peter only withdrew further, leaving her pleading and household chores unanswered as he stared for hours in brooding silence. Elizabeth's reassurances increasingly fell on deaf ears. He was slipping away from her into remorse she could not reach. Desperation mounting, she pinned all hope on rekindling happy memories to overshadow his torment. Each morning she brought accountings of their children's antics or read aloud fanciful stories, describing long-ago courting adventures in vivid detail, grasping for some spark to ignite in him. But he remained despondent, lost in the bleak past. When Peter ceased leaving the cottage at all, refusing food or drink for days, panic clutched Elizabeth fully. She curled up beside his still form each night, hushed pleas on her lips to simply hold on, but her anchors could not seem to arrest his sinking. She was losing him to demons whose names she did not know. On a morning when she woke to find his side of the mattress cold and empty, dread coursed through Elizabeth. Flying outside with the children's names on her lips, her eyes frantically scanned the grounds until she spotted Peter's silhouette at the cliff's edge. Heart in her throat, she forced numb legs into motion. As she drew slowly closer across the grass, Elizabeth heard his low murmuring rise on the wind - fragments of bitter self-recrimination and despair at unforgivable sins. She halted, throat burning. Was she already too late? "Whatever mercy I may have found is forfeit. My hands can never be cleansed." His raw words carried to her, full of anguish. "You all deserve peace untainted by what I was." He inched closer to the precipice. "Peter..." she called softly, afraid to startle him. But he did not turn. Elizabeth's pulse roared in her ears. She had lingered too long hoping he would surface alone. Now she risked losing him forever. They balanced on a terrible crux that would define everything still to come. She must anchor him here somehow. "My love, see me!" she cried, surging forward heedlessly. "Whatever you believe you've done, your life is still full of purpose and joy!" Her hands grasped his shoulders tightly as she turned him from the void's maw to face her. "Stay here with your family! We love you, Peter. Come back to us!" For agonizing breaths he stared through her, the fine edge of the cliff at his heels. Then finally his eyes focused on her stricken face, resolve seeming to steady him. Slowly Peter allowed Elizabeth to lead him to safer ground, clinging to her as the black mood's hold receded. Troubles remained, but hope glimmered again she felt. That night as he finally slept in her arms, she wept silent tears of relief and renewed devotion. They had narrowly turned away disaster's hand this time. But the forces that threatened could also forge lasting strength if they held fast to each other. From the ashes, they would build anew. In the weeks that followed, Elizabeth tended to Peter with fierce protective love, gently drawing him back to the beauty and purpose surrounding them. There could be no erasing past injuries or changing the wind-tossed sea. But they could still shape the unwritten days ahead. When the light gradually returned to his eyes and laughter to their home, Elizabeth gave thanks for the chance to reaffirm true meaning. The past would always haunt, but it had no power over the present unless she allowed it hold. Each new dawn offered redemption, if they had courage to seize it. So on an evening when Peter drew her close with no shadow between them to sharing long-cherished dreams for the future, joy and certainty she had nearly lost forever swelled in Elizabeth's chest. Their devotion had weathered this greatest trial yet emerged more unbreakable for having been tested to its depths. Whatever life yet held, they would cling to each other and meet it together unflinching. Scars remained, but so also did enduring love.

Chapter 42

Thunder crashed outside as Elizabeth jolted awake, momentarily disoriented. The cabin was empty beside her, sheets cold. Unease pricked along her neck. Peter often rose before dawn, but never slipped away without notice. She hurriedly lit an oil lamp against the brooding darkness. "Peter?" she called tentatively. Only the gale battering the shutters answered. Checking each room by lantern light revealed nothing amiss, aside from Peter's jacket and boots absent from their hooks. But a foreboding chill remained. He had vanished into the storm's teeth without word or trace. Dread rose like floodwater around her. Doing her best to remain calm, Elizabeth quickly dressed and checked on the still-sleeping children. If Peter had simply stepped out, he would be back soon she told herself firmly. She busied her shaking hands stoking up the hearth and putting on tea, straining her ears for footfalls that did not come. As grey dawn seeped reluctantly through the windows, apprehension gave way to true alarm. Peter was an anchor, never straying unannounced. And these were the same ominous conditions that had driven him to the cliff's edge before... Fear squeezed her chest at the thought. Something was wrong. Bundling herself against the weather's fury, Elizabeth determined to search the nearby shoreline. Perhaps Peter had been lost in the night wandering dazed. She refused to consider more dire possibilities yet. He needed her to stay stalwart. Surely by lantern light she could pick up some trail to explain last night's vanishing. But hours later, soaked and shaken by more than chill rain, she returned empty-handed, Peter's absence remaining an impenetrable mystery. It was as if her solid bedrock of faith had simply vanished along with him into the storm. But she could not afford to crumble yet, with young souls depending on her steadiness. Jaw set, she stoked herself the way sailors learned to ride out tempests - hunkering down to batten hatches and brave the worst until tides turned. Over the uneasy days that followed, Elizabeth maintained a facade of normalcy for the children's sake. But inside she wavered between desperate hope Peter would reappear any moment and grim acceptance he had likely met some tragic end alone in darkness or waters that had claimed him before. Their little world was upended once again by forces beyond understanding. Rising gossip surrounding the disappearance tested her composure further. Lewd speculations seemed to swirl in every hushed conversation and averted glance now. Staying upright against such malice was exhausting. But Elizabeth remained resolute - she would shield their family's dignity and honor Peter's memory, whatever version ultimately proved true. Her unwavering faith in the man she loved could withstand even this. Their story did not end here. Weeks passed without answers, only deepening mystery. Then late one rain-soaked night, a timid knock roused Elizabeth from fitful dreams of seeking and finding not. Heart lurching, she hurried to unlatch the door with trembling hands. But it was only a sodden stranger clutching a shell-studded box familiar as her own skin. Wordlessly he pressed it into her grasp before disappearing back into darkness and deluge. The compass. Peter's sole keepsake and talisman. She sank to the floor cradling it, tears finally spilling free. There could only be one meaning - Peter was gone, for good this time. Whatever cruel sea had tried claiming him before had succeeded at last, helped perhaps by his own willingness to surrender to its embrace after years wrestling inner demons. Part of Elizabeth had clung desperately to implausible hope, but now stark truth crashed over her. He would not be coming back. Hunched there on the cold plank floor as her world crumbled, she felt torn between anguish at being left untethered and grateful release that Peter had escaped final victory over his tormented mind. Perhaps this was a form of peace for his spirit, however agonizing the manner. She must try to take comfort his suffering was ended while cherishing the gift their time together had been. Though alone again, she was stronger for having been forged alongside his strength. The rest was just wretched circumstance, not a reflection on their marriage. He had clung to her and redemption as long as he could. Over subsequent days, Elizabeth grasped for purpose and routine again like a lifeboat. Though grief and unanswered questions yet churned within, its rough familiar planks helped steady her. She need only endure one wave at a time, however towering. For the childrens' sakes she must remain seaworthy, keeping their little craft pointed ahead when she could just as easily go under. If she focused only on each small task of living - baking bread, mending clothes, singing lullabies - the pain could not overwhelm her fully. So gradually, imperceptibly, the cottage came back to life as Elizabeth found her rhythm again in its well-worn grooves - solitary, yet bearing the lingering imprint of Peter's steady devotion surrounding her. The humble rooms still echoed with his deep laughter by the fire, the porch still creaked where they had sat dreaming. His absence surrounded her constantly, but it was no longer a specter battering down hope, simply a bittersweet tide now carrying her into unknown waters. She would cling to what yet remained and sail on as he would have urged for their family's sake. The years ahead held ache still, but even that could not erase the profound happiness they had carved from hardship and redemption. That joy would light her way forward as brightly as the compass points guiding lost sailors home. She need only remember how to read its language again as the sole map to strange shores. This time she knew she did not travel alone after all, but carried his sturdiness within to steady her course. So on a blustery grey morning as she watched her son amble the cliffs carrying his father's old walking stick, Elizabeth let grief wash through her transmuted to gentle melancholy. However suddenly ended, their story held beauty free from regret. The compass points gleamed yet to guide her ahead, and she would follow their charge faithfully - raising their children with abundant love, shouldering the days with courage, and remembering always that though love leaves, it does not ever truly leave us. Its light lingers lifetimes. She need only carry the memories onward and teach their children to do the same someday. Though tides swept some dreams away, hope pointed towards fresh horizons now.

Chapter 43

Elizabeth paused to catch her breath atop the hill crest, gazing down the sloping trail to the remote seaside village nestled below. Nearly ten years had passed since she received the cryptic unsigned letter pleading she come quickly. Mary was dying and had confession to make regarding the past. Part of Elizabeth had wanted to ignore the abrupt summons, leaving the wounds of that time safely scarred over. But in the end, she realized this might be her sole chance to understand the events that had inexplicably spirited Peter away, never to return. She owed it to his memory and the questions that still haunted her to make this journey, however painful. The village was small and unfamiliar, much changed since her youth. She made her halting way through the narrow streets, directions clutched in one hand. The lanes and cottages all seemed to blur together in unfamiliarity. How much had life reshaped this place and those who inhabited it, herself included? It was another world from the reckless innocence they had shared. At last she located the nondescript cottage flanked by withered gardens. Hesitating on the step, Elizabeth steeled herself before knocking softly. The frail wisp of a woman who opened the door was almost unrecognizable as the pretty carefree Mary from memory. But the eyes were still bright and searching as they rested on Elizabeth's face. "You came. Thank the saints." Mary's thin voice rasped with feeling. "I have wished so often I could take it all back..." She broke off coughing into her shawl before beckoning Elizabeth inside weakly. The air smelled of medicinal herbs and candle wax. Death was near. Settling creakily at the table, Mary gripped Elizabeth's hand with surprising force. "I must unburden my soul before it's too late, though you've no reason to believe me." Her eyes pleaded for grace. "Just know I never wished real harm, only to win justice." Trying not to betray the storm of emotions churning inside her, Elizabeth kept her voice calm. "Tell it plainly then. I cannot promise absolution, but you have my ear." She held the frail hand gently, letting long unspoken truths finally emerge. Halting through wheezing breaths, Mary recounted an unthinkable history - how obsession in youth had twisted to bitterness at abandonment and led her to plot revenge on callous Peter by posing as her own deceased twin sister Clara. But the lies intended to torment instead destroyed lives. By the time she realized the damage wrought, Peter had vanished into the mists, fate unknown. "Not a day goes by I don't regret it all." Tears slipped down Mary's sunken cheeks. "I thought only to wound pride, but destroyed the pure love you had found." She gripped Elizabeth's wrist feebly. "Can you find it in your heart to pity a foolish jealous girl?" Elizabeth sat stunned in the wake of these revelations, a thousand emotions churning through her. The woman before her was culpable, yet also victim of her own reckless passion. They had all been young and foolish once. Who was to judge what roads led them here? She squeezed Mary's hand lightly. "The past is buried. I am simply grateful to finally understand." Nodding acceptance, Mary sank back, seeming to shrink before Elizabeth's eyes as the weight fell away from her spirit. When she spoke again, her voice was barely a whisper. "I do not know what became of him after. My own stubborn pride kept me from stopping the avalanche before it was too late. But I swear to you, I played no role in his end." Looking into the sunken eyes, Elizabeth knew she spoke truth. Mary had only been misguided, not monstrous. And the time for blame was long gone. They had all changed beyond reckoning from those brash youths who expected the world's secrets to unlock at their demand. Life proved more complex. "I believe you wished no true harm." Elizabeth's voice held steady conviction. "All is forgiven now. Let the past finally rest, Mary. It served none of us well, but cannot be undone." She squeezed the bony hand, feeling its frail grip finally release the misjudgments carrying her here. Their story together was ending gently. Long after Mary finally slipped into labored sleep, Elizabeth remained keeping vigil by flickering candlelight as darkness fell outside. They had walked such different paths since parting ways doomed by hasty errors. But she felt only gratitude that the truth allowed old ghosts to be laid down in peace at long last. It was enough. In the small hours before dawn, Mary's breaths slowed and ceased, face smooth and untroubled by the first faint light. Elizabeth sat unmoving, emotions spent. So much wreckage caused by impulsive youthful lusts and imagined slights. She and Peter had clung to joy nonetheless for a time. But even the wise could not evade fate. She pressed a gentle kiss to the cool wrinkled brow in somber farewell. Their tangled story was over now. After the no-frills funeral, Elizabeth placed a modest bouquet of white blooms by the fresh grave, mind far away. She did not look up at the sound of footsteps approaching slowly. A weathered hand reached down to tightly clasp her own. Glancing over in surprise, she met the kind eyes of Mary's elderly aunt, now caretaker of this place holding so much faded history. "You knew her long ago I think. She regretted the harm deeply." The old woman spoke almost in a whisper. "But the soul's journey holds more than we see. I hope you found some balm here." Elizabeth could only nod silently, throat too tight for speech. With a final comforting pat, the woman left her to the gravestones and restless sea. Alone on the windswept hill, Elizabeth let the tumult of revelations sink into her marrow. Nothing could undo the suffering planted or lives cut short by imprudence. But laying the past finally to rest here between whispering grass and granite brought unexpected peace. They had all faltered and fallen, but were together dust and memory now - forgiven and remembered. She touched Peter's name engraved in her heart. Wherever he journeyed, she prayed he had found similar grace. Their story was woven of more than its darkness. Turning her face to the clean sea wind, she let it carry grief out over the cliffs as she began the long walk home. Their time together held joy unmarred by its end. She would cling to that, leaving judgment behind in the barren earth. What lay ahead was still unwritten, a blank page. In her heart, she felt Peter urge her gently onward. And though the unknown path kept some shadows, she did not feel them as threats now. Even darkness held discovery for those willing to seek. She would carry on, a life freshly hers to shape day by day however she willed. It was enough. More than enough.

Chapter 44

Elizabeth hummed softly as she kneaded the bread dough, gazing out the window at the sun-dappled cliffs. A week had passed since her journey to lay old ghosts to rest, and it seemed some shadow had lifted from the cottage and her spirit. The unrelenting heartache of Peter's absence had finally begun morphing into softer melancholy. She would always miss his steadying presence, but the raw wound was mending. Letting go of regrets and misplaced blame had allowed fond memories their proper place again. She smiled recalling Peter teasing her as she baked, stealing a kiss with floury hands. A bittersweet pang yet echoed, but it could not erase the moments of grace and love they had shared. Her heart was slowly learning to lean into that warmth again after so long hunkered against storms. Knocking at the door startled Elizabeth from reminiscing. She peeked out to see a stranger shifting impatiently, face obscured under a battered hat. Unease pricked at her as she unlatched the door cautiously. "Can I help you?" The man swept off his hat, revealing weathered features and piercing grey eyes that jolted her heart. He was the very image of Peter from their youth. Elizabeth stumbled back in shock before anger erupted. "If this is someone's twisted idea of a joke, I'll not stand for it! Be gone, sir!" But he raised his palms pleadingly. "No jest, ma'am. Peter Maxwell sent me before...before the end." His voice dropped. "I swore to find you and deliver a warning he died too soon to give." Elizabeth froze, thoughts churning wildly. Some hoax seemed likely, yet how could this stranger know what Peter called her in tender moments? And his visage truly was haunting... She studied his face distrustfully, but saw only earnestness there. "Speak then of what you claim to know." With an anxious nod, he removed his cap and began hesitantly. "I knew Peter these last years on the lonely isles where broken men wash up. We became as brothers until his final day." His eyes took on a distant sheen with memory. "Before the sickness took him, he made me vow to carry a message to you." He grimaced. "There are men who yet wish you harm for old deeds, men who hounded him even in that forsaken place until he fled to protect you. He begged me warn you before they fulfill their vengeance." Rough hands twisted the battered hat in agitation. "I fulfilled my sworn duty. Now you must prepare and take care." Mind reeling, Elizabeth tried to reconcile the stunning details with guarded skepticism. This man clearly believed what he said, and his pleas echoed the protective spirit she knew so well in Peter. But phantom threats from old forgotten quarrels? She shook her head warily. "You spin quite a tale, sir. But I know of no one seeking such retaliation now. Our life has been quiet." Letting out a frustrated breath, he grasped her hand firmly. "Please, you must heed what I say! Peter knew the lengths they would go for revenge. He sacrificed all to hide from them, but could not elude forever. If you do not take this seriously, calamity will follow." Dark brows drew together in emphasis. "For the love Peter bore you, be on your guard!" Elizabeth wrestled with clashing reactions. Part of her recoiled at this sudden ominous warning from a face that nonetheless stirred tender instincts. But how could she ignore Peter's concern, however improbable or outdated? She had erred before in underestimating threats. This time she must pay heed. Features softening, she squeezed the stranger's weathered hand. "Very well. I cannot discount Peter's care for me, however dubious its cause." Meeting the fervent grey eyes steadily, she added, "I will proceed with caution for my family's sake." Nodding grimly, he donned his hat. "That is all I ask. Peter hoped his silence would protect you, but fear should not rule." He hesitated on the threshold, brow furrowed. "Guard yourself yet keep faith. Dark plots have a way of bringing light if met boldly." With that enigmatic assurance, he disappeared down the cliff path, leaving Elizabeth unsettled. In the following days, she found herself wrestling between instinctive skepticism and nagging disquiet. The maid busied herself ensuring doors and windows were secured each night, yet her sleep grew increasingly troubled. What if the warning held some validity from the vanished past? But no matter how she wracked her memory, no enemies or scores unsettled came to light. The island years seemed almost a distant fever dream now. Still unease lingered. When the dawning weeks brought only calm and no signs of trouble, Elizabeth began to relax again, chalking up the strange encounter to overactive fears. She managed to mostly ignore the prickling at her neck on lonely stretches of beach or shadowy lane. Their corner of the world was still serene, whatever phantoms the messenger had awakened. No corporeal danger revealed itself. Until late one afternoon as she crested the hill above the market, Elizabeth spotted a unfamiliar hooded figure asking questions of a shopkeeper, who shook his head and turned away. Without seeing the man's face, every instinct within her suddenly screamed that he did not belong here. Dropping her basket, she yanked up her shawl hood and slipped into a winding alley out of sight, heart racing wildly. Peering around the corner, she watched the figure continue down the lane away from her, his odd lumbering gait stirring vague recognition. Where had she known someone who moved that way, with shoulders hunched like a battering ram? The island again fluttered at the edge of memory, just out of reach. Hardly daring to breathe, Elizabeth trailed the stranger at a distance as he made his way from merchant to tavern to dock, seeming to be on a mission of inquiry. By now, she was certain he was no benign visitor. When he disappeared into the sailors' pub, she slumped against a shadowed wall, mind churning. Her thoughts flew to the children back home vulnerable and unwarned. Elizabeth longed to race to them immediately. But she could not lead this phantom from the past straight to their refuge. Better to divert attention from the cottage entirely. She must play the decoy, staying visible so he did not lose the scent. Jaw set with maternal resolve, Elizabeth straightened and retied her shawl loosely, letting the breeze catch it. Then she set back down the lane boldly, ensuring she was never quite out of the stranger's line of sight as she went about errands and lingered chatting with villagers. She felt his eyes tracking her, haunches primed to attack whenever she let down her guard. As evening dusk descended, though, icy doubt crept in. She had perhaps acted rashly on vague suspicion. What did she truly know of this man's motives? He had not approached or explicitly threatened her, merely asked general questions. The messenger's warning rang hollow suddenly - had her own fears conjured the rest? Doubt swiftly eroded her defiant certainty. She had only imagined attack and instead made herself the hunted prey. Weariness and confusion overwhelmed her. Lost in self-reproach, Elizabeth did not notice the lantern flare behind her until a heavy hand clamped down on her shoulder, making her cry out. Whirling around, she found herself staring up at the looming shadowed figure, his familiar guttural voice confirming all her worst fears. "Thought you could evade me forever, witch? I have only awaited my chance for vengeance." Then the reflexes of a mother defending her young kicked in. With startling fierceness, Elizabeth clawed and kicked against iron restraint until she broke free. Blindly she dashed away into the night, feet flying over the darkened paths by childhood instinct alone. She had only one thought - to lead danger away from her family's door. Their safety was all that mattered now.

Chapter 45

Elizabeth paced the cottage floors, weariness and frustration churning inside her. Three days had passed since her frightening encounter on the lane that ended with the ominous stranger's abrupt disappearance once she broke free. He had clearly seemed intent on harming her for imagined past grievances. Yet in the aftermath she began questioning if she had acted rashly, letting old phantoms and rumors rule her response. The man had not actually harmed or threatened her aside from the cryptic remark before she ran. Perhaps she had conjured additional menace in her panic. But why had he grabbed her so forcibly? None of it made sense, leaving her restless and on edge. When another knock finally came at the door, every nerve jolted. But peering out cautiously revealed only the same weathered face as before, grey eyes anxious beneath a drooping hat. Elizabeth opened the door warily, unsure whether to welcome or scorn him after the chaos sown. Ushering him in, she crossed her arms. "I think it time you explained yourself fully, sir. The other night, what did you hope to gain by the tale you fed me?" The man removed his hat, worry lines creasing his brow as he studied her. "My lady, I meant no harm, only wished to help as I swore to Peter I would." He raked a hand through grey-flecked hair in agitation. "But I see now my approach only spread fear, not aid. I am sorry for the distress caused." His shoulders slumped. "I will trouble you no more." Seeing his remorseful sincerity, Elizabeth felt her defensiveness begin softening. "Wait," she entreated, motioning to a chair. "I know you believe you carry some mission from Peter. But I require the full truth before deciding if you are friend or fraud." She sat across from him, composed but unyielding. "So speak plainly now. No more veiled tales." The man's expression turned inward as if wrestling some internal battle. When he met her stare again, shame and defeat had replaced hesitance. "You deserve the truth after my blundering interference," he began slowly. "In fact Peter and I were hardly acquainted. I met him but once when my ship docked on the isle where he had washed ashore." He looked down, abashed. "But I revered him even from that brief encounter - his courage and character were clear as light. When I heard he had passed, I vowed to honor his memory somehow, however foolishly." His eyes implored her mercy. "I spun fiction thinking it would grant me purpose. But I see now I have only overstepped, to your detriment." Though Elizabeth still felt the sting of deception, she reached over to clasp his hand in forgiveness. "Your intent was good. Let us speak no more of it." At her gentle absolution, his weathered features relaxed into humble relief. But doubts still plagued her restless mind. "Before you go, grant me one truth - was there ever any real man I should fear?" The grey eyes met hers solemnly. "None beyond the ghosts we imagine. You have lived an exemplary life." He rose and bowed deeply before donning his hat. "Thank you for your grace, my lady. I wish you only safety and joy hereafter." He turned to the door, shoulders less stooped now. Watching him shuffle down the lane, Elizabeth released a slow breath, feeling the knotted tension within her begin to unwind. There was still mystery about this stranger's motives, but she sensed no malice in him. Some souls simply longed to be part of tales larger than their own. He had meant well honoring Peter's memory, however awkwardly. She wished him well on less fanciful ventures. In the days that followed, calm returned to the cottage as the events took on a dreamlike quality - strange but no longer menacing. Elizabeth focused on the comforting rhythms of life before her - children's laughter, clifftop strolls, quiet evenings alone only with memory's bittersweet company. It was enough. She had survived worse storms and emerged whole. Until late one grey afternoon when another knock intruded on her solitude once more. Opening it warily, Elizabeth was surprised to find the sheepish man from before, cap twisting in his hands. She opened her mouth to politely dismiss him again, but he spoke up earnestly before she could begin. "Please my lady, do not send me away just yet. I know I have no right to ask your trust after my foolish deceptions, but I have one final thing to share that may be of use." He extended a weathered journal, pages warped by ocean brine. "It was Peter's from those lonely exile years. I found it when I...visited the island." His eyes silently pleaded for a last chance. Reaching hesitantly for the journal, Elizabeth felt unexpected emotion swell within her. Her fingers traced the faded binding reverently as she recognized Peter's sturdy script covering the pages. She had thought all remnants of him lost forever. Looking up into the stranger's hopeful face, she summoned a tremulous smile. "Thank you for this gift beyond value." Relief broke across his features as he nodded and backed away. "Use it well then. My spirit is at peace knowing his words are returned to your hands." He inclined his head in farewell before turning and departing with lighter steps now. Elizabeth clutched the journal to her chest, almost dizzy from the sudden overwhelming prospect of hearing Peter's voice again from beyond the grave. Here were the missing years and pieces of himself he had spent so long secreted away. A tangible second chance she had never dared dream of. Hands shaking, she began reading the stained pages with fresh tears and laughter. The entries recounted his early days marooned battling despair, glimpses of tropical beauties surrounding the ragged castaways, moments of grace and camaraderie in the camps, demons that haunted still. But interwoven were remembrances of her - her name scribbled in the margins absently, passages reliving tender moments from their past, brushstrokes painting the vision of her that gave him strength. He had clung to her memory anchoring his tired spirit when all else was stripped away. When Elizabeth reached the final entry written in a hurried scrawl, she could almost hear Peter's gravelly voice urgently sharing what might be his last words to her. He recounted fleeing the island camps under darkness, sure unknown enemies tracked him still. But he declared his only purpose now was making the passage home, certain that she awaited. The last lines spoke with stoic hope across time and distance: "Our story does not end here, my love. I will find you somehow, someday. Our compass points north together always." Clasping the journal over her heart, Elizabeth let long-restrained tears course down her cheeks. She could nearly see him vividly standing before her now - weathered face gentle yet resolute, strong arms that had cradled her through every hardship open again. If she listened closely, the wind through the cliffs whispered with Peter's low laughter. Their time together had been cut short by fate's fickle hand. But that vitality yet lived on in her and this small cottage brimming now with his spirit. She need only infuse it into each new day.

Chapter 46

Elizabeth paused before the weathered clapboard door, the faint din of voices and clinking glasses audible from within. This was the fourth disreputable gambling house she had tried that night, guided only by the vague journal clues suggesting Peter had frequented similar places those final mysterious days. Each one stirred more uneasy doubts that she was too late - the patrons and owners proving either tight-lipped or legitimately ignorant when she inquired about him. But she could not stop now. The children were safe with her cousin's family. And she had sworn to follow this ghostly trail to whatever end, no matter how Peter's memory emerged changed. Adjusting the hood of her travel cloak, she slipped quietly inside, scanning the dingy taproom. It was crowded with rough, hard-edged types, far removed from her sheltered home life. She garnered curious looks and muttered comments, but kept her eyes fixed firmly ahead as she edged up to the bar. The surly proprietor raised an eyebrow at her but poured the ale she ordered before moving down to other patrons. Sipping discreetly, Elizabeth listened in on conversations around her, interjecting casually whenever there was an opening. "Come around here often? I had a friend once, Peter Maxwell, used to frequent these parts..." Most shared nothing useful, but she persisted, describing his features and shipwork. After enough time she learned to filter out crude jests and grumbles about a nosy newcomer shattering drunken reverie. She had weathered worse. When the fourth grizzled seaman shook his head dismissively and turned away, though, despair crept up Elizabeth's spine. This dusty den of iniquity had proven just as much of a dead end. She had exhausted the paltry leads, gambling away her only hopes of finding answers What else remained to cling to? Dropping a few worn coins on the counter, she was rising to leave when a scarred hand unexpectedly clamped down on her wrist. "Not so fast, missy. I've got a tale to spin that might be of interest." Elizabeth looked up to meet the hard grey eyes of an elderly sailor. Stale breath and days old whiskers enveloped her as he leaned in. "Only it'll cost you, hearing truth often does. What's it worth to you?" Elizabeth hesitated, resentment rising at this crass opportunism. But her need to finally understand ultimately won out. She untied her coin purse and passed a few more silver pieces over, steeling herself. "Tell me then what you know - and speak fact, not fiction." Pocketing the coins with a gap-toothed grin, the old salt nodded. "Aye then, truth it is." He stared past her rheumily. "I knew your Peter alright. Good man mostly, till he got in over his worthless head." A cough rattled his chest before he continued. "Always fond of games and spirits, he was. After some sorry business elsewhere, he washed ashore here, half-mad and with debts chasing. Threw himself into darker pleasures - cards, drink, women." The watery eyes met hers frankly. "Reckless living only works awhile. But he wouldn't heed no warnings, not even with thugs at his heels. A man on fire can't feel the burns till it's too late." He shook his grizzled head regretfully. Elizabeth reeled as this seedy account upended her image of Peter's stoic dignity in exile. But deep down it resonated believably - an anguished soul in hiding might well seek numbness and perilous escape. She found herself nodding for the man to continue, braced for the worst. "So one night the demons came to roost. Drunk as a sot by the third hand, Peter had gambled half the gold he didn't have. When he lost the rest, the dealer and his cronies followed him out back..." His voice dropped, rough with remembered menace. "I heard the scuffle and bones cracking but didn't dare intervene. They made sure the debt was settled permanent-like." The blunt words seemed to pierce and crack open her heart as Elizabeth listened numbly. However dressed up in romantic memory, this was the unvarnished end Peter had stumbled to - bleeding out nameless in an alley over someone else's gold. She pressed the heel of her hand hard against burning eyes, willing back useless tears. However desperately she still wished to change its course, their story's conclusion could not be denied or outrun. Better to face fate's reckoning here than keep chasing phantoms. Numbly laying a few more coins in the man's gnarled hand, she managed a thin but sincere "Thank you" before pushing away from the bar's oppressive grip. The journey to closure was never easy or graced with dignity. But the depths of truth were better than endless fruitless shadow-boxing with the past's ghosts. She was relieved to feel grim calm settling over her as she stepped into the cold night air. It was over now. The long road home stretched empty ahead. Elizabeth drew her cloak tighter against the chill, but did not shiver. Even stripped of romance or mystery, Peter's love and spirit yet traveled with her, familiar voice gently admonishing her not to dwell on sad finales but to sow goodness ahead. She could nearly picture his roguish wink and crooked grin before fading again like mist. Their story together lived on within her, and always would. She need only open her heart to share that cherished memory, turning it to light and wisdom passed on. As the carriage jostled forward, wisps of old dreams floated by ungrasped to join the fading stars. Dawn approached, clean and unwritten. Elizabeth did not glance back. The future's blank page awaited boldly seized. With her family's joyful din filling the cottage again soon, she was ready to live it fully, letting time wash grief's sharp edges to smooth memory stones. She would have smiles to share when she placed wildflowers on two half-forgotten graves come spring. Mystery could haunt only what she refused to shine light's grace on bravely. Her story moved forward filled with purpose.

Here is a 3500 word continuation of the story: Chapter 47 Elizabeth glanced down at her dirt-stained breeches and scuffed boots, barely recognizing herself. But desperate times called for throwing propriety to the wind. With Peter's fate still unknown after vanishing amidst the seedy gambling dens, she had decided disguise and cunning offered her only chance of unraveling the mystery. No one would willingly share secrets with Peter's genteel widow. But as a rough newcomer hustling card games, she might learn something of use. Or so she hoped. Adjusting her cap lower over pinned-up hair, she pushed through the creaking doors into her third disreputable taproom that night. Smoke and raucous laughter enveloped her as she made for the corner tables where dice and cards promised insider gossip as well as coin. She kept her shoulders hunched and gait swaggering as she'd observed of the dock rats. Just another green lad chasing fortune's favor, or so she must appear. Settling onto an empty stool, Elizabeth ordered ale and studied the other players slyly through its bitter foam. Their crude banter and mocking jabs at the young pup in their midst helped disguise her lack of cardsmanship. She played along clumsily, letting her pile of coins slowly shrink amidst grumbles about beginner's luck running out. They were surely on guard for trickery from new faces. It was enough to simply blend in for now, listening for any talk of Peter. After an hour of playing the hapless fool, she felt one weathered sailor take the bait, his grin flashing gold as he leaned in avuncularly. "Say lad, you look to be needing some tutelage. I'd be happy to teach you a trick or two if you don't mind losing a few more shillings." With an exaggerated wink, he began slyly stacking the deck while the others chuckled. Elizabeth played along dutifully, letting her last coins slide across to him over the next round. But as the group's attention drifted back to their own hands, she put on a show of crestfallen dismay. "Bugger it all, that was my whole week's pay gone!" She stood quickly, wavering as if drunk, and clutched the cheating sailor's shoulder, slurring. "Least you can do is buy your star pupil a drink, mate. I'm sure you've bled enough lambs tonight." Guffawing at the spectacle, her mark waved his hands acquiescently and called for two ales. As they sat side-by-side, Elizabeth kept up a show of wide-eyed naivete, strategically needling him about his obvious mastery of cards. "I bet you've taken many a fool's last coins before me, eh? Probably know all the desperate souls around here trying to gamble their troubles away..." She shook her head ruefully, priming him to expound. When a fresh hand started, the sailor leaned in confidingly. "Truth is, I used to run with a real cunning chap, could stack the deck quick as a blink." His voice dropped. "Old Peter Maxwell. Probably the best hustler around before his number came up bad. No one had his skill or nerve." The hard eyes glinted with remembered camaraderie. "We made quite the pair cleaning out sots and layabouts. Shame how it ended..." Elizabeth's pulse quickened, though she kept her face casual. "Poor bastard. I heard talk of him before - sounds like he lived too hard and fast." She clinked their bottles together conspiratorially. "Here's to devils getting their due." As the night wore on, she slowly drew out more details between hands, her new friend boasting happily of past schemes and conquests. The stark picture emerged of Peter feeding his own self-destruction in these halls, dangerously untethered. But even this unvarnished truth was better than silence. She had found the missing fragments at last. His memory could rest, if not wholly at peace. Nearing midnight, sensing she had gained all she could, Elizabeth made exaggerated yawns about early work on the docks. Clapping the sailor on the back in gratitude, she promised to return to practice her card skills if they ever met again. Though inwardly ready to shed this charade forever, she kept up the swaggering performance until safely away down the fogbound alley. Leaning against a damp brick wall in the shadows, she let out a long slow breath. The truth was never as hoped for, but it was done now. She had filled in the last haunting gaps in Peter's vanished final days. There would be grief still, though now more for the anguish he must have endured than her own loss. He had been unraveling, trapped by remorse and fear. But she could finally lay the past's lingering power to rest, remembering the vital living man she loved, not how he perished. Their story did not end tragically. Peeling off her cap and ruffling sweat-dampened hair, Elizabeth felt the night breeze cool against her skin. The sagging drunkard's disguise had served its purpose, winning her truth if not dignity. She was ready to shed the artifice and return home to mend the parts of her spirit left bruised by chasing difficult answers. A bath, clean clothes and the childrens' unfettered laughter awaited. For tonight, she had done enough.

Though mystery would always shroud Peter's final fate, she knew him safely now free of torment in memory's sanctuary beyond time and wounds. And she would share with their children the stories of their father that glowed bright as compass lights - tender smiles, deep laughter, hands clasping hers steady against the storms. That enduring love guided her forward, rather than fruitlessly mourning all she could not understand or change. The past would haunt only what she refused to illuminate with grace. It was time to begin again. Drawing her cloak tight, Elizabeth slipped from the concealing shadows into the misty night. The road ahead seemed less forbidding now. However uneven and obscured at times, her journey with Peter through joy, loss and redemption had led her here. She walked on with purpose. Though sometimes difficult, the truth had set her heart free to embrace life's fullness again, mystery and all. That was enough.

Chapter 47

Elizabeth pulled her cap low and collar high as she slipped through the dark alley's mouth into the muffled din and haze beyond. She had come tonight not chasing shadows of the past, but decisive final truth - whether her elusive husband yet lived or had perished as the wall of silence suggested. One high stakes game to lay the mystery to rest, whatever that revealed. She steeled herself against hope and heartbreak alike. The back room she entered was thick with tobacco smoke and tense silence as a dozen rough players focused on their cards and dwindling piles of coins. Hard faces sized her up briefly before dismissing the unknown youth to their risky business. Elizabeth took the last open seat, keeping her eyes downcast like a proper newcomer. She would bid her time mixing with these cutthroats, listening for anything more that might illuminate Peter's fate. Patience had served her well enough thus far. So she played the first few hands conservatively, letting her pile slowly shrink as she grasped the rhythm and stakes of this shadowy world. The men grumbled and swore steadily as luck turned against them, bravado barely masking desperation. Even without looking up, she gleaned ample gossip between games - cheating scandals, ships lost at sea, Sheriff raids expected soon. Useful intelligence should trouble arise, though so far indistinct. Finally after losing a few more hands intentionally, Elizabeth decided to risk engaging one grizzled mariner beside her who had been muttering foul curses under his breath all night as his coins dwindled. She made a show of pushing her last few bits forward precariously, shaking her head ruefully. "Gentlemen, I fear this is my retirement hand, whether for good or ill!" As expected, her neighbor took the bait, turning to study her patronizingly. "Poor lad's had hard luck tonight, I see. Well don't lose heart yet." He lowered his voice conspiratorially. "Truth is, these fine fellows tend to forget their manners once gold is involved." With a wink, he pulled a hidden card from his cuff, showing her a brief flash. "A swift learner can still gain the upper hand. Follow my lead if you ken..." Several hands later, aided by the sailor's subtle tricks, Elizabeth's pile had grown back Healthily as the others blustered in disbelief. She made certain to press her new mentor for any useful gossip she could coax between games. His grumbling provided little insight, but she remained patient. Each hand likely brought her closer to some revelation if she was vigilant. Fate rewarded her persistence several long hours later when a hulking brute of a man joined, immediately drawing wary looks from the other players. He was introduced grimly as Mr. Stokes, owner of this fine establishment. Elizabeth kept her eyes averted like the others, only studying him discreetly through her lashes. But she noticed his left hand was mangled grotesquely, making shuffling and handling cards awkward. Her mind filed this vital detail away for later use as the game progressed tensely. The players behaved warily, as if wolves acknowledging the bear in their midst. When Stokes began winning hand after easy hand, though, mutters broke out, quickly silenced under his glowering stare. But bristling tension pervaded the cramped room now. These men would only tolerate obvious cheating so long, proprietor or not. Elizabeth bided her time, sensing an opportunity approaching. Finally after losing a particularly large pot of coins to yet another of Stokes' improbable hands, she allowed her youthful bravado to overrule restraint. Slamming down her empty mug, she pointed a quavering finger, voice raised gratingly. "Now see here, I may be new to such fine games as these. But I know a bully and a cheat when I see 'em clear enough!" Stokes' eyes snapped toward her, blazing with menace. But around the table she caught the other players' nods of approval and relief that someone had voiced their silent outrage. They straightened in solidarity, weathered faces set stubbornly now that the challenge was raised. Cracking her knuckles, Elizabeth pressed on, emboldened. "I ain't blind. Your dealing stinks of trickery, friend." She waved contemptuously at his misshapen paw. "Ain't sporting using that deformity to stack the deck neither. Why not let me shuffle and deal next hand so we all know no snake's at work?" Murmurs of agreement rose around the table as the bristling men endorsed her bold proposal. For a fraught moment, Elizabeth thought Stokes might lunge at her directly as his face purpled alarmingly. But at the crew's implacable glares, he reluctantly conceded, shoving the deck toward her bad-temperedly. "Go on then. But you'll regret this insolence, whelp." The table seemed to release its collectively held breath as Elizabeth began shuffling thoroughly. For the first time since she had entered, the game's outcome now rested solely on fortune's whim, not manipulation. As she dealt evenly around the circle, the hands proved fair and modestly sized for once. Stokes noticed the men's mood lifting and shot her a black scowl that promised later retaliation. She tensed, prepared for the inevitable confrontation ahead. When her turn came around next, Elizabeth flipped over her cards, revealing a winning two pairs over the others' hands. As she reached to pull the sizable pot of coins over, a vice-like grip seized her wrist suddenly. She looked up slowly to meet Stokes' volcanic glare. "You think yourself mighty clever don't you, boy?" His grip tightened enough to grind the small bones together painfully as she refused to cry out. "But you'll regret this night sorely." With his other meaty hand, he flung the rest of the cards and coins away violently, then clutched the front of her shirt and lifted her bodily towards the back door. "Time you learned what we do to insolent upstarts around here." Trying not to let stark fear show in her face, Elizabeth braced herself as he half-dragged her outside. She struggled futilely, tears pricking at her eyes as she heard the crash of a fist against flesh behind her. But Stokes was in a mindless rage now. He slammed her small frame brutally against brick wall, massive hands closing around her throat. "Won't talk back so smart now will you, boy!" Just as black spots started swimming across Elizabeth's vision, the choking pressure released suddenly. She collapsed limply, gasping for breath that seared her throat. Blearily she made out two figures scuffling nearby, one still hulking, the other leaner but vicious in attack. A familiar gravelly voice that jolted her heart shouted, "Get off away from him or you'll get more than a bloody nose, Stokes!" As her vision cleared, Elizabeth saw none other than Peter - thinner and grizzled but him beyond all doubt - pinning the larger man against the alley slats by his neck. "I heard you were back to your old ways bullying lost souls. But you'll face me now." He glared before landing a sharp blow across Stokes' jaw that made him reel away. Turning hurriedly to Elizabeth still slumped raggedly on the ground, Peter knelt by her, calloused hands cradling her face with exquisite tenderness, eyes searching hers desperately. "You damned fool, what madness drove you here risking your life this way? Did you think I would not find you?" Despite the harsh words, his voice broke with emotion as he gently helped her stand. Leaning heavily against Peter's stalwart frame, letting delayed shock take over, Elizabeth finally registered through her daze that the impossible had somehow come to pass - her lost husband was here, solid and real against all reason. As tears streaked her dirty face, she clutched him tighter, afraid he might vanish back into memory. "You were dead...I had to know..." she manages to rasp thinly past the garrote's damage. His stern expression softened as he tilted her face up. "Oh Lizzy, always leaping into the lion's mouth. I disappeared to protect you from my shameful state, but should have known you would chase the truth blindly." He tucked her head beneath his bearded chin. "Forgive me for striking out alone. You deserve the full truth now." Half-carrying her away from the groaning Stokes, Peter led them out of the dank alley down the deserted midnight streets to a small shack on the wharf. Once inside, he stoked a humble fire and tended gently to Elizabeth's cuts and bruises before offering a simple meal. Then with her head cradled in his lap as she fought exhaustion, he began to speak of all that had passed. "After I became mired in addiction and peril, I could not bear you seeing what I had sunk to..." His voice remained steady, if thick with remorse. "I thought vanishing completely the only noble amends. But I have regretted that choice every day since." Strong hands stroked her hair softly. "It was you who saved me, Lizzy. I just had to realize I could still come home even the lowest wretch to find your heart yet open." Nestling closer, Elizabeth lifted a hand to his bearded cheek. "The past matters not. You are here now, that is everything." Tears filled Elizabeth's eyes as she gazed up at her beloved husband, still scarcely believing this was real after so many years missing and grieving him. "You have nothing to ask forgiveness for," she whispered. "It was I who should not have endangered myself recklessly pursuing ghosts." She placed a hand over Peter's heart, feeling it beat steadily beneath her palm. "All I care about is that you are alive and safe again. We have suffered enough apart - let the rest fade away." Peter covered her small hand with his own weathered one, his eyes glistening. "You ever were the wise one, my love. Our pasts may be tangled, but this moment now is what matters." He leaned down and kissed her tenderly. "Come home with me," Elizabeth implored, sitting up to caress his bearded cheek. "The children have missed you so, and your cottage waits still." Hope flickered across Peter's tired features. "I dare not hope any welcome remains for this prodigal wretch..." "Always and forever," she vowed fiercely. "We shall be a family again." Peter enfolded her in his strong embrace, and Elizabeth felt the last missing piece of her heart slot into place. The storms had passed, and from the wreckage, their love had endured, strengthened and tempered. Now at long last, safe harbor awaited. They had found their way home.

Chapter 48

Elizabeth awoke to daylight filtering through the small shack's grimy window and the comforting weight of Peter's arm draped over her. For a blissful moment, she forgot the years of longing and loss separating them, feeling as though they were still carefree newlyweds with a bright future sprawling ahead. Then she shifted slightly, her bruises throbbing, and reality returned bittersweet. Turning, she studied Peter's bearded face relaxed in sleep - more weathered now, with new creases and a perpetual furrow between his brows, but still so beloved. Her heart swelled, even as she grieved for all they had endured apart. What mattered most was they had found their way here despite every obstacle. As if sensing her gaze, Peter's eyes blinked open. He reached up to tuck back a loose strand of her hair gently. "I scarcely dare believe you are real, Lizzy - fear I'll wake to find you a dream." His voice was gruff with emotion. "But I swear here and now, I will not waste our second chance." Taking his rough hand in hers, Elizabeth pressed it ardently to her cheek. "This gift of having you back is more than I ever dreamed might come to pass." She kissed his battered knuckles lightly. "The past can remain buried. You need only look forward." Sitting up slowly, Peter kept her hand clasped in his. His grey eyes were grave. "I wish it were so simple, my love. But I have much to atone for still." He gestured around the dismal shack. "You should not have found me mired in this squalor, too ashamed to come home." His jaw tightened. "I know now I cannot outrun the debts haunting me, only try to make amends." Though her heart ached, Elizabeth nodded. Redemption was never easily won. "I understand, Peter. Make peace however you must. But please do not think your family will reject you. We yearn only to have you home." She touched his cheek. "You shall always have a safe harbor with us." Leaning into her palm, Peter's expression softened. "Your faith has been the one true compass in my darkest days. I confess I do not deserve such devotion after abandoning it for far too long." He clasped her hands earnestly. "You and our children should have been my sanctuary, not spirits that tormented and shamed me." "The past is done." Elizabeth spoke firmly now. "What matters is who you are still - a good man who fell into shadow, but found his way back." She smiled through sudden tears. "Our family is not whole without you. Come home to us, Peter. Please." A lone tear slid down his weathered cheek as he murmured hoarsely, "Granting me yet another chance I do not warrant..." Pulling her close, he buried his face in her hair. "I swear I will spend my remaining days proving worthy of this family I have missed so much." They clung together wordlessly until Peter finally drew back, dashing the moisture from his eyes gruffly. "Well then, I suppose there are two small whirlwinds awaiting my return." A spark of anticipation lit his expression that had been absent far too long. "Best gather my affairs here and face the onslaught on my old bones." That afternoon as Peter shore up loose ends from his wayward years, Elizabeth made discreet inquiries for any news of the intimidating card den owner Stokes or where to find the local magistrate. Though her ego was bruised, she could not let the villain's cruelty go unanswered. Her courage had won Peter back, after all. And for him, she would see justice done properly. By dusk, Peter had collected his meager possessions, settled accounts, and bid his transient acquaintances goodbye, while she finished her own errands with head held high. Then finally, for the first time in endless years, they departed that wretched place side by side, scars healing and hope rekindled. The road ahead remained unsure, but navigating it together made all the difference. As Peter's boyhood home peeked into view on the horizon next dawn, Elizabeth felt him tense beside her anxiously. She squeezed his hand and smiled encouragingly. "No matter what, we are home as long as we are together." Nodding gratefully, he helped her down from the carriage, shoulders braced. The cottage door burst open instantly, children spilling out with joyful cries. They nearly knocked Peter over with exuberant hugs before turning shy, the intervening years suddenly real again. But he ruffled their hair and coaxed them inside with gentle humour. The healing had begun. That night after the children were long abed, Elizabeth found Peter standing absently before the cold hearth, fingers tracing old scorch marks. Coming up silently behind him, she wrapped her arms about his solid frame, cheek pressed to his back. "Happy to be home, sailor?" Turning, Peter cradled her face, eyes lit with wonder. "You were right, Lizzy. This is still home as if I never left." His smile deepened playfully. "But I confess, it is far better now with my beautiful wife nearby." And he drew her into a kiss that sparked that hearth back to roaring life. In the idyllic weeks that followed, Elizabeth watched with joy as Peter slipped back into the rhythms of life at the cottage - tilling soil, fishing, playing with the children. With each passing day, she felt his spirit healing and unburdening further. He smiled often now with a deep contentment she used to know. Their family was finally whole again. Until late one evening when a knock jarred the cozy scene. Exchanging wary glances with Peter, Elizabeth opened it cautiously to reveal the local magistrate flanked by deputies. "Pardon our intrusion ma'am. We are here to collect your husband Peter Maxwell. There are serious charges against him." Though Peter surrendered willingly, it was still an anguished scene as they led him away into the rainy night. Elizabeth remained strong, buoyed by certainty of his innocence. With faith and fortitude, they would endure this test too. Their devotion was stronger than any flickering shadows now. She would cling to that light until he was safely home in her arms again.

Chapter 49

Elizabeth busied herself kneading bread dough, gazing out the window occasionally to where Peter was repairing the sagging barn door under the warm afternoon sun. It had been several months now since he had returned home, slipping gradually back into the rhythms of daily life with them. Watching him work steadily, humming some sea shanty to himself, Elizabeth smiled softly. The initial tension and awkwardness between them had faded day by day as Peter opened himself up humbly to his family once more. He no longer hid away from shame, but faced each challenge with good cheer. Her trust and pride in him swelled daily. When he glanced up to catch her eye through the dusty window, his boyish grin made her heart skip just like old times. He was still the same man she loved beneath the new layers time had accrued. With each passing season, it felt more as if he had never left. Turning her attention back to the rising dough, Elizabeth sighed contentedly. Their world was whole again. The gossip in town about Peter's sordid past had faded to disinterest as he kept his head down, working diligently. She had done her part too, facing down malicious whispers with calm faith in the man she knew, not wild tales. Let their actions speak louder than slander. Soon the cottage door banged open to admit two whirling dust devils - their son and daughter returned from school. They chattered happily about their lessons and friends as Elizabeth sliced bread and jam for their snack, smiling as they recounted antics and adventures. She blessed the everyday joy of this family daily. Glancing up from his scribbled drawings, her son paused hesitantly. "Ma, why do the other children say such nasty things about Pa? They call him a scoundrel and worse." His young face was troubled. "I know Pa's not like that." Sighing, Elizabeth smoothed back his unruly hair gently. "People do not easily forget rumors or first impressions." She took both children's hands. "But we know who your Father truly is - not the broken man he once was, but the devoted husband and parent before us now. Time will change narrow minds in the end." The solemn little faces before her nodded, faith restored. That night after the little ones were snugly abed, Elizabeth sank gratefully into Peter's embrace before the dying fire. His voice rumbled softly behind her. "I know I have damaged our good standing hereabouts, and for that I am sorry, Lizzy." His arms tightened around her waist. "I will work twice as diligently to prove myself an upright man to any who doubt." Turning to face him, Elizabeth cradled Peter's bearded cheek tenderly. "Pay no mind to petty gossip. I never questioned loving the man before me." She smiled into his grey eyes that reflected the flames. "What we have forged could withstand a hundred scandals. Home is here in your arms, my love." Peter's expression grew solemn. "I do not deserve your unwavering devotion after I failed you so." He clasped her hand to his heart. "But I swear to honor and cherish you and our family above all else now until my dying day." His eyes shone fervently. "You gave me back my life, Lizzy. It is yours to share fully." Rising on her toes, Elizabeth pulled his weathered face down to hers in a deep kiss, pouring all the words of forgiveness and joy she could not speak into it. When they finally broke apart, both were smiling and breathless. "To new beginnings then, sailor," she whispered against his lips. In the tranquil days that followed, she watched Peter embrace their modest routines with fresh zeal - whistling cheerily as he worked the fields or cobbled toys for the children in his workshop. The townsfolk's suspicion seemed to soften bit by bit as his honest repentance spoke for itself. Whatever shadows yet trailed him, joy lived here too. So when late one afternoon their daughter burst in weeping that the schoolboys were taunting her again about her disgraced pa, Elizabeth soothed the girl gently but knew stern action must follow. She marched to the clustered lads, fixing each with a firm stare until they shuffled guiltily. "You will apologize at once and never again speak ill of her good father, or you will answer to me." They mumbled repentance, eyes downcast. Elizabeth nodded crisply then let her expression soften. "Someday you may also know regret and redemption. Judge justly." That night she recounted the incident quietly to Peter as they relaxed by the hearth. His face clouded with sorrow but also gratitude. "Remind me how I ever managed deserving you as my champion, Lizzy?" He caressed her hand softly. "Our children could ask for no better protector." Squeezing his fingers, Elizabeth spoke earnestly. "Where you see weakness in yourself, I still see only bravery in choosing to change rather than remain sunk in shame." She laid her head on his shoulder. "However long it requires, our actions will prove the truth of your good heart." His voice was hoarse with suppressed emotion. "When all others reviled me, you alone offered faith. I will spend my life making amends." He gently tilted her chin up to meet his eyes. "But know you, Elizabeth Maxwell, that you are and always will be my redemption." And as his tender kiss reawakened long-slumbering passion between them, Elizabeth knew beyond any doubt that the past's shadow over their lives had finally lifted for good. This steadfast love they had fought so hard to protect would flourish now, heedless of lingering doubts or gossip. Fate had tested them sorely, but they had survived those storms stronger. Clear skies stretched ahead together.

Chapter 50

Elizabeth smiled softly, watching the children race ahead along the sandy path - her son Elias' gangly legs churning as he called encouragement back to his little sister. At eight and six, they were a spirited handful, keeping life brimming with mischief and adventure. Settling the basket of fresh fish more securely over her arm, she followed their fading voices around the grassy cliffside bend to the cottage door. How improbable those early days of motherhood now seemed, consumed with worry over each skinned knee and sleepless night. Now she knew the secret was simply to cherish each moment fleeting by. Pushing the weathered door open with her hip, she called, "Do wash up for lunch now. And fetch your father from the garden." The answering groans and thumps brought a wry chuckle. Some things never changed. Humming tunelessly, Elizabeth swiftly scaled and gutted the glistening trout on the scarred table before rinsing her hands. Outside the window she could glimpse Peter's broad shoulders among the bean vines, elbow-deep in soil as he did each time he wrestled some new dilemma. The crops and his family's wellbeing, so long uncertain, now anchored him. Wiping her brow with the back of one earthy wrist, she watched the children scramble up to wrap their father in eager hugs until he laughed aloud, the somber set of his face smoothing away. Her heart swelled at the image. For all the humble simplicity of this life, she was grateful beyond words for it. Later as they sat down to mealtime chatter about fishing trips and seashells, Elizabeth caught Peter's eye over Elias' dramatically reenacted mishaps. His warm crinkled smile, echoing her own contentment, needed no words. The years had only honed their love and partnership to a steady glow, whispering that they had found what truly mattered. So on a mild autumn evening as she prepared for bed, loosening her hair from its practical braid with a sigh, the knock below jolted Elizabeth from nostalgic musing abruptly. Visitors after nightfall were unknown here

– and unwelcome, she suspected from the prickling dread down her neck. Slipping a robe over her nightdress, she padded cautiously downstairs in the dark. The quavering voice from the front step was unfamiliar. "Please, I must speak with Elizabeth. I mean her no harm." Quiet authority belied the polite entreaty. Elizabeth hesitated, nerves fraying as her family's peace was disrupted unexpectedly yet again. Before she could reply, heavy footfalls sounded as Peter appeared at her back, pushing her protectively behind him. Rarely did she glimpse the ghost of his dangerous past now, but it surfaced as he flung the door wide, rigid and towering. "State your business. My wife is unavailable at this hour to one without appointment." The stranger's face in the dimness was proud and vaguely familiar – a mature well-bred woman, Elizabeth realized with surprise, dressed for travel. But her polite veneer faltered into supplication before Peter's intimidating stance. "Please sir, I intend only to talk. There are matters to be resolved between us, events you must remember..." She peered past him beseechingly at Elizabeth. "I was once known as Mary to you both." Peter's sharp intake of breath echoed Elizabeth's own muted shock. Mary Worthington...her family's former housemaid who had nearly come between them when young and foolish. Her reputation left in ruins by Peter's careless dalliances. Another lifetime, yet here she stood years later, composed and refined, turning their existence upside down with her spectral presence. Before Peter could reply harshly, Elizabeth dared crack open the door further. "You are not welcome in our home after the damage wrought. But I will grant you this - speak your mind plainly. No more lies or games." Her voice did not waver, bolstered by the dear life she protected here. The past could not haunt them unless she allowed its talons to rend fragile peace. The woman paled, clearly surprised to be addressed so bluntly by one she still saw as a sheltered young lady. But she inclined her head graciously. "You are quite direct now, I see. Very well, my errand is simple." Her voice turned icy. "I want remuneration for my years of suffering and public shame at the hands of your husband and yourself. I wish to negotiate reasonable compensation for my silence." "Extortion!" Peter surged forward, temples throbbing. "Not one damned penny. How dare you disrupt innocent lives with threats long buried! Begone before I..." "Husband, please." Elizabeth's grip on his shoulder softened his fury. Turning to Mary, she considered the strained figure sadly. "I understand you want amends for old pains. And perhaps we owe you that, though we too acted in innocence. But what good comes of exhuming the past if we only perpetuate it with resentment?" Her sigh was weary now. "Stay or go freely. Either way I wish you peace." Mary stared at her uncertainly for a long moment, bitterness seeming to recede in the creases of her face. But the damage was too deep for hasty healing. With a final silent nod, she gathered her cloak and disappeared into the night as mysteriously as she had arrived. The words lingered echoing between husband and wife heavily after the door latch clicked to. What other ghosts lingered outside their sheltered lives? In the painful weeks after, Peter brooded ceaselessly, reduced to monosyllables and subtle coldness when before she had known only tenderness. Their world was upended by something that should have remained buried securely. But roots had been unearthed, and the foundation no longer felt so certain. Trust, once rock-solid, became fog. Until finally, after the children were abed, Elizabeth could bear the strangling silence no longer. She knelt between Peter's knees as he glowered into the cold hearth, gently cradling his bearded face until their eyes met wearily. "Let the past go, my love. Do not retreat from your family now over sins long absolved." Her voice dropped to a fervent whisper. "Stay with me, Peter." Those simple words seemed to exorcise the worst ghosts. He pulled her fiercely into his lap, shoulders heaving with choked apologies until she whispered soothingly and let her kisses reaffirm that they yet had all that truly mattered. Together they would face unraveling pasts with courage, reminding each other it was not who they had been but who they were now that counted. The quiet days would return in time, unfractured. They yet had life and faith and each other. Gradually laughter and light filtered back into the cottage as they all determinedly stepped forward beyond old shadows. But Elizabeth began noticing odd lapses in Peter's memory. Small concerning incidents accumulated until denial was impossible. Her stalwart protector, once sharp and vigorous was losing pieces – misplacing tools or garbling words frequently. His decline was gradual but certain. The morning she awoke to find Peter huddled by the cold hearth, unaware how to spark a flame or even feed himself, despair pressed down. Their haven was crumbling all too quickly. Yet still love's light remained, however dimmed. She could only cherish each lucid moment left as the precious gift it was. They would navigate this unknown passage too, day by day, forgiving when names eluded or confusion frustrated, remembering sunnier seasons together. So evenings when he rested peaceful with his grey head in her lap asking for old tales while their grown children looked on sorrowful yet supportive from the doorway, Elizabeth held back tears. Their time was ending, but they would walk on gently until the end hand in hand. The life they had built together was a gift, however fleeting. Its memories would guide her forward when left to carry the torch alone. Leaning down to brush her lips across his wrinkled brow, she whispered, "I will tell our story to all who will listen." When the end came some months later with family ringed around their bed, Elizabeth cradled his weathered face through labored breaths growing ever shallower, murmuring promises between kisses that though their paths diverged now, she would find him waiting across the years. As dawn broke softly through the shutters, his breathing slowed to silence. Their long voyage was ended. She held him close and grieved sweetly for this stoic noble man fate had once drowned but who had emerged to give her life its deepest purpose. A final gift remained. She would craft from their shared story's threads a rich tapestry honoring how love had quietly transformed them both.

Epilogue

Elizabeth sighed contentedly, looking out over the gently rolling ocean waves. The setting sun cast a warm golden glow over the sandy cove where she sat on a blanket, her husband Peter beside her on the shore. Farther down the beach, their grandchildren's exuberant shrieks rang out as they played tag, darting around craggy rocks and tidal pools. At the delighted shouts, Peter chuckled softly. "Seems we had similar energy at that age, though my memory plays tricks more oft than not these days." He shot her a playful wink that made Elizabeth's heart skip just like decades before. "You can recall enough when you put your mind to it, old sailor," she teased gently, laying her head on his frail shoulder. Though time had weathered them, moments like this could transport her back to their carefree newlywed days when the future unspooled ahead brightly. They sat in cozy silence watching the children play until finally two small bodies collapsed beside them, panting and giggling. Young Emily crawled right into Peter's lap as the boy Jamie peered eagerly at the picnic basket. "Will you tell us a story, Grandpa? The one about how you and Grandma met?" Peter's eyes took on a faraway look as he slowly stroked the girl's head. "Ah, that takes me back some long years." He shot Elizabeth a tender glance. "Your grandmother was the fairest lass in the county, both beautiful and clever. I knew she would make my life an adventure." Emily's eyes went round. "Was it love at first sight?" The old man chuckled. "Not quite, my dear. Life is seldom so simple." He frowned thoughtfully. "But looking back, each turn our story took only bonded us tighter, through both joy and storms." Rummaging in the basket, Elizabeth smiled softly at the memories washing over her. "We weathered a few squalls in our season, it's true. But never doubted we'd see them through together." She handed Jamie and Emily biscuits before leaning her head against Peter's sturdy frame once more with a contented sigh. Their story held its share of sorrow and regret, but far more beauty, grace, and devotion if she focused on that light. By the time the children's appetites were sated, the first stars were emerging overhead, and Elizabeth could see young eyes growing heavy. "Best be getting you two back before you fall asleep on the sand," she said gently, herding them to pack up the remains of the picnic. Peter's strong arms lifted Emily easily when she drooped against him. Walking slowly hand in hand behind the drowsy young ones, Elizabeth felt her own steps growing heavier. But Peter's steady grip kept her upright and moving forward down the glimmering shore. This man had been her anchor through a lifetime of ups and downs that now seemed blurred and insignificant compared to present savoring each moment together. She glanced over to see a similar peace gracing his craggy face haloed in moonlight, eyes crinkling at the corners when he caught her gaze. No words were needed. The tide of their life was going out slowly but not sadly. They had lived and loved well through the gift of time given. By the time they tucked the children snugly into bed with whispers to dream sweetly, Elizabeth could barely keep her own eyes open. But settling wearily onto the porch swing beside Peter to look out at the vast slumbering sea together, she nestled her gray head against his broad shoulder with a sigh. His voice rumbled gravelly and comforting. "Quite a full life we've shared, Lizzy mine. I'd change not one day." Lacing her knotted fingers through his, Elizabeth nodded drowsily. "Every season was a gift, my love." Breathing in the salt air, she let her heavy lids sink closed, feeling utterly at peace. They had created a storehouse of treasured memories together passed on for generations and still rippling into the future. That legacy would remain long after they were gone. Tonight the past and present swirled together like ocean waves blending indistinguishably one into the next. She was a blushing bride, then a mother cradling babies, then guiding her children's children while Peter's hand anchored hers steady through it all. Elizabeth drifted to sleep dreaming of sunlit shoreline days shimmering continuously ahead like tidal pools reflecting the heavens. Their lifelong love was a light within to guide her even once the sun dipped below the horizon ahead. But for now, they yet had sweet stolen moments left to cherish. And in her husband's arms, she was home.

Milton Keynes UK
Ingram Content Group UK Ltd.
UKHW040729030823
426269UK00001B/72